T0065198

KING of SARA

L. STITT

authorHOUSE

AuthorHouse™
1663 Liberty Drive
Bloomington, IN 47403
www.authorhouse.com
Phone: 833-262-8899

Published by AuthorHouse 08/05/2020

ISBN: 978-1-7283-6825-2 (sc)
ISBN: 978-1-7283-6954-9 (e)

Print information available on the last page.

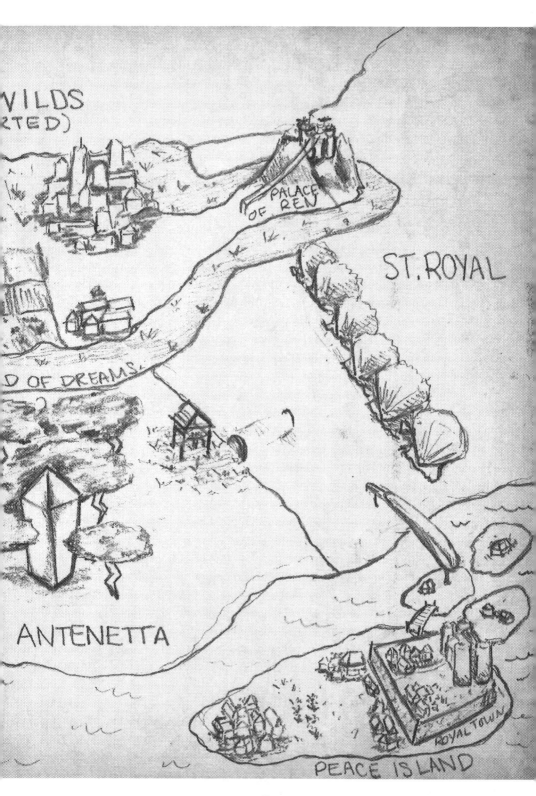

WILDS
(RTED)

PALACE OF REN

ST. ROYAL

D OF DREAMS

ANTENETTA

ROYAL TOWN

PEACE ISLAND

I

PEACE ISLAND

The whole world around us begins to shake. Desperation is in everybody's eyes. Our world is no longer green pastures of sunflowers or breezes that taste of sea salt. The pastures turn black as the ground cracks open, and red veins dance through the thick magma bursting from the depths of the island's crust.

This is not how I thought it would all end. I look over at my friend Sione, and I see it in his eyes, the fear that we might actually fail. For months, we have been running to prevent this very moment. We gave it our all. Is it really going to end like this, even before we get to play our hand? After all we've done, is this how it really all ends?

"Come on, you cowards, this is no time to be scared. We still have time to save Peace Island," says Tuy.

"But how? Everything is in flames!" Sione exclaims.

"Tuy is right," I say. "The worst has yet to come. We can still stop it!"

"The castle was the first place that was hit. So, we should probably head there first," says Tuy, standing back in his rightful place as commander of this mission. Wasting no time, he takes off in a full sprint. I get ready to follow him, but Sione grabs my arm.

"King, this already isn't looking good. Maybe we should just focus on evacuating the island."

"We are not running away. We will not let anyone or anything push us out of our home."

"But, what if—"

"I understand you're scared. I am too. Our world is falling apart. But just because our greatest fear is right before us doesn't mean we should give up. We can't be cowards forever. One day, we are going to have to change for the better."

"Well, maybe one has to be a coward in order to survive."

After I hear the word "survive," I suddenly feel hot, hot as the red veins of magma that are closing in on us. Sione is a soldier just like me. We both have dedicated ourselves for the last couple of months to this mission. But right here at the end, he wants to run away because it has become too tough? We should be ready at any time to lay down our lives for our island, for we took the soldiers' oath. It makes me so mad to see that he hasn't changed after all we have been through, that he is being so selfish, that he has forgotten what is at stake. A life that is worth saving, even if it means our deaths.

"Sione..." I mumble under my breath, my body still growing hotter.

"King, calm down, you're glowing!"

His voice shakes. I look down and see soft white specks of light encasing my body. I frantically try to brush off the glowing white specks, hoping they will float away in the light breeze that brushes my cheek, but they cling. I fall to my knees and grab my head as it begins to pound viciously. My breathing is shallow and the world around me is losing focus. Tears pour from my eyes at the sight of my own weakness and fear of the inevitable. I turn to Sione, who is sobbing as he tries to get to me, but some type of force field keeps him out.

He bangs on the dome that has shrouded me in its devious care. I grab my chest, which burns as hot as the magma surrounding us, and beat at it, trying to stop the inevitable. But the white light that has encased me is too heavy. I lower my head and fall to my knees as another tear runs down my cheek, and at that point, it begins.

The red veins in the magma crackle and break free, straight up the middle of Peace Island, and our world splits in two.

The pulsating energy aura no longer encases me and, shaking, I fall face down onto the scolding ground. All I can see around me is destruction. Every time I breathe, the pungent smells of brimstone, melting bones, and burning flesh twirl in my lungs. It is unbearable. I just want this all to end.

Lava sweeps toward me. My body is so stricken with fear that I am unable to move. I see my home split in the middle, houses destroyed, greenery burned, and my neighbors dead. This is not the island I know.

I must stop this from getting any worse. I don't want to see the leftovers this disaster leaves after it is done with its feast. I stretch my arms wide and try to feel the calm breeze of our home. I close my eyes to this new world, this world of flames, and I'm back on Peace Island.

The endless miles of sunflower fields, so high that you could get lost in them. The tall mountains where we harvested golden apples in the spring. I feel the sand between my toes as the sunlit water tickles my heels. At night, the sea becomes a field of stars, and I swear I can hold them in my hands.

The town's straw-topped huts glow in the distance like fireflies. Lanterns light up the fronts of shops and homes. Though it's late, children still run through the streets as mothers try to haggle with Old Man Tim for his delicious cream pies. There are no frowns on people's faces, except for the Tree Stump Drunkards who have lost all their money again gambling. However, their smiles soon return as they become merry from the spice of olmalga berry tea, and they quickly forget about their empty pockets.

The village smiles and above it smiles the royal palace in all its splendor. Its ivory and red pillars and marble carvings softly reflect the night. Only the highest of the high can see the inside, but the outside is enough to make one become lost in wonder.

Then I remember my home, not this crumbled mess before me. My intact home on the outside wall of the Royal Town. Though it isn't as luxurious as those on the other side of the wall, I was blessed to be a little better off than most villagers. I've never had to worry about food or necessities. I have also been able to have a good life without needing to adhere to strict codes and worry constantly about my status, like those in Royal Town.

Though the Lower Village and Royal Town were two different worlds and feuded at times, we could be seen coming together during the Salt Festival. The lower and high class can be seen joining hands and singing our folk songs. The women participate in bake sales as the men try to show off their strength, which the village men usually win since they're used to working with their hands.

Come to think of it, the night of the Salt Festival is where this all began. Sitting on this burning world, I sadistically laugh at myself. I guess

I should have gone to the bathroom instead of running to Tuy's beck and call.

"King, let me talk to you for a second," Tuy whispers in my ear. I exhale deeply and give a quick scan around the Salt Festival before following him. I swing off my helmet as we get to our destination behind the old oak tree near the edge of town.

"This better be good! You know Commander Lin doesn't like for us to leave our post, even if it's an emergency—which reminds me, I really have to pee," I say, shuffling my feet back and forth.

"Well, you're going to have to wait a little while longer, because trust me, you'll want to see this."

I raise an eyebrow to Tuy, wondering what could be so great that he is willing to be punished by Commander Lin. He leads me to one of the many enormous bushes surrounding the tree. Once he pulls back its branches, I peek over his shoulder, only to gasp. In front of us was a young girl who appeared to be unconscious. Her golden skin shimmered in the moonlight as her long golden brown hair stuck to the sweat falling from her face. After taking her all in, I couldn't believe who I was seeing, it was none other than the princess, Luna.

Tuy moves deeper into the bush, but suddenly the ground around Luna caves in, and the world below swallows them whole.

It's only a minute, but it feels like hours that I remain stunned and immobile while trying to think of a plan. However, once again Tuy proves that he is fully capable of relying on his own resources to get out of situations. Before I can spring into action, he swings a grappling hook from the sinkhole, catching a jagged rock near the top. He climbs out cradling the princess on his side. Like a hero, he moves with great precision.

Just once I want to know what it feels like to be on his level. To be needed.

"Are you okay?" I ask Tuy.

"Of course, King. Am I ever not okay?"

"Well, how did you get out of there?"

"I've always told you, you need to always be prepared. Basically, keep your utility belt on your uniform at all times," he says with a smile that I can't quite digest. "But I'm not worried about me. I caught the princess as we were falling, but she still is in shock. Honestly, I am too. Such a strange place for a sinkhole to appear. Strange things are starting to happen on our little island."

I shrug my shoulders, as I too find it weird. When I lean in to look at the princess, her breathing is slow and shallow. Though come to think of it, she was like that before she fell into that hole. "Well, let's just take her back to the palace; they can treat her there," I suggest.

Tuy exhales heavily and lowers his head as he says, "You truly do not have the spirit of adventure. There are so many questions to be asked and answered, and all you can think about is a doctor."

"Well, I'm sorry that I'm concerned with this poor child's health," I hiss, then bite my lower lip.

But Tuy only chuckles. "It's okay, King. She will be fine; trust me, I know. But if taking her home makes you feel comfortable, let's just take her back."

"Exactly," I say sternly, but with a hint of doubt in my voice.

As we head back toward the palace, I look over to Tuy, who has the princess cradled in his arms, covered with his coat, as if to protect her identity. Royals of Peace Island are never allowed outside of the innermost circle of Royal Town until they reach the age of sixteen. Everyone says that the high elders spend that time training them to act and speak like royalty. That they fear if they get a taste of the relaxed outside world, they will not make good rulers in the future. Which is complete hogwash if you ask me. How will you be able to serve the people if you waste your teen years, your maturing years, behind a wall among people who answer to your every beck and call?

As we walk, I can't help but ponder on Tuy's statement about questions that need to be answered. What adventure could possibly come from a lost princess? "Tuy, what did you mean by the spirit of adventure? And what possible questions should I have been asking?"

"There is no reason for me to answer that question when you are only seeing with your eyes." I must have been looking at him like he was crazy, as a warm chuckle escapes him. He pauses on the street underneath one of the paper lanterns and stands in its embrace. "You should not rely on your eyes so much. The heart is your greatest asset and sense. King, things aren't always as they seem. Sometimes it's better to approach situations blind. You will understand, one day, the power of following your heart and listening to that faint voice inside of you."

Now as I see my neighbors and friends dying, I wish I could hear the voice you were talking about.

As we reach the palace, the doors fly open before we can even state our purpose, revealing a distraught woman in royal attire—the queen. When she sees the princess, she flings herself upon Tuy, pulling Luna from his arms as she begins to sob.

Though I am a Peace Island soldier, most of us have never seen the royal family in close vicinity.But just like her picture on our money, she is a beauty. Thick lashes surround her dark green eyes. As she sobs for her daughter, her jet-black hair sticks to her once-golden cheeks, which must have grown pale from worrying. After placing a few more kisses on her daughter, she finally finds her composure and turns her attention to us. She does not speak, even to ask about the poor girl's unconscious state, but simply nods for us to follow her.

We enter the castle, passing guards stationed at every corner. The best way to describe the elusive inside is *gold*. From the top to the bottom, it looks like somebody dipped the palace in a bucket of gold paint. The floors are even embedded with jewels. The weirdest part, though, is that all the windows were covered with thick curtains. It has to be past ten PM, so the yellow super moon must be out. I have never known a Peace Islander who would miss the opportunity to bask in the yellow moon's radiance and absorb its longevity-increasing minerals, waking up with perfect skin the next day.

"Tuy, do you think those rumors are true?"

"Which ones? That my lord and my lady are vampires, or that they're able to hoard all of their money by burying and engraving it in their home?"

"Both."

"Well, I'm going to say no to the first, and…" Tuy pauses, looking past me at our surroundings. "Let's just save this conversation for another time. Too many powerful eyes and ears are around." He winks.

"Young Tuy and young King," the queen sternly whispers. We jump at the sound of our names, being as we never told her what they were.

"My husband is behind these doors. He would like to have a word with you," she says as she turns and walks off deeper into the castle, still cradling her daughter. Tuy and I stand in silence for a moment, confused. I mean, we did just save her daughter, and you would think we would have at least received a thank you.

"Well, that was weird, but there's no turning back now," says Tuy. He pushes open the door before I can come up with a reason why we should just leave.

We enter what appears to be the king's study, but there is no time to examine our surroundings, for our land's ruler is right before us, sitting in a grand purple velvet chair. Although a row of guards blocks us from a clear view, I still can get a feel for him. Unlike his wife, he looks nothing like his picture on the money. The king is a feeble, sunken old man, a lot older than the queen.

After a moment, we are ordered by one of the guards to approach his desk, so we do. His majesty is looking through what appears to be someone's journal. He continues to flip through its pages before suddenly letting out a heavy sigh and putting it to the side, and finally, our eyes meet.

"Well, if it isn't the other King." At our majesty's words, I don't know if I should laugh, cry, or be afraid. I take a peek at Tuy, and to my surprise, he has a huge smile on his face.

"See, this fellow gets it," the king says as he points his wrinkly, shaking finger toward Tuy.

"Of course, my lord, there is quite a rumor going around that you have an impeccable sense of humor." I look at the both of them with great confusion, feeling like the butt of their joke.

"Don't appear so grim, son. I know there are a lot of rumors about us out there, but only ninety-five percent of them are true," says King Vernon.

"So, what about the other five percent?" I choke out, trying my best to be calm.

Suddenly the king's face changes, and I think I might have gone too far, that I failed miserably in my attempt to open up. Then King Vernon jumps across his study with a great agility that seems impossible for a man his age. He lands directly in front of me, and we are now looking eye to eye. While he was sitting in his chair, he seemed much smaller, but up close I can see he is in amazing shape for an old man. And now I know it: imminent death.

However, instead of sending me off for execution, he opens his mouth very wide, but not too wide, just enough so that I can still make out his words as he says, "Well, you want to see my teeth?" He and Tuy burst out in laughter. Once I remember how to breathe, I let out a sigh of relief and laugh along with them.

"Well, kids, I called you to my study to thank you for returning my daughter." King Vernon slowly bows his head, and I feel the tension in the room from the other guards. Tuy takes a small step towards the King, kneeling, "you don't have to lower your head to the likes of us." However he persists, "I have been very worried about my daughter lately. Before her disappearance, she had not been eating or talking as much. She refused to participate in her lessons and stayed to herself. It was like she was a completely different person.

Then, speaking of the devil, Luna races in the room. "Why, hello, dear. Did you come to thank these young men?"

"No," says the princess coldly.

"I do apologize. Clearly, you see what I was talking about."

"King—"

"Sir King, dear."

"Yes, father. Sir King, please accept this." Luna holds out a silver necklace with a strange pendant attached. Flustered by her sudden gift, I wobble slightly as I kneel to receive it.

"How kind of you, princess, but don't you think that necklace is quite peculiar?" says Tuy.

"You see, I don't find it abnormal at all. I find it intriguing how the crystal pendant is almost lifelike, as if the broken butterfly wings are encasing the orb inside of its body and holding on for dear life. Some days if I look hard enough…" At that moment, the king clears his throat and glares at his daughter. The little girl's face grows dark as she turns back to Tuy. "I think it's very pretty," Luna says as she places her small token of gratitude around my neck.

"Thank you, my lady." I smile at her, which she responds to with a cold stare before pushing past me and exiting out the room.

"Luna… Luna…" her father calls after her, but she does not answer. "I do apologize. As I stated earlier, she has not been quite right in the head lately. But once again, I do thank you for returning my daughter. Peace Island is in great hands because of soldiers like you. I will be sure to let your superior officer know. These men will show you out." Suddenly we are surrounded by the guards in the room, who block our view of the king. They extend their hands, directing us to the exit. As I turn to leave the study, I catch one last glimpse of him. He sits back in his chair, and once again feeble and with the face of an old man, filled with the wrinkles of time.

On the walk back home, Tuy and I are quiet. The palace was an overwhelming place. A place of mystery with a haunting atmosphere. Though most people wonder what happens behind its walls, I don't think people really want to know. Our visit was on the normal side, but there was still a strange feeling in the air that I do not want to return to.

As we exit Royal Town and get back on familiar streets, I stop dead in my tracks.

"What's wrong?"

"Nothing. It's just, I feel really weird all of a sudden."

"Well, you never did get a chance to go pee…"

"I'm serious, Tuy. I feel…. I feel…" While I try to express the current wave of sickness washing over me, my head begins to spin and my vision blurs. I see Tuy's lips moving but I hear no sound. Suddenly, I lose my balance and the world around me goes black.

Death. Destruction. Everything that lies before my eyes at this very moment is something I saw the night I passed out after leaving the castle. As the white specks of light continue to encase my body, cuts appear along my arms as if something is trying to escape from me. As if the vision I had that night is detaching from my mind and breaking free through my skin, coming to fruition, destroying my present world.

I suddenly wake up in a cold sweat. All-white walls surround me and tubes run along them, all leading to me. I move slightly and can tell, from the enormous number of lumps pressing into my back, that I am in a hospital bed. Frantically I start to pull the IVs from my arms, but to my surprise, all the monitors surrounding me begin to blare. Nurses come flying through the door. I try to leap free from the lumpy bed's embrace, but I am thrown back down without a word and the nurses yank four long tan straps from the side of the bed, holding me down. I squirm so hard, the restraints dig into my skin. I tell them that I must head for the situation room, that a great evil is coming to Peace Island and to the world. However, no matter how much I kick and scream, no one listens to me. The doctor finally appears in the room, and I try to plead my case to him, but he just ignores me. He takes out a long needle, sticking it into the side of my neck, and again my world turns dark.

"Yeah, I don't know what happened. He was fine and all of a sudden he fainted."

"And did you hear about yesterday? They said he was in a rage, babbling conspiracies."

"He must have hit his head pretty hard."

I wake once again to voices, this time in a calmer state. "Hey. If you're going to talk about me, do it outside."

"Oh look, the loon is awake," says Sidney.

"Ha-ha, very funny," I say.

"Well, you were the one spitting fire and brimstone prophecies," says Sione.

His statement causes me to reflect on my fit of rage and the dream that caused it. It was so real that it felt like I was there. To see our world split in two and everyone dead.

"King, you okay?" asks Tuy, who has a serious expression, unlike the others. He walks closer to me and places his hand on my chest. "Wasn't the orb on your pendant gold?" Tuy moves his hand toward it, only to pull it back while letting out a cry of agony.

"What happened?" Sidney exclaims as she runs to Tuy's side.

"Nothing, just felt a shock."

I know he is lying, as I feel the warmth of the necklace that just burned him. I see his hand is now covered in blisters.

"Alright, guys, I need to talk to King in private."

"Thank you for visiting me."

Of course, we are met with looks of suspicions from Sione and Sidney. But they shrug it off and tell us their goodbyes. Sione says he was hungry and ready to leave anyway, only to turn around and give us a wink. As the door shuts behind him, I look at Tuy. "What was that wink all about?"

"You haven't heard the rumors?"

"What?" I say as I give him a strange glare.

"I'm just kidding." Tuy chuckles while he begins to treat his hand with medical supplies left on the table from my earlier fit.

"Burned you?" I ask.

"Yeah, weird, isn't it?"

"Being as necklaces don't usually burn people, yes. But, knowing where and who I got this thing from, I can't say I'm surprised." We both laugh despite the seriousness in the air.

"So, this vision you had?" he asks.

"What makes you think it was a vision? I haven't had any since I was a kid."

"Well, did it feel real?"

"Too real."

"King—"

"No, it can't be a vision!" I cut him off, once again fighting against the straps that hold me down.

"Calm down. Was it that bad?"

I can't find the words to answer right away. Why would I want to put on his conscience the horrible things I have seen? A part of me wants to deny what I had seen. I want it to all be a dream, but deep down I know everything I have seen will soon be our future.

"In this vision I had, our island split in two. There were dead bodies everywhere. Houses were on fire and the ground was slowly being covered in lava. But it was very strange, it didn't appear to be caused by a natural disaster. I stood in the middle of it and then these white specks started to float all around me, but as they encased my body, they burned and cut at my skin."

"So, what makes you think the disaster was unnatural?"

"Well, before I came to, I heard the faint sound of a malevolent laughter and saw the cloak of an outsider, embellished with the emblem of the moon and sun," I whisper, to which Tuy replies by drawing his sword.

II

THE CASTLE

Tuy raises his sword high in the air and I know I should scream or think of a plan, but I just shut my eyes and pray. I feel the breeze of his swing, and with a swoop, the straps restraining me fall to the floor. I open my eyes to glare at him. "How about a heads-up next time!" I exclaim.

"I will next time, only if you show some courage." I continue to glare but I can't find the words to argue. Deep down inside I know he is right. "Anyway, let's go, we need to inform the king."

"There's no way he will believe us."

"We'll never know unless we try."

I sigh heavily as Tuy helps, more like forces, me to get out of bed and get dressed. After sneaking out of the hospital, once again we stand at the grand entrance of the palace. I thought being my second time it would feel less intimidating.

"You better find your courage soon, because this is only the beginning."

"Of what?"

"You'll find out in due time."

"You know I hate things like that, more than receiving this creepy necklace." I groan as I pull at my unwanted gift and stomp my feet behind Tuy in protest.

"Gentlemen, I didn't expect to see you back so soon. Let's not make this a habit." King Vernon lets out a boisterous rumble from his throne.

"We do apologize for imposing on you again, sir, but this could not wait," says Tuy.

"Oh dear, bad news before my morning tea. Well, go ahead lay it on me."

I creep closer to the throne and somehow manage to croak out, "I think our little island might be in danger."

The king's grand smile starts to fade and his wrinkles fold, showing the stress he holds. "Huh, I had a feeling."

His majesty turns around and nods for us to follow him out of the room. Once again, we are led through the palaces' mysterious halls, until we come to a stairwell that curls so far down, I cannot see the bottom. Without saying a word, King Vernon leads us deeper into the castle.

Once we reach the end of the steps, we come to a long hallway with a large door at the end. Above the door, I can read "Center" written in the ancient language of Peace Island, but the rest of the words I cannot comprehend. As I enter, I'm blinded by the lights on the other side of the door. The room is all white and people are walking around in white coats with golden gloves. However, they are not the strangest thing in the room.

"Your highness, what is this place?" asks Tuy.

"The Neuro Center. It's where we get a deeper look into the mind, particularly minds of the special inhabitants of Peace Island," says the king. "I brought you here because my daughter told me two days ago that she too had a dream where Peace Island was in danger. She said it felt so real that she could taste the tar and soot in the air. You saw our island splitting in two, did you not?"

Shocked, I just stare at the king for a moment. I have yet to tell him the details of the danger that was coming to Peace Island or even the fact that I had dreamed it. "How did you—"

"There are a lot of things you do not know, King. But we can discuss that later. Now, time is of the essence. I want to get a deeper look into your mind, if you would allow me. I want to know if what you saw was a vision or just a dream."

"You know that I can—"

"Yes, young King. I know all about your childhood and the little things that make you special. But don't worry, no harm will come to you. You are our own, and a soldier."

"Do I have to go into one of those machines?" I ask, pointing to a contraption full of wires.

"Why yes, it's only natural," squeaks a strange voice from behind me. I turn around to see a short woman who wears a red coat with black gloves, unlike the others.

"Umm, hello," I stutter.

"Oh yes, hello. Where are my manners? My name is Dr. Carrington. I will be the one looking into your mind. Now, don't worry, the Neuro Machine isn't dangerous at all, at least in this stage," she says with a nervous laugh.

"This stage?"

"That's not important. All you need to know is that it is perfectly safe. It uses a high frequency of something called 'Gamco waves.' These electronic waves plunge deep in your subconscious, transmitting an electromagnetic signal, like the ones used for the Tube, so we can see archives of your memories, dreams, and other things. But don't worry, we won't snoop too far. Just in your most recent archives, so we can physically see this reverie you had."

I take a deep breath in this strange, bright, white room I have somehow got myself trapped in. I'm reminded of my mother, for she told me to take care of who I let inside. *The wrong type of people can change you if you are weak in spirit.* I always thought of it as a figure of speech, but at this moment, I become wary of her seemingly harmless words. "Sir, please just trust me. I know what I saw wasn't a dream," I say to the king, trying to weasel my way out of having to go into the Neuro Machine.

"Forgive me, but it seems that you misinterpreted my order as a request. As your Chief in Command, I order you to get into that machine, for the sake of Peace Island," the king directs sternly, all of his compassion disappearing.

"Yes, Sir." I speak reluctantly, and right away the attendants and Dr. Carrington take me further into the lab. We reach a dome waiting room filled with windows and long purple couches. The attendants hand me a white shirt and pant set as I'm instructed to change in the lone bathroom in the waiting area. I feel my hands shaking as I strip off each piece of my uniform, leaving me vulnerable. I shuffle out of the bathroom, and sink into the purple couch, throwing my balled up uniform beside me.

I become lost in thought but am brought back to the real world as Tuy puts a firm hand on my shoulder to try and calm me. "You okay?"

I look out the large window in the waiting area, which faces a beach hidden behind the castle. "Yeah, just a little nervous." With each crashing wave, I take in a deep breath to calm my nerves. "Thought our island only had three beaches," I say.

"It makes you wonder what else they are hiding from us."

"Well, from the looks of this room…I'm going to say a lot."

"Mr. Zale, we are ready for you." I slowly get up and follow Dr. Carrington back into the blinding white room from earlier. I'm taken up the stairs to one of the strange machines, this one had its own room and is connected to an observation room that I could only see through a window in the wall. I'm instructed to sit in a chair as a large helmet is placed on my head with a hundred long tubes sprouting out of it, and in front of me, there is a blank white screen.

"Alright, we are about to get started," says a voice behind the observation window to my side. I take a deep breath, but before I can respond, a purple gas is emitted into the room. I suck in its lavender scent and instantly drift off into what must be my subconscious.

"Young King… Young King…"

"Who's there?"

"My, oh my, don't tell me that you have forgotten my voice."

"M…Mo…Mother?"

"If that's who you want me to be, then I shall be."

Suddenly the dark space is splashed with color and I arrive in a quaint village by the river.

I begin to walk the streets along the river, which is hugged by small, colorful cottages. Flowers spring up from the cobblestone sidewalk every time I take a step. I reach the center of town, filled with fruit and vegetable stalls, little shops, and a giant fountain in the middle of it all. Then it hits me: where are the people?

I run up to one of the shop windows and peer in, only to find it completely empty inside. I go to the next shop and that too is empty. I try yanking at the door, but it is locked. I run farther into the village, and once again I am surrounded by colorful cottages. I go up to one and knock, but nobody answers. I cautiously peer through a window only to find it just like the shop, empty and inaccessible.

"Hello! Is anybody here?"

"Farther…"

"What?" I turn around frantically, trying to find the mysterious voice that came out of nowhere. I search my surroundings, but nobody is there.

"Well, what do I have to lose?" I head deeper in the village until I reach the edge, coming face to face with a dark wooded area. I can't help but mumble, "Of course, because it's not a nightmare without a dark forest."

As I make my way into the woods, I become unsure of my decision. Though it was clearly day a few seconds ago, it is now pitch black. However, I continue walking, wondering what I will find on the other side. Then, suddenly, I fall.

"A sharp-edged cliff, really?" I scream as my body breaks free from the darkness of the forest to the light and mist of a great waterfall. I hit the water hard, sending me deeper into a blank state of unconsciousness.

"We don't have long. Are you really going to spend our time together sleeping?"

"Whoever you are, just leave me alone."

"Why? I thought we were having fun."

"Yeah, taking me to a deserted village and throwing me over a cliff is not really my idea of fun. Can you please just tell me where I am?"

"Well, in your mind, of course."

"I guess that explains why it feels like I'm floating in space."

"Oh, if it's bothering you, is this better?"

The gripping blackness is erased from my eyes and I'm back in the Neuro Center beneath the castle. I exhale deeply, figuring I just had a bad dream. I look toward the large screen in front of me, but for some reason, it's still blank. I move my head to see the window where the doctors were doing the analysis. As I get a good view of the observation room, it appears to be empty. I squint my eyes to make sure— it might be the tint on the glass playing tricks on me— but there is no doubt that it is completely empty.

"I know you're there." I exhale deeply and wait to hear the voice that has been haunting me for what feels like hours, only to be met with silence. "Of course, when I'm looking for her she isn't there." I close my eyes, hoping to drift back into sleep, but instead, I am startled by the sound of blaring alarms.

My eyes fly open. The room is now silhouetted in red flashing lights. I jump up and race to the door, trying to escape from the blaring alarm. I frantically pull on the door, but it won't budge. I pull so hard that I feel like my arms will rip from my very being. The alarm gets louder and my ears are starting to bleed; I bang on the door and yell for help at the top of my lungs.

"What happens when help won't come? Will you rely on your own strength or will you constantly rely on others?"

"What?"

"When will you stop only existing, and begin to live?"

Sweat drips down my face at the return of the mysterious voice. As the alarm becomes even louder, I feel myself starting to lose control. "I don't know what you are talking about. I know you're the one who set off the alarm, can you at least stop that, please? And then we can sit down... or float around, whatever you want to do, and talk!"

"Not this time. I want to see who you truly are."

I just want to wake from this nightmare. I knew I should have listened to my mother when she told me to be careful of who I let inside. "Let me out of here! I'm tired of playing this game with you!" I yell, only to once again receive no answer. "I know you're still there! Answer me! Hey! Whatever you are, let me out of here, right now!" I fall into a fit of rage. "Fine, then. If you will not let me out of here, I'll tear this little fake world you created apart."

My body temperature rises as I feel an ominous breeze. I reach for the metal handle on the chair I was sitting on. I pull at it, a foolish attempt, but enough is enough. I cry out in agony as once again my arms feel like they will tear from my body.

"Come on, stupid bar, break free!" I holler at the top of my lungs.

The wind under my curly hair blows stronger, and then, unexpectedly, my vision is blacked out. But I continue to pull at the bar, unfazed by my loss of sight.

"Aren't you afraid?"

"Why? I have great power right now, so why should I worry about sight?" With explosive power, I finally pull the metal bar free from the chair.

"What good is it to gain the whole world if you lose your soul?"

"Whatever," I huff, swinging the bar around me, hoping to hit the main window and escape. "This world isn't real, so if I have to destroy myself in the process, why not? I will wake up from this."

"Hmm, I guess that is true to some extent, but instead, why not learn to control your power and have both? Having sight and power, you would be even stronger and could see what you are destroying. You now have power but no direction."

"Enough!" I cry out. I swing the metal bar and hear shards of glass falling around me. Finally, I know I am free of this world.

"Son, don't become like me" says a different voice, deeper than the first.

At the word "son," my limbs are immobilized and the darkness around me begins to lift.

"Very funny, changing your voice to a man's, but I have no father."

"I know," says the voice as it fades.

After my vision is fully restored, I collapse at sight of the destruction I have caused. I am no longer in the Neuro Center but in my dream of the island splitting in two. However, this time, I am floating above the island and—

"Alright, Mr. Zale, you did an amazing job," says Dr. Carrington as she lifts up my chair. "Is this real?"

"I'm Sorry?"

I repeat myself once again, only to feel my body shake and tears well up in my eyes. "Did you see what I saw?"

"Why yes, it was just as you described. But you do not look too good, are you feeling okay?"

I can only smile as I lower my head and whisper, "Good."

"Come on, son, I'll take you to the recovery room. I think you might have had an allergic reaction to the anesthesia."

"I think so too, and please don't call me son."

"I do apologize. Come on," says Dr. Carrington helping me into a wheelchair. I am taken down the hall. My mother was right about being careful of who or what I let inside.

"King, you sleep?" Tuy calls out behind the door of my recovery room. "Yes."

"Good!" he says as he swings open the door and plops on my bed.

"That meant don't bother me."

He just ignores me, staring me down with his signature stupid smirk. "Well, you obviously weren't sleeping."

I shake my head, pushing it back into my pillow. As I fall deeper into its plushness, I try to make sense of everything that happened. Maybe I had a bad reaction to the anesthesia and it was all a dream, but what if it wasn't? If what I saw comes to pass, I don't think I could live with myself. Unsure of my future and what I am becoming, I feel the warm springs of my mind finally escape down my cheeks. I squeeze my eyes shut to try and keep any more tears from falling, but in the end, I completely break down.

As I wallow in my fears, Tuy places his hand on my shoulder. "King, the king is coming!" I quickly wipe my eyes and sit straight up. Tuy gives me a comforting smile, as if to say he is with me.

"Young King! I heard you had some complications from the anesthesia. I presume that you are doing better now? Having your friend back by your side and all."

"Yes, sir!" I exclaim.

"Excellent, then you will not have a problem doing me a little favor."

"Of course, as a Peace Island soldier, your wish is my command."

"Good, get dressed and Bartholomew will take you to the situation room. Tuy, you follow me."

"Yes, sir!" Tuy salutes, then turns on his heels to leave with the king. I plop my head back down into my pillow, fearing Dr. Carrington might have lied to me.

"Mr. Zale, please hurry, we have no time to spare," says Bartholomew as he pulls me up from my bed. He takes out my clothes from a small drawer in the corner and then starts to grab for my white pant set.

"Uh, I got it," I say, yanking my pants from his hands.

"Oh, don't be shy. Seen one, you've seen them all." He lets out a haughty chuckle.

"Really, it's okay," I say, continuing our tug-of-war match.

We stare each other down for a moment, neither letting go. "Very well," Bartholomew says and walks out of the room. What a weirdo. I finally get myself together and head out the door to find him waiting for me. He looks me up and down, obviously still mad, but nods his head as if to say "follow me." I can't help but snicker quietly as he leads me to the situation room.

"Young King, your seat is up here by me," calls a man dressed in a gold and black military suit. I walk toward him a little reluctantly, as I have never seen him at any of our military meetings.

"General Claude. Nice to meet you, son," he says, reaching for my hand. As we shake, I gaze deeply into his eyes, and I realize who he is. I've only seen him once in my life, when I was six. I remember him coming to my mother's home, asking to speak with her for a moment. My mother told me to go to my room, but as she turned her face from me, I saw her smile fade. After they went into our home's office, I snuck back out and peered through the crack in the door. The fear that shot through my veins that day didn't leave me for months.

The general seemed to be in a rage. He paced back and forth as my mother sat on the leather olive reading chair. He finally stopped at the briefcase he had carried in and pulled out what appeared to be a metal cane. When he extended it, electricity started to flow along its length. I remember him standing in the open window and looking at the night sky as he lit a cigar, sucked a heavy amount of nicotine into his lungs, and blew it back into the cool air, the sparks from the metal rod continuously glowing around him. He asked for my mother's hand, my worst fears coming to light. He swung the rod in the air with great gusto and just as quickly swung it back down.

I snatch my hand from General Claude, as I can't and don't want to remember the rest. We are met with strange glances from the council, but I could care less. I grip my fists out of frustration that I cannot avenge my mother. I might not be able to strike him, but I give him the evilest side-eye known to man. I turn on my heels and go to my seat. Bartholomew scoffs, obviously already annoyed with my antics.

"Okay, everyone, let's calm down. The king will be in in a few. Until then, please enjoy some of the delicious refreshments we have prepared," he says, raising his hands in the air and trying to lighten up the mood. Conversation starts again as the council begins to stuff their faces, but I continue to stare at my hands.

"They should have used a stronger antidote," the general mutters under his breath.

"What did you say?" I growl, cutting my eyes back at his despicable face.

He leans closer to me. From the corner of my eye, I see Tuy place his hand on his sword. "You shouldn't be alive."

"Who are you to tell me if I can or cannot be alive?"

I expect the General to grow angry, but instead I am taken aback by his response. His eyes turn red and well up with tears. I look at his wavering gaze as I try to understand.

"The king is entering!"

All the councilmen stand, but as I get ready to join them, I am pushed back down by the general. He pulls me toward him, using the standing council as our shield. He places his face right next to my ear. He is so close that I can feel his heart beating. "King, trust no one. You are destined for greatness, so much that it scares others, and they want to destroy it. Trust only in yourself. She will come for you." After whispering this, the general releases his hold on me and stands up and greets our lord as if nothing happened. I tilt my head at Tuy, who seems just as confused as me. Not to alarm anyone, I catch my breath and stand to greet the king.

"Keep it together until we get out of the castle," Tuy mouths across the table. I nod to him and turn my focus back to King Vernon.

"Good evening, council. I have called this emergency meeting because something has been brought to our attention by two of our soldiers." King Vernon motions us to the front.

I move to the podium and look back at General Claude, who shakes his head slightly. Do I believe what he has told me? Or do I do my duty as a Peace Island soldier and tell them everything I saw, and I mean everything? I reach for the mic with my clammy palms, but as I put it near my mouth it starts to shake. I introduce myself, stuttering. The council receives my pathetic introduction with disinterest and I can feel the doubt in the room.

Suddenly a hand lands on my shoulder. I turn around and see Tuy. He gives me a wink and grabs the mic, and as always, introduces himself with cool composure.

"Good evening, everyone. I am Tuy, a soldier of the Outer Wall . The king has called this meeting because my friend here came in contact with someone who had received secret information that suggests a great calamity will be coming to Peace Island."

Chatter grows heavy in the room, many questioning how this secret messenger learned of the coming calamity.

"We think this coming destruction will not be caused by God, but by a man who wants to be God."

The air in the room grows serious. One of the older members stands and asks the question that it seems everyone fears. "Then you must be talking about the Dark King?"

"Yes. It will be him."

Then without warning the room goes into an uproar. Chatter is all around, many already losing hope and others trying to strategize and wanting to evacuate the island. Bartholomew and General Claude try to calm the room. In the midst of all this, I look toward the ground. I wonder why Tuy didn't tell them the whole truth. And where did this story of the Dark King come from, and who is he?

"Maybe it was he who tortured me in my dreams," I whisper to myself.

"It's all that child's fault!" cries one of the council members, throwing a glass cup at my head. "We must kill him if we want to be spared."

"That is quite enough," King Vernon says in a booming voice that echoes throughout the situation room, causing all the rowdy old men to take their seats. "Mr. Ebon, do not forget your place."

"A bunch of barbarians," a quiet voice says from the back of the room. "I'm the one that learned about this calamity through a vision I had one night. Unfortunately I told my favorite guard, who also has loose lips, as he told King. Thus King did his duty as a soldier and told my father, Therefore, I'm the one who had the vision, so I guess you should kill me," snaps the princess.

At Luna's entrance, Mr. Ebon lowers his head so far that if it went any farther, the mahogany table would have swallowed him whole.

"Well, Mr. Ebon?"

"I do apologize, princess; I was way out of line. I jumped to conclusions without knowing the truth. Please forgive me."

"Just this once."

The king smiles at his daughter and nods, agreeing with her decision. Tuy clears his throat and continues, "Thank you, Princess. We should not be fighting, but planning how we will face him. He does not know we know of his return, so we might have a chance at beating him at his own game. I think we should get help from the mainland, as he will probably try to conquer their regions as well."

"I agree. You both may take your seats now," says the king. "Council, we will put together a small team to go to the Emperor of Kasai and share this information with him. Young Tuy, I am entrusting you as the head of this team. You and the members of your choice will be leaving at daybreak tomorrow morning. Is that clear?"

"Yes sir!" Tuy salutes the king and bows to the council and princess before exiting. I follow right behind him, also saluting and bowing, but before I leave, I make eye contact with Mr. Ebon, who scoffs at me. I might be a coward, but I'm no wuss. I look him dead in his face and scoff right back at him. As I turn from his astonished face, I see the princess giggling. I smile at her, but the cheerfulness doesn't last long as her famous blank expression swiftly returns. Awkwardly, I look away and leave the room.

The door shuts behind me and I start to walk down the long corridor. "It feels like I have been trapped in this castle for a whole week."

"You have," says a small voice behind me. Startled I spin around, only to see the princess.

"Come on, kid! You have to stop doing that."

"Shouldn't be such a chicken," she says, sticking her tongue out at me. I can't help but laugh which makes her face scrunch up.

"Sorry, it's just that you really should start showing some emotion. I didn't know you could make such cute faces."

"Very funny. That would have hurt my feelings if I actually was the princess."

"What?" I whisper. The princess's eyes glaze over as she heads down the hall, presumably back to her room in the castle.

"Wait!" I cry after her, "have I really been in here for a whole week?"

"Yeah, it took five days to enter your mind. They said you're very strong-willed, King, or somebody just put one serious lock on your memories."

"Why didn't one of the doctors tell me?"

"Nobody tells people like us anything."

"People like us?"

"Dreamers. I'll show you later, for there are eyes everywhere." The princess turns on her heels, vanishing down a long staircase at the end of the hall.

"King, let's go!" Tuy yells from a balcony on the floor that leads out of the castle. I break into a full sprint for the exit, finally able to escape this castle's hellish web.

— III —

DEPARTURE

As Tuy and I finally return to my home outside of Royal Town, we both let out what feels like an eternal sigh. We stand in the entrance, neither of us saying a word.

"Um, you guys okay?" asks Sione. "Also, where have you been? We went to the hospital and nobody could tell us anything!"

"Let us relax for a minute, but please, call Sidney for me. I have some very important information to share with you both," Tuy says.

We convene in the living area. Sidney has arrived, and like Sione, she seems uneasy. I look around the room at my friends. These poor souls don't know what is coming for them. Deep down I wish I didn't have to tell them. If I don't tell them, they could continue to smile, to love, and to laugh without fear. But I guess I would be stupid to think like that. There is no such thing as perfect peace, only hope, so that is what I will give them.

Tuy opens his mouth and I know he will not sugarcoat my vision or the message from King Vernon, but I don't want anyone else to have to deal with this fear that is plaguing me. I remember the look in the eyes of the councilmen, especially when the elder mentioned something about a Dark King.

"We have just left the Palace. His highness has given me and King a top-secret mission. For this mission I will need to assemble a small, elite team of soldiers. Of course, you two were the first to come to mind. You might not have the skills that some of the others do, but you have the heart and the ability to blend in with the mainlanders."

"We're going to the mainland?" Sidney jumps up from her chair.

"What exactly is going on that requires us to leave the island?" Sione asks calmly.

Tuy lets out a deep breath and I know it's coming. "Well—"

"I had a vision!" I blurt out. "One of the emperor's right-hand men is corrupt and trying to lead a coup d'état against him. The day I passed out, I saw it all. He wants to take over Trinity in order to be the new emperor and rule Kasai through a dictatorship." At my statement, their mouths fall open. The emperor's family has been in power for over fifty years and has the highest favorability rating.

Sione and Sidney mumble together, asking who would want to do such a thing. I catch Tuy staring at me. He leans toward me and whispers in my ear, "What was that?"

"I just wanted them to have some hope. It's not like I lied. A man fueled by envy is coming to take over. I just figured that they would have more hope and less fear if the man was unknown and not the man you spoke of in the meeting. Also, who wants to know that their home is going to split in two? Think about it."

Tuy drops his head and grins. "Okay. I guess everyone doesn't need to know. But you've been hiding a lot of things lately, haven't you, King?"

This time I turn my head fully, looking him straight in his eyes. There is no way he could know the things that I actually saw. "Well, looks like we both have a secret," I whisper back.

He smirks at me. "Everybody deserves secrets, as long as it doesn't get in the way of our mission."

"Uh, lovebirds?" Sione waves his hands to break Tuy and I free from our staring contest.

Tuy sarcastically replies, "Very funny, Sione. Alright, since both of you have been briefed, we will leave in the morning for Trinity. King Vernon has enclosed in this letter an analysis of King's vision, and it is to only be opened by the emperor. Sidney, I am entrusting you with it, keep it close." Tuy places the burgundy velvet letter case, monogramed with the king's seal, in Sidney's shaking hands.

"Now, listen here. This mission will be dangerous, for we will not only be fighting against flesh and blood. We have all heard stories of the vicious and wondrous creatures that live on the mainland. Trust no one. Many will seem like friends but change their faces when it is time to kill. Once again, I have chosen you all for your hearts, not your skills, for something tells me this mission will require more than brawn. Sidney, we will need brains. Sione, we will need weapon expertise, and King—" at my name, Tuy pauses, and his voice becomes softer as he almost whispers, "we will need your compassion." I am not convinced that is what he really sees in me, but I know I am needed on this mission. For it was my vision, and if I can stop it from happening, then I will.

My chest grows tight and I drop my head. Why would anyone do such a thing? Is it jealousy? Vengeance? Or just pure evil? Also, why have I never heard of this Dark King the council members spoke of? The way that Mr. Ebon talked, it seemed as if he has tried to destroy Peace Island before or at least came into contact with us.

These are the times I hate the seclusion of our island. Though I guess, just like I wanted to give Sidney and Sione hope, the king wanted to give his people the same by shielding us from the evils that lurk in the other regions of Kasai. I wonder if I should have told them. I shake my head as I start to regret the lie I told. This whole situation just grows more confusing by the hour. My vision makes no sense, the castle has some top-secret lab, and there are secret letters, voices in my head, and not to mention the princess who says she's not the princess. I cry out to the heavens and throw my head back over the top of my chair, my brain feeling like it will explode.

As I open my eyes, the others are starting at me, rightfully so. "I'm going to bed. Got to be well rested, for we have a long journey ahead of us," I say avoiding eye contact as I run off to my room and shut the door.

I plop down on my bed and stare out the window at the full moon. It shines brightly, illuminating all of my trinkets and photos. I crawl under the ivory sheets and wrap myself in a cocoon, only leaving my eyes exposed. Hearing the sound of the sea from the open window as the palm trees sway peacefully back and forth, I treasure this moment, as it is the first time all week that I can breathe easy.

As I continue to stare at the moon, I think back to when Tuy drew his sword after I mentioned how the person in my vision wore the emblem of the moon and sun. Though I didn't see that persons face, I guess the council elder was talking about him. I look into the blanket cocoon at my own necklace, the one the princess gave me. Tonight the orb is a swirl of blue. I haven't told anyone that it changes colors, or that sometimes I can feel it pulsating. I'm already weird enough I don't want to lose the few friends I have.

I close my eyes, feeling myself drift off. I roll over on my right side trying to block out the moon's clear light. As I prepare to sleep, I pause at my mother's picture on the bookshelf in the corner of my room. I miss her. I gaze at her long silver hair, not from age, but from birth. Her pale purple eyes twinkle back at me. The islanders use to call her a monster, but she always felt like a goddess to me. I giggle at the thought of my mother being a goddess; maybe she would have been more like a fairy. She was always fluttering from here to there and even though she was clumsy, she had her graceful moments. I find myself wanting to reach out toward her picture, foolishly hoping she would grab my hand.

The lucid rays behind me suddenly become blinding. I can see nothing around me but the photo of my mother. I wonder what is happening, and I become a little annoyed that my time of calm only lasted for a few minutes. Then I see it. Another moon that shines brighter than the one in the sky is hanging from her neck.

Suddenly my room goes black.

I sit straight up in my cocoon and swing my head toward the window, only to see a woman in a flowing pale pink dress, which shines as bright as the moon, standing over me. I try to scream but no sound comes out. I look around frantically and try to run, but I am unable to move from my bed. I have no choice but to give my attention to the woman. Tears fall down my cheeks, as she is the spitting image of my mother, but how could she be?

"Mother?" I call out with a trembling voice.

"I see you're still a scaredy-cat."

"No, I'm not," I reply in a boyish fashion. I catch myself and cover my mouth, reminded of how my mother always picked on me for being scared of everything.

"I know this is frightening, King. My poor child, you have had a trying week."

My tears cannot be contained as I know she is my mother, and if I am seeing her ghost, she must be dead. "Mother, what happened to you?"

My mother busts out laughing as she whacks me upside the head. "I'm not dead, son! You're just dreaming."

I let out a sigh of relief. "Were you the one who was talking to me in my dreams?"

"Nope. Look, King, every voice in your head is not your friend."

"Why? Who did the voice I hear belong to?"

"I can't tell you that," my mother says with a perplexing look on her face.

"Why can't anyone tell me anything? I'm tired of it all! I fear for tomorrow so much, mother." I scream as I am finally freed from my bed, allowing me to swing my body forward and fall into her warm embrace.

"For the evil that is coming to Peace Island, or do you fear what you could become?"

At her question, I squeeze her closer and wipe my tears. I have no answer. I just want to hide from this time in my life.

"Young King, sit up straight. This journey will be the hardest thing that you will ever face. But there is greatness inside of you. You are a strong young man, you just have to believe in yourself. I've always told you that life is not easy."

I drop my head as I feel the tears upon my cheeks again.

"Hold your head up! I named you King because I always believed you could become one. You must learn to be unshakable and a leader. You can stop the one coming to destroy your island and you will. Also, when she comes for you, accept her by any means necessary."

At my mother's last statement, I roll my eyes, as I now have something else to worry about. "Great, more stress. How will I know this person I must accept by any means necessary?"

"Let's just say it's a person who is like day and night. Sweet yet sharp as a whistle at times, but other times, hmmm, is 'scantily clad' the word I'm looking for?"

"Mother!"

"What? I'm just speaking the truth," my mom says as she crosses her arms and throws her nose to the ceiling, showing a face of disdain. "What can I say, I don't really care for her. She caused a lot of problems. But even I am confused about how she has returned and why in such a form. King, please find this out for me. Actually, you need to know this more than I do. Find out her purpose."

"But… I still don't understand. What does this have to do with me or Peace Island?"

"This journey you are setting out on is so much greater than the storm coming to your island. Learn all that you can while you are on the mainland. You must find the truth if you want to save your home. That is why I can't say much. If you don't overcome this yourself, you will never become who you were born to be. I know you can do it, King. I love you." My mother places a kiss on my forehead before fading away.

I open my eyes, and I'm back in my sheet cocoon. I look at my mother's photo and turn to the moon, which once again shines like normal. I find myself smiling. I thought I would never see my mother's face again. Even though I only saw her in my dreams, a tear falls down my face, for my dreams are not dreams at all, but reality manifested in my deepest subconscious. My eyes grow heavy as I finally drift off into a real sleep, still feeling the kiss my mother placed on my forehead. Her parting gift of luck for the journey ahead of me.

The next morning, I wake to loud banging from the kitchen. I groggily get out of bed. My head is pounding, for the last twenty-four hours has been a nightmare. I walk into the kitchen to see Sione swinging knives and spatulas in every direction. He had a pot on every single eye and about five pans in the oven.

"Oh! Good morning, King. Did I wake you?"

"Nah," I respond cheekily.

"My bad, man. Just want to make sure we have enough food for the journey ahead of us. You know how I get when I'm hungry."

"Yeah, I know." I plop down on the sofa in the living room smiling at him. "Well, while you're at it, be sure to make some of your jelly bombs."

"Already in the oven!" he exclaims, twirling around the kitchen like some sort of fairy, making me burst into laughter.

My smile fades, though, as I feel guilty that he has to blindly go on this dangerous adventure with us. I never thought I would find someone who was more cautious than me. I look at the ceiling and remember what got us this house to begin with. I was too scared to commit to an 80% deposit on my own. Sione had been searching for a place as well, but they wanted a deposit plus first month's rent. So, we both decided to go with the 80% deposit, splitting it 50/50, even though the rent at my place was higher.

Now we are just two wary soldiers living together. It's been a good five years. But I just hope he can find some type of bravery, because something deep in my heart tells me we will be pushed to our limits.

I can see he is already worried, food supply my butt. Sione always cooks to calm himself down. When we had to capture a giant koi that was tormenting beachgoers, he fainted not when he saw the fish in its entirety but when he saw its whisker. Now, he has to go against this Dark King. I look over to Sione, who is whisking some more jelly bombs at the speed of light, and I know there is no way I can tell him the truth behind this mission. This coward has to protect his fellow coward.

"King, you going to stare at the ceiling all day or are you going to start getting ready? Tuy said we have to meet at the Rainbow Bridge at 0800 hours."

"Oh yeah." I sit up and flail my hands, ruffling my hair as I cry out, "This is so crazy!"

"True, but if somebody was planning to kill you, wouldn't you want to know?"

"Huh?"

"The emperor's coup d'état …"

"Right, that." I take a deep gulp as Sione looks at me suspiciously. Avoiding eye contact, I hurry to my room but I can feel his gaze still upon me. I've got to be a lot more careful.

Rainbow Bridge, 0800 hours

"Gentlemen and my lady, beautiful morning, isn't it?" General Claude exclaims from the front gate of the Rainbow Bridge.

"Yes, sir, it is!" Tuy waves as we approach. Once we reach General Claude and two of his men, he begins to pace back and forth, looking all of us over. After a good two minutes, he stops directly in front of me. I tense up. Then suddenly he breaks into an awkward laughter and claps his hands, taking us all aback.

"Perfect team you have assembled here, young Tuy."

"Thank you, sir."

General Claude smirks as he throws out his hand, into which one of the guards places a scroll and a key. He unrolls the letter and reads its perfect calligraphy aloud in a booming voice:

Dear Young Soldiers of Peace Island,

I would like to commend you on your bravery. The road ahead might seem dangerous and uncertain, but I bid you to not think of it as such, but as a new beginning for your lives. Seek the spirit of adventure. You will be representing Peace Island to the mainland, and I expect you to perform honorably. May all your encounters be dignified and filled with love. I know the road ahead is scary, but I am so proud of you all. May God be with you and our Island.

Signed,

King Vernon

After he finishes, we kick our heels together, saluting and exclaiming at the top of our lungs, "Yes, sir!"

I am so sorry, King Vernon, but I think we might have fallen short.

General Claude nods his head and gives Tuy the keys to the ocean monorail that connects our island to the mainland. I've only heard stories about the monorail, I would have never thought I would be one of its passengers. Yet, I have no time to daydream as the General yells for the gate to be opened. The Rainbow Bridge has not been opened for years. The outside island used to hold a small port town until it was overtaken by a swarm of honeybees. I scoff at the memory of the attack, which was ludicrous, but a great threat to our peaceful island…. *Or our naïve island. This poor town knew not what was coming for it, nor all the hidden signs they missed.*

"Wonder if we'll see any honeybees," I whisper to Sione, laughing lightly.

"If I was you, I wouldn't be laughing. I told you, everything is not as it seems."

Sione and I stare at Tuy for a moment as we both let out a sigh. "Do you always have to be a downer? Can't we have a little bit of fun on this trip?" Sione mocks.

"Sure." He smiles, but his eyes say otherwise, more like *Sure, if you want to be killed.* Sione stares at Tuy's back, giving him the evil eye.

"I guess he does have a point, we should be serious from now on," I say as I pull on his arm.

"Yeah, whatever."

"Alright, soldiers, are you ready?" exclaims Tuy.

"Yes, sir!" we shout at the top of our lungs before sprinting off into our future, letting the Rainbow Bridge lead the way. I see General Claude and his men waving goodbye in the reflection of the sea, but I also see as their smiles fade as he crosses his heart, and I am no longer worried about trivial things such as honeybees.

— IV —

THE PORT

Sione collapses on the ground as he tries to catch his breath. Sidney shakes her head at how out of shape he is. "Alright, let's move out," says Tuy.

"Wait a minute, we just ran ten minutes straight, can't we take a break? I have some jelly bombs in my backpack if anybody wants some."

"Sione, when are you going to start taking this mission seriously?"

"I am taking it seriously! And, I'm lugging more gear then all three of you combined.

"Well that was by choice. We already stopped on the bridge three times and practically took a morning stroll by the lake, so I don't want to hear anything else about a break!" Tuy moves inches away from Sione's face. "Do you understand?"

To which he has no option but to answer "Yes, sir," as he is a rank below; we all are.

Once we finally enter into the abandoned port town, I manage to get close to Sione. "You okay?"

"Yeah, sorry if I'm holding you all up."

"You're not holding us up, you're so important to us. There is no way we all could carry as much stuff as you."

"So basically, I'm a pack mule." I can't help but laugh out loud at Sione's statement.

"Be careful, Mr. Sour Pants might catch us."

"Oh, right. Hey, Sione, Tuy has a lot on his plate, being the leader and all."

35

"I know. But the guy has to loosen up a bit. I have no idea how you two are friends. What could you possibly see in him?"

"Everything that I'm not."

"Hey, don't say that, King. You have so much power. I mean, you're kind of a loser like me"— I cut my eyes at Sione, who smiles and places his hand on my back— "but you're not as big of a loser as me. You are brave at times, and I believe once you really find your place in this life, nothing will be able to stop you. Then Tuy will be the one looking up to you, like I do."

"You look up to me?" I ask in surprise.

"Yeah, you're like my big brother. I want you to shine on this mission. So, I will promise to give 110%, but I will have to drop an occasional joke, whether Mr. Sourpuss likes it or not, because you know I hate silence," says Sione with the cutest expression on his face.

"I know." We chuckle, causing Tuy to turn around. We straighten our faces, as we have sort of fallen behind while we were chatting. But all is good; he just turns back around and we both smile and catch up with the others.

While we walk through the deserted port town, I feel bad for those who lost their homes over a problem that just doesn't make sense. An eerie sky hugs the abandoned homes, marts, and fishing boats covered in moss. What used to be covered in life is now dead and corroded.

"How could something as small as bees cause this?" questions Sidney. We all look at each other, but my sight stops at Tuy, and I remember what he always says, that everything is not as it seems.

Suddenly he draws his weapon, followed by Sione and Sidney, and they point them straight at me. I fumble at my side, trying to reach my sheath, but it is missing. I quickly move my hand to my back, but my second sword is also gone. I frantically move my head from side to side, searching for where it could have fallen, and I remember the lake where we had previously stopped for water. Was my own team behind this? Did they render me defenseless in order to take out the freak?

Before I can think any further, I feel my feet taking off, back toward the lake. The others cry out behind me. Maybe General Claude was right, that I shouldn't trust anyone. I run for five minutes straight until I finally see the lake in front of me. I search for my swords, and there they are on a large rock.

Shaking my head at my stupidity, I reach for them and strap them back in place. I take a moment to catch my breath. The beautiful valley in front of me is covered in white birds. "Was this whole thing a setup? And why me?" I whisper to myself, but suddenly tiny hands cover my eyes and the beauty in front of me is blocked out.

"You really are an idiot," says a snarky voice.

I jump up and slap the hands away from my eyes, then draw my sword and place it to the speaker's neck. However, I do not follow through with my strike. Instead, sweat pours down my face as the sword falls from my hands and I let out a low-pitched yelp.

"My lady, I am sorry. I didn't know it was you," I say as I kneel before the princess.

"That's okay," she says as she taps me on my head. "Just glad to know you have some type of bravery."

I scoff at her statement, but as I catch myself, I throw my hands to my mouth. Then it dawns on me: what is she doing out here?

"Um, if I might be so rude as to ask, why are you here?"

She looks at me for a while and I can tell she is searching for the right words. "I'm joining your team."

Or maybe she wasn't searching for the right words.

I stand up, put my sword back in its sheath, and place both my hands firmly on the princess's shoulders. "Absolutely not. As a Peace Island soldier who has committed his life to the king, I cannot allow that, for I know your father would not be pleased. Come on, I'm taking you back across the bridge."

"So you still trust my father after the men he sent you on a mission with turned on you? Where do you think they got those orders from?" the princess asks with sarcasm unsuitable to the circumstances.

"How do you know about that?"

"I've been following you all this whole time. I also know that your friends weren't stabbing you in the back," she says as she moves closer to me. "What are you so afraid of, King, that you fear everyone is out to get you? You were so overwhelmed by your fear that you missed the monster your friends were drawing their weapons to slay."

"What?" I cry out.

"A Fera was right behind you and you didn't even notice it. Instead, you ran off like a coward." The princess laughs. "It seemed like they were having a really tough time—"

I turn from her cruel sarcasm and dash off, back in the direction of my friends. Like the fool I am, I have to slap back the tears running down my face. Now is not the time for fear. I am so embarrassed with myself that I can feel the heat rising in my cheeks. I just hope everyone is okay.

Yet, When I finally make it back to where the group was, they are nowhere to be found.

"Ahhhhh!" I hear Sidney cry out in the distance, from near the old shipping dock, along with the sound of Sione's large double axes swinging. I turn and run. Once I am there, I see it: a Fera.

"Weird, isn't it?" the princess asks from behind me, causing me to fall on my butt. I try to figure out how she kept up with me, but I don't question her. I point to the mutated organism in front of us.

"A Fera?"

"Yep, *Apis mellifera*, also known as the western honeybee— or my favorite, as they call it in the western plains, a killer bee."

"Why is it so big?" I stutter out. I can't move my eyes from the insect, whose body is as big as a toddler, with wings the size of fishing ships and a stinger and fangs pure as silver and sharp as a blade. I look to the princess, as she has grown silent, only to find that she is gone. I lower my head and exhale deeply, turning my attention back to the Fera. I now know that this is only the beginning, that on this journey there will be many unexplainable things.

I take a moment and breathe in the port town's stale air, pushing my thoughts to the back of my mind. Then I draw my sword and charge ahead.

"King! Where in the world did you go?" Sidney roars.

"I'm sorry. I left my sword at the lake," I say reluctantly, now standing side by side with my comrades. I dare not tell them the real reason I ran away.

Tuy only cuts his eyes at me and turns back to the issue at hand. "Let it go. He's here now, so let's get back to slaying this beast." He jumps for the Fera, swinging his sword, but he is pushed back by the gust from its wings.

Sione runs to assist. "Here it comes again!"

All the focus is snatched from me as the giant bee begins flapping its wings rapidly. The air vortex from those wings was so great that the abandoned boats sway at the dock and the sand from the shore twirls into miniature tornados. "It is creating a sandstorm! We should move to some type of shelter!" yells Sidney.

As I look around for cover, I spot the old fishers market on a tall hill. I yell to the others to follow me. At first, I can tell they are hesitant, but as the beast flaps harder, the sand storm grows, making sight almost impossible. I signal them by pointing in the direction of the ruined giant fish statue that sits in front of the market. As they nod their heads, I feel I have gained at least some trust points back. We scale the edge of the shipping dock, getting out of the beast's line of sight. We cut in between abandoned beach houses and through the upper hills.

"It's following us!" yells Sione.

Sidney peers through the gaps in the trees. "Smart little insect, isn't it?"

Turning around, I can see that a Fera has been keeping up with us steadily.

"It's spotted us! Get down!" yells Tuy, and we all hit the ground just as the Fera sends what appears to be a metal dart straight for us.

Sione's head shoots up from the grass. "Really, he can shoot darts from his stinger? Are you serious?"

We continue to run from the beast until we finally reach the old marketplace. Sione runs forward and bashes his shoulder into one of the boarded-up windows to make a hole. We all hurriedly climb through. Tuy motions for us to go upstairs. We move past the abandoned carts and evaporated fish tanks filled with decaying carcasses. I cover my nose, as the smell is so pungent it becomes hard to breathe. After we head up the old wooden staircase, Tuy pulls on a door, only to find that it has been locked. Sione pushes me to the side and tries to pry it open with his large build, but to no avail. Sidney then takes Sione's axe and breaks the lock with precision. We file into what used to be an office and shut the door, letting out a sigh in unison as we fall onto the paper-covered floorboards.

The room we sit in is dark and overlooks the market through a glass window. It holds three desks, and another door to the back of the room probably leads to the owner's office.

"I don't care what anyone says, but that does not look like a bee infestation to me. It might look like a bee, but that is not a bee," says Sidney as she finally catches her breath.

"Infestation..." mumbles Tuy.

Sione sprawls out, kicking his feet. "Oh man, just dealing with that one was enough. There is no way we can take on more of whatever that thing is!"

"Feras."

"What?" the others exclaim together.

"It's called a Fera. I think it's a mutated western honeybee, or as the princess said, a killer bee."

"The princess?" all three of them exclaim together again, and suddenly it hits me.

"Yes, the princess," I whisper, my words hitting the bottom of my stomach. How could I have forgotten about that poor child?

Before my heart can communicate with my mind, I leap up and push my way past the others, fly through the door, and head down the old wooden stairs. Sione calls out, telling me it is too dangerous and that she will be alright, but how does he really know? Filled to the brim with adrenalin, I do not go the way we came. Instead, I use all my strength to break through the ebony front doors. My attack is so forceful that shards of wood fly forward and take out five Feras, and I know I have done it.

I stand on the staircase of the market and hear great gusts of wind, created by the Feras' wings, coming from the east. I figure they would come for me since I have taken out their friends, but for some reason, the swarm stops and hovers over the far-off wooded area before making numerous vicious descents. "She has to be over there," I think to myself.

I yell back to the others that the princess is to the east, before I take off for the woods. I sprint so hard that it feels like my legs will fall off and my vision becomes blurry, but I don't care. That poor child is all alone. No matter how rude or tough she might try to seem, she is still a child. As my legs continue to get heavier, I let out a painful shriek that echoes through the woods, but I finally see her.

Her long hair shines in the light that falls through a hole in the small cavern she hides within. No matter how strong she wants to seem, I see the tears falling from her eyes as she clutches her knees to her chest. The sound of tornados from the Fera's flapping wings gets closer and before I know it, one of them descends upon her, aiming its metal stinger at the cavern entrance and preparing to shoot. But before it can, I reach it.

I leap in the air, cutting its head clean off. I fall back down to the earth covered in blood. Before I can catch my breath, five more appear. I breathe in the pungent salt-filled breeze and take a moment to hear the waves crashing around the small isolated island. I feel fear, but instead of being a hindrance it fuels my soul. Neither the princess nor will I die here tonight, for our journey is only beginning. I take out the sword that I carry on my back and go to work. I cut off wings and heads, stab hearts, and at one point I even cut off a stinger and use it against its owner. By the time I kill the last Fera, the eastern woods are splattered in blood. I let out a sort of inhuman roar to the heavens, and afterward the sound of the waves returns and it becomes quiet for a moment.

I slowly turn my head to the princess, who only looks at me with a blank stare. What has this poor child seen that the images of war do not even frighten her?

"You're not scared?"

"No. Why would I be?"

"You were crying a few minutes ago."

"Well, they are dead now, so what's the point of crying?" Once again the princess's nonchalant attitude takes me by surprise. I still can't quite put my finger on it, but something is not right about her. Nevertheless, the Feras are dead.

"Well, at least they are taken care of," I say as I try to knock blood clots from my uniform. "Yeah, that batch," says the princess quietly.

"How…many of them are there?"

"Well, when I snuck into the research hall under the castle I read a report about the Feras, and it said they created twelve different batches."

"Alright. Well, I just killed six here, and three earlier, so there are only three left. No big deal." I count on my fingers and shrug my shoulders.

The princess twitches as she wrinkles her brows like an old man. "Batches, King."

"Oh…" I feel myself blushing.

"So how many were in a batch?"

Not even flinching, she coolly answers, "A thousand."

My eyes grow huge. "Okay, we'll go over the details later, but we have to get off of this side of the island." I grab the princess's arm and head back toward the others.

"Wait." She pulls, trying to break free from my grip, "After we find the others, are you taking me back to the castle?"

"Of course. Where else will you go?"

"I want to stay with you."

Though we're in a dangerous situation, I can't help but laugh out loud.

"I am serious. I have to come with you if you want to live!"

"I can take care of myself. Thanks, but no thanks. Let's go," I say sternly as I grab her hand. But once again she frees herself and takes off into the woods. I call to her, but she does not turn back and all I can do is let out a frustrated groan. "I'm never having children!" I yell as I run after her.

As I move farther into the eastern woods, they become denser. Suddenly, a branch breaks under my foot and as odd as it sounds, I fall straight through the ground. But a vine catches my leg, dangling me upside down, and I don't see the ground but the sky, which is now beneath me while the woods appear above me. They look like they are encased in a glass globe which I hang from by the thick green vine.

I start to flail. I am so over these strange happenings.

"Help! Princess! Help!"

As abruptly as it caught me, my vine is caught and I am pulled back up through the woods. Yet once more I glance down at the sky beneath me. This time I see a beautiful waterfall in the sky and a young woman sitting on the edge. She has blue hair, a golden crown, specks of gold covering her body, and only jewels covering her chest. She smiles at me and of course, I smile back.

As I am pulled to reality, I find myself soaking wet. I splash about in an out-of-place pond, trying to catch my breath while ripping vines off of me. Looking behind me, I see the princess. I grab her shoulders and ask if she is okay, but she just giggles and says she is the one that saved me.

I shake my head at her foolishness. "Please don't run off like that. I know you want to experience life outside the castle, but now is not the time. Soon this world is going to get dangerous, so you should go home where it is safe."

Princess Luna tilts her head to the side. "Safe? Well then, why would you send me back to an island that is supposed to split in two?"

I smack my forehead and let out another sigh, having forgotten that she had the same dream as me. She continues to smile and then says something

I know she wishes we both didn't hear. "For the good of the island and my parents, I should stick close to you, especially since you're the one that is going to cause it."

Gasping, she covers her mouth, and for the first time I see her flustered.

"Who told you that? Was it in a report?" I yell and shake Luna by her shoulders, and the poor girl begins to cry but manages to crack out a few words.

"No, it wasn't, she just told me."

"Who? Dr. Carrington?" I try to ask calmly as I let go, seeing that I am scaring her.

"No," She quietly replies, and it hits me.

"Is this person a woman? Is she covered in gold, and does she have blue hair?"

Rather than answering my questions, Luna falls straight back into the pond, as if something has taken ahold of her, and submerges herself completely under the water.

"Princess!" I dive underneath the cool water and feel around for her.

The necklace she gave me begins to pulsate and I hear a voice telling me to open my eyes. Once I do, the water has turned to a crystal-clear blue.

"Behind you," says a voice. I turn around and there she is, the woman from the sky. Her light blue hair encases me and I feel sucked in by her amber eyes. She once again smiles at me and I smile back, but then I remember Luna. I remove my focus from her, trying to resume my search for the princess, but she catches my chin and shakes her head, as if to say the princess is not here. I flail in fear at the thought that something has happened to her.

The blue-haired woman laughs and holds my face between both of her hands. We start to float up and I get a peek of the golden jewels barely covering her chest. My cheeks grow warm underneath the cool water and it hits me. "The scantily clad woman," I think to myself, except, unintended by me, my inner thoughts were somehow said aloud and they vibrate through the water. The blue-haired woman's eyes begin to glow a faint pink color and I wave my hands in front of me.

"No, I don't think that. That's what my mother said."

Her eyes go back to normal. She sticks her nose up in the air, pouting, and for the first time speaks. "Humph, figures."

"So, are you the woman?" I ask her.

She nods her head up and down at me and says, "But first let us move from this place. And don't be alarmed, my appearance now is not what you see. Here I am amber and gold, but above the surface, I am golden but young." She places a kiss upon my cheek before lifting me to the surface.

As I emerge from the pond, I stand straight up and try to catch my breath, only to look down and notice I am carrying something: Luna.

For a moment, I just stand there with the princess in my arms, confused beyond belief. I think about everything: the necklace, her knowing the truth behind my vision, and how she reacted to me telling her about the blue-haired woman. I don't know how, but I do know one thing– she must come with us on this journey by any means necessary.

As I finally make it back to the fisher's market, the sound of the Feras is becoming louder. I call out for the others, telling them to come outside quickly, that we must make a run for the monorail station. As I anxiously wait for them, Luna opens her eyes and looks up from my embrace. "King, I'm scared." Of course, I want to agree, but I know I must appear strong for her.

"It's going to be okay. We will get to the other side safely."

"No, not that. I know we will make it off this island—heck, I know exactly how far we will go—and that makes me scared for the journey ahead."

I stare at Luna, wanting to ask her how this whole thing will truly turn out. *I wish I had more than ever at this moment.* But instead of seeking knowledge about my future, I become concerned only for the princess and push curiosity about my fate to the back of my mind.

"If you really don't want to do it, you don't have to," I say. "That woman with the blue hair might be a part of you somehow, but she does not control you—"

"Yes, she does."

"No, she doesn't. Nothing can control you but you. You decide your own future by the choices you make. She might lead you down an unknown path, but there are moments where you are awake and she is asleep and that is when you are the one in control. And another good thing is that the blue-haired woman seems to be very kind."

For a moment, the princess looks up at me with her famous blank stare once again before she says, "Well, that's all a matter of perspective."

Before I can ask her to go in detail, she closes her eyes, and I look up to hear the others calling my name as they run toward me.

The crew gives me a good once-over and I can see that all of them are a little afraid to ask what has happened to me, even Tuy. But I don't blame them. My once clean uniform is now torn and covered in blood, and I smell of the deep forest as I hold a delicate flower in my arms.

"Are you okay?" asks Sidney boldly.

"I fought off some Feras and saved the princess. You know, the usual," I choke out sarcastically in an attempt to lighten the mood.

"Oh. I see." Sidney chuckles awkwardly before becoming serious again. "Well, we'll have to put our journey on hold and return her highness to the castle."

Everyone nods in agreement, but my gaze falls to the princess, who is squeezing my uniform between her tiny hands, and I hear her whisper that she wants to go on this adventure. I peer deep in her eyes to see if it is really her decision or if the blue-haired woman has once again taken control, but they shine back to me with childlike innocence. At that moment, we are in this together.

"No, she is going with us," I say sternly.

Startled, Sidney goes on the defensive. "Absolutely not!"

"King, are you insane!" Sione says. "One, if we allow her to go with us, that is like, treason on so many levels, and two, we cannot risk her getting hurt."

I try to tell them that they don't understand and that she must go on this mission with us. But both Sione and Sidney stare at me like I am crazy. They decide to ignore me and reach for the princess, but I hit their hands away and move back.

Tuy has yet to say a word. The air starts to grow cold, and for a moment, nobody is saying anything. Only the sound of the far-off waves to the west and the Feras incoming from the east can be heard, until Tuy cuts the stale atmosphere, calmly asking me, "Why?"

"I think—"

"No. You know."

"I know that she can help us. Just trust me right now and I promise

I will tell you everything in time. Please just trust me," I say, feeling passionate tears well up in my eyes.

"Absolutely not—" Sidney starts before being cut off by Tuy.

"Fine. But if anything happens to her, remember it will be on your conscience, not mine."

"Are you insane? She's just a child."

"Sorry, guys, but I have to agree with Sidney on this one."

"Well, I am the commanding officer on this journey, and I say she can come if King believes it is for the best."

Sidney takes a moment to assess the situation, and the choice she ultimately makes is one that I was ready for. She draws her sword, pointing it at me while standing firm in her beliefs. "Well, I believe you are in the wrong, and as a soldier in good standing, I have the right to correct you if you appear to be going left. It is only common sense that we return the princess!"

"My, how the winds are changing," Tuy says as he looks up toward the sky, smiling. "Everything is not as it seems, Sidney. All things happen for a reason. It might seem strange to you, but there are some powerful forces at work that you cannot see, so let them be and put down your weapon."

"Both of you have lost it. We are not taking her into what might turn into a war zone!"

Sione tries to get all of us to calm down but to no avail. Sidney continues to point her sword straight at me, and Tuy does not move his glaring eyes from her, and I dare not loosen my grip on the princess.

Sidney's eyes grow wide as she calmly says, "Very well then." Swinging her sword at me, she causes me to drop the poor girl on the ground. Luna lets out a loud cry as she grabs her arm.

"Are you insane?" Sione screams as he swoops between me and Sidney and picks up Luna. He whispers to me that he is sorry and he believes in me before running toward the monorail.

Sidney tries to run after Sione, but I trip her and wrestle her to the ground. We struggle under the hot sun, pebbles cutting into our skin. I tell Tuy to follow Sione. As he takes off, I can't see him, but I hear his steps falter as he slips something in my pocket, before fully leaving me and Sidney behind. I continue to try holding Sidney down and making her see my way, but she refuses to listen. Then I hear my mother's words—"*by any means necessary.*" I pin her down and place all my weight on her, keeping her from moving or throwing punches at my face.

"I am sorry, but the truth is we lied to you. This is not a mission to warn the emperor of a coup d'état but to warn him that the Dark King might be returning. In my vision, I saw our island splitting in two and everyone dead. I promise you, in time it will all make sense. But if things start to look bad on the home front, you know what to do. Now please forgive me," I whisper before I reluctantly swing my arm back and punch Sidney in her face, knocking her out cold.

I drag her back into the fishing market office and head for the owners' office in the back. I kick it open and it reveals a chic office filled with unpolished but expensive vases, paintings, and trinkets. I place Sidney on a leather couch in the corner, then take my bloody uniform off and place it over her. The sight of my comrade leaves a sour feeling in the bottom of my stomach. I cross my heart as to ask for forgiveness of my sins.

I continue to look at her, knowing it will be a great while before I am allowed to see my homeland again. Before I leave, I search around the office to make sure it is safe, that there are no Fera eggs lying around or any other of Peace Island's strange secrets. The room appears to be okay, but just in case I set up booby traps. I reach for a trap in my side pocket only to pull out a small metal device, it's like nothing I've ever seen before.

"Tuy…"

I continue to examine the metal circle before it starts to vibrate, throwing it, it starts to speak. "King, this is a notifier, I know it is seems strange, but this will help the others find Sidney. Place it near her and before you go, press the red button on top, and make sure you hear it beeping." Says Tuy's voice from the little metal circle.

After a few minutes I find myself walking in circles. I just need to calm myself down. I look over at Sidney again and stop in my tracks. Something behind the owner's desk is glaring off the buttons on my uniform. I peek behind the desk and let out a silent gasp. Piles of money and gold bars are just sprawled out, probably left behind from the manager's attempt to escape and salvage his riches that were obviously obtained through corruption. I hesitate for a second, before I fall to the floor and begin picking up the fallen dollars and stuffing them in my bag. Once I get to the gold, I find myself contemplating. One bar has to weigh at least five pounds. I settle on taking only two, and decide to leave some dollars behind. I don't want to be seen as a traitor and a thief.

I finish filling my backpack and pick up the notifier, pressing the button I place it delicately near Sidney. I head out of the market and once outside, I don't even turn around as I grab a flare out of my cargo belt and shoot it in the air. And just like that, my new life begins.

I can hear the Feras coming in from behind me at full speed. I know I can't cut through the woods, because more than likely that is where their nest is. I assess my surroundings, the forest to my right and the town to my left. And then it hits me. My dream, the one I had in the Neuro Center—I must have been seeing this town.

I remember falling from the cliff, so I decide to cut through the small, quaint neighborhood. Once I am farther in, I see a canoe along the river. It's in bad shape, but it floats. I hop in and head for the monorail station that connects the fishing village to the mainland. As I continue on, I notice that the air around me has calmed down and that I no longer can hear the Fera. My mind goes to Sidney, but I shake away the thought of what I have done. I start to paddle faster and then I see it, the top of the monorail tracks. Yet, at the same time as I dock the boat, a blue flair goes off where I had set off my red one. Panic shoots through me. I didn't expect the Recovery Team to arrive in this area so quickly.

My cheeks grow flushed and not even the cool tears running down them can cool them off. I roughly wipe my tears away, once again turning from my past, and dash into the fog that covers the monorail station docks. I look for the entrance to the station. The fog is so thick I can't see around me. I feel through the air and eventually find the stations opening and railing to my left. Then the automatic sliding door flies open and I fall down the stairs onto the platform. I grab my back in pain and am met with laughter. I jump at the appearance of three shadows in front of me, but once my sight clears I recognize Tuy, Sione, and Luna. "What are you guys still doing here?"

"We couldn't possibly leave you," Sione scoffs, "and remember, the general only gave us one key to operate the monorail."

"Oh yeah. I forgot about that."

"I'm glad you jumped, but calculated jumps are even greater." Tuy smiles at me. I reply with an arrogant smile to his obvious shady comment.

"Alright, guys, before we go, we should regroup," Tuy says next. "Especially since we have a precious new addition."

We huddle into a circle and Tuy pulls out a map of the mainland and other important notes for our journey. He tells us that our end objective is the same, but this mission is now a rouge one. Once the kingdom realizes the princess is gone and the treason we have committed, we are in this game alone. "But at the end of it all, the kingdom will realize we did all of this for our island. Even if we have to get messy and break protocol to get it done."

At Tuy's last sentence, Sione and I look to the princess.

"Little girl, are you sure you can handle this journey? It's going to be scary," Tuy says, turning his attention to her. "You might even see the monsters that only come out at night."

"I'm fine. I find it all quite interesting. I too am doing this for our island. Even if I am killed in the process, we must get this message to the emperor."

"My, my! Don't talk like that. There is no way we will let anything happen to you," Sione replies with a warm smile, which quickly fades as he stands straight up and grabs me by the collar. "The letter! We forgot that Sidney was the keeper of the letter for the emperor!" Sione throws his hands in the air, then grabs his head and falls to his knees.

"Calm down. You think I would have forgotten that?" I pull the letter from my backpack and give a silly grin, which is greeted by the others cheering.

However, soon our cheers fade. We all sit in our perfect circle, nobody saying anything because we all were thinking the same. No matter how brave you are, running toward a potential war zone can make you weak at the knees. Finally, though, Tuy finds his strength and stands up. He nods and motions for us to get on the long-abandoned monorail.

"Does this thing even work?" Sione asks as he straps himself in the conductor's seat. Luna's eyes grow large seeing him there. Tuy and I can't help but laugh at the astonished look on her face.

I also get settled into a seat, right next to Luna. "He might be a scaredy-cat, but believe it or not, he sails the *S.S. Peace*."

"He is a captain?"

"No, he just sails the boat," I say, and we snicker.

"Alright, everybody ready?"

"Yes!" we all reply as Sione throws the monorail into full throttle.

— V —

ANTENETTA

The monorail comes to a creaking halt. We exit the station and step right onto a beautiful, quiet beach. Unlike the abandoned port town, the beach greets us with a bright sky and fresh air. For a moment all I can do is look around with my mouth wide open like some country bumpkin. Here I am, standing at the threshold of our peaceful island and the mainland with its vast cities, people, and cultures. Only very few Peace Islanders venture to the mainland; I never thought I would be one of them. I sneak glances at the others, who are also looking around. Huge rock sculptures and seashells covered in neon green moss have captured their attention. Further inward Luna is sizing up a large cluster of rocks that creates a tunnel, paired with a small wooden sign that reads: Antenetta Border – 5 miles. I decide to make Luna my prey and feed my excitement on to her. I slyly walk over to her and playfully shout, "Exciting, isn't it?" Of course, I hope to get some type of reaction out of her, but she only replies with a blank stare.

However, what feels like a good minute of killing my inner child, she at least speaks. "We should be moving on if we want to beat the worst of the storms." I look at her in confusion, as there isn't a cloud in the sky.

"Mhm, you have a lot of knowledge for somebody who isn't allowed out of the castle until she turns sixteen," says Tuy, appearing behind us out of nowhere.

"I like to read," Luna replies simply as both of them make some weird eye contact only to be broken by Sione jumping into our little huddle.

"Storms?"

"Right now, we are on a beach belonging to St. Royal, who we share a treaty with allowing us to pass through their region freely. However, we are not going to St. Royal, the city you see past the giant seashell wall. We are heading toward Antenetta, the city through the tunnel in front of us. We need to get to the dock in time to get a Wing Runner."

Tuy has completely confused Sione and me, and the realization makes him throw up his arms in anger. "Were you two not listening when I briefed you?"

Our heads fall in unison, as nobody ever really listens to Tuy's drawn-out hero monologues.

"Well, now we know, so lead the way," Sione playfully pokes, and I agree skipping hand in hand with him toward the tunnel.

"Wait!" Tuy yells. "Antenetta is not an easy place to enter. If you knew what was ahead of you, you wouldn't be skipping like you're about to walk into a city of rainbows and flowers. Come on, guys, don't tell me you know nothing about the mainland."

There is a long pause as Sione and I stare at each other. We both look back at Tuy and simultaneously shrug our shoulders and throw our hands in the air to illustrate our lack of knowledge.

Truthfully, I never have been one interested in the outside world. I figured I would just live a peaceful, boring life. Have a family and maybe even raise a dog. However, though I didn't know it at that time, the moment I had stepped on that beach I stepped into my destiny.

I should have turned around.

"That's cute." Tuy smirks at us. "Well, Luna, it looks like it's going to be a long trip. We don't only have to watch our own heads but we have to watch these guys as well." Sione and I scoff at his remark. "Okay, men and a little lady, how about we get this show on the road? All the things you don't know about the mainland you can find out on the way." We groan at Tuy's statement as we drag our feet along the sandy beach.

Once we pass through the five mile long tunnel of rocks, it is just as Tuy said, shocking. The sky is full of storm clouds. No vegetation grows as the ground is black, almost burnt, and for as far as the eye can see there sparks a parade of lightning bolts, though no rain. "Tuy, what is this place?" I ask.

"Antenetta, the land of the Eternal Storm."

"Eternal, as in forever?" asks Sione.

"Yes."

"How do people live here? Because I'm pretty sure building a house in a storm of lightning isn't exactly safe," I say in a shocked tone.

Tuy shakes his head. "They live underground, idiots. We are at the border; the city is farther in. What have I told you about only trusting your eyes?"

"Sorry," we mutter.

"Yeah, yeah, yeah. Come on, we don't want to miss out on getting a Wing Runner."

Sione and I look at each other with an uneasy feeling at the bottoms of our stomachs waddling behind Tuy like two helpless children.

Finally, we come across a small house and a wooden dock on a strip of grass facing the plains, miraculously untouched by the lightning. Upon the dock are what appear to be floating plastic bubbles with seats and some type of projected electronic map. The bubbles are attached to a machine with three dual exhausts at the back that resemble angel wings. Then on those exhausts, a ten-foot metal rod sticks straight up in the air. I can only guess what that's for. Once again my stomach feels queasy.

At the Wing Runner docking station, we are greeted by a redhead woman in a tight red spandex suit, a little too tight, so much that I cover Luna's eyes only to have her swat my hand away.

The woman notices this. "Think what you want, but when you work aboveground there's no 'taking chances' when it comes to being struck by lightning out on the Plains of Thunder. You should be worried about yourselves, traveling across the plains with those pieces of metal on your uniforms. You all are definitely on a suicide mission."

"Let me apologize. We are not from around here."

"Even so, it is a little too tight," Sione says under his breath, only to be greeted by Tuy's hand covering his mouth.

The woman looks us over one good time before rolling her eyes at our strange quartet. "Sorry, dears, we just closed. There's only one Wing Runner left and I need that to get home."

"We can't ride with you?" I ask.

"Nope. It's a solo."

"So, what are we supposed to do?"

"Go back to the beach. I sleep out there plenty of times when the storms get too bad."

Before I can come back with a reply, the redhead pulls off on her personal Wing Runner, the high powered wing shaped exhaust leaving behind a trail of grass particles.

"Well, that didn't go according to plan," Tuy says. "Okay, guys, let's try being nice to the people we meet on this journey. It will make our trip a lot smoother." He plops his butt on the grassy outskirts of Antenetta.

"We have to keep moving," says Luna in a small voice.

"Sorry, I think it would be impossible to travel across those plains by foot. If we get struck—"

"No, King, she is right. His highness probably knows his daughter is missing by now."

"Are you crazy, Tuy? We will die if we go out there!" Sione exclaims.

"Not necessarily. In the olden days of Antenetta, when the Eternal Storm had only been occurring for a month, the people still lived aboveground. In order to get around, the people enveloped themselves in plastic suits while holding giant conductors that reflected the lightning."

"So what you're saying is we have to wear those ugly spandex suits Red had on?"

"Yep. Funny how karma works. I'm pretty sure she has some extra ones in this dock house."

"What about our uniforms?" I ask.

"Leave it. Also, all metal, leave it, even our pots and pans." At Tuy's words, Sione makes an extremely sad face.

Inside the dock house, which is only slightly bigger than a coat closet, we're able to find spandex suits that will fit all of us. I even find a suit with a hood to hide the princess's identity.

"Okay, so what about this conductor?"

Tuy, smiling sadistically, pulls back an old brown cloth that was under a junk pile of scraps. "Simple. All the parts we need are right here."

"Dude, those look like old umbrellas," Sione says, with which I had to agree.

"True, but they are more than that. They are conductors. The metal top sucks in the electromagnetic energy, but spits it back out once it travels down the rod to the plastic handle, stopping electrocution of the body. The inside of the rod is actually some type of energy converter."

After Tuy's lecture he must feel the atmosphere of befuddlement, as he throws his nose up in the air and hastily hands us all conductors while letting out some groggy words under his breath. "Basically, just don't let go of the handle," Tuy finishes before turning and stepping out of the docking house. Of course, we follow.

As we stand at the edge of the plains, I make my way to Tuy's side. "Are you sure this is going to work?"

"It's been at least a hundred years since his method was used, but what choice do we have?"

For a good moment, I just stare into his eyes. I wonder why he agreed with the princess to carry on instead of setting up camp on the beach. I also wonder why he agreed so easily to her joining our journey. Why it always feels like he knows something I don't know, or that he always knows exactly what I'm thinking. But one thing I do know is that he and Luna are right, we have to keep moving.

The lightning storm is increasing in size and power; we had to move out quick before it becomes something Tuy called, a Bo, a storm so bad the entire plains are covered in lightning, blinding and killing anyone who walks through. We raise our conductors and step out onto the plains. "Remember the plan. No matter what, don't let go of the plastic handle. We head north and at the abandoned church, we make a sharp left and head to the crystal watchtower, and through there we will find the entrance to the city. Let's go!"

After Tuy's briefing and its concluding battle cry, we all split, zig-zagging in separate directions, except Luna who was being carried by Tuy, piggyback. I run for what seems like hours through harsh wind and blinding lighting. But though the storm feels like it will swallow me whole, at one moment I know I've run straight through its eye, it's so calm. I guess even eternal storms have their peaceful moments.

I continue on, unable to hear or see the others over the gaudy thunder and heavy rain, until I finally spot the Crystal Tower. The grand structure glistens and stands tall in spite of the harsh, eternal storm. As I move closer, we reform as a group and run in a diagonal line to the entrance.

"Made it," Sione says under his breath as we hug one another inside the tower's strong embrace.

Going in, we are greeted by two men in sleek black armor, made of some type of material I've never seen. "What is your purpose here?" asks one. I start to take out our passports, but Tuy speaks up as Luna makes strange faces by his side.

"My friend's daughter is sick and we seek help from Dr. Lisa." He rummages through his bag and holds up a forged letter, while Luna accompanies him with heavy panting and a slight cough.

The Border Patrol looks over the letter, then to Luna, then to me. "What's wrong with her?" he asks me. I tense up.

Where did these forged documents come from? And how are Tuy and Luna so in sync with their acting? I take a peek at Sione, who is sweating profusely. He shakes his head slightly as if to say he knows nothing about what is going on, either. I look over to Tuy, and now I know that two can play this game I have been playing. I compose myself and go along with their lie. "She has a nerve disease and only Dr. Lisa can help." Tuy hands me two more documents and I scan them over before saying, "here is a note from Dr. Carrington, and here are our passports."

The BPs give the document a look over and whisper among themselves. One of them suddenly shouts, "They have the Grand Patrol's highest seal, they are clear! Sorry, we didn't realize who you were. Please, this way," he says, leading us to the entrance of Antenetta.

We follow the BP down a tunnel-like stairwell, then to an elevator that takes us even farther underground, to a grand marble gate guarded by men with heavy artillery. "Right this way." As we enter, I'm taken aback. Beneath those lighting plains is an entire civilization. Before my eyes are skyscrapers and even a high-speed monorail, with cars that don't emit exhaust, but some type of blue dust. People from all walks of life parade in the streets, shopping, laughing, eating, and just living. One would think because they're underground their country would be underdeveloped, but it is far from that.

"Isn't she a beauty? The port town of Antenetta," says the BP walking us to a sleek black car.

"Port town?" I ask.

"Yep, and it's exactly as you think. This is the town all the ships from across the nation arrive at, at least once. Right through the underwater valve. I figured you knew, since you all have Level 0 clearance."

I look to my left, and I see three large valves with an enormous amount of water rushing out of them. I can't see where the water goes, but the hole is big enough for ships to pass through. I let out a nervous sigh. "Of course. Sometimes my geography gets mixed up. I thought it was the town farther down that had the underwater valve. Such…such an amazing technology," I stutter, trying to cover my slip of the tongue and wrap my head around what an "underwater valve" is.

"It happens to the best of us."

"I guess you all were surprised—" Sione starts, but is cut off by Tuy.

"Surprised that we came through the storm entrance without an announcement a week in advance."

"Nope, not really. A lot of your guys have been coming through off the record the past month."

"This town must suffer from an officer who has such loose lips," Luna says under her breath.

The BP stops in his tracks and looks to me. "What did she say?"

But I have no answer. Luna has put her act back on and starts to cry, asking for water.

"Sir, we don't have time for this. We need to get her to her appointment," Tuy says as he pushes past the guard and opens the door to the car waiting for us. I follow his lead, picking Luna up and placing her in the car. I turn to the BP and say "Thanks for everything," as I close the door. Sione and Tuy join us inside and our driver speeds off.

Once we lose sight of him, we let out a unanimous sigh, except for her highness.

"You guys, what did I say? In order for smooth travels, let's try being nice to those who are helping us. That even goes for you, princess." She responds to Tuy's comment by rolling her eyes.

"So where are we going?" asks Sione.

"To see Dr. Lisa."

"Um, why are we actually going to see a Dr. Lisa?"

"Because she is my sister." Tuy doesn't even bat an eyelash as he makes his startling revelation.

I grow hot because, once again, he's been keeping something from us. "For this mission to run smoothly, you can't keep—"

But before I can finish my sentence, the cab comes to a stop and he gets out with the others, completely ignoring me.

A beautiful, slender young woman with thick dirty blonde hair and brown eyes is waiting for us. "Well, well, well, I'm surprised to see you back here so soon."

"I told you I was going to start visiting more often."

"What is it?"

For a moment Tuy and Dr. Lisa have a staring contest, which Tuy loses as he sweeps off the princess's hood, revealing her identity.

"Yep! This has to be the stupidest thing you have done in your whole life. Please tell me she's been authorized to be here with you."

"Let's just say yes."

Dr. Lisa lets out a stressed groan, tilting her head for us to follow her inside. She leads us up a staircase to a sunroom filled with trinkets and plants. There are even lights on the outside of the windows that shine inside, creating artificial sunlight. We crowd around a window seat while Dr. Lisa serves us some warm jasmine tea. "So, whose bright idea was it to kidnap the princess?"

"Oh no, we didn't kidnap her. She sort of just tagged along," I say.

"Well, if that's the story we're going with—"

"Not a story, she did tag along."

She clicks her tongue at my response. "Okay! No need to get your feathers in a bunch. You're a fiery young man, I see."

"Who, King? Please, he is scared of his own shadow," Sione says. I cut my eyes at him.

Tuy waves his arms in the air, trying to get back some control. "Alright, guys, let's calm down." We all finally do, but no one dares to make eye contact, for our emotions are running high.

"I wasn't kidnapped," says Luna.

"So why did you run away?"

"Because she told me to."

I peer at her from behind the others and shake my head slightly, warning her not to reveal our small adventure in the woods.

"She?"

"It's not important. I just felt like I had to come on this journey after I found out King and I shared something in common."

"Very well, but do you understand how much trouble you are putting these young men in? You should return home before anybody finds out you left your region. Then again, I guess it's too late. Once you passed into our land, your father would have been notified."

We all put our heads down awkwardly as Dr. Lisa thinks, and then it hits her. "Wait a minute—how in the world did you cross the border with the princess? And nobody was alarmed? What is going on here?"

"Calm down, sister. We have this under control," Tuy says.

The room grows silent again and now is my chance. "Actually, I would like to know as well. The general gave me, Sione, Sidney, and you passports. Where did you get this 'grand seal' from?"

"The general and I talked about it earlier when you two weren't around," says Tuy, avoiding eye contact.

"When? We have been together this whole time," Sione chimes in.

"I can see a lot of black auras in this room," Dr. Lisa says. "Black is the color of secrets. We all have secrets, but too many can tear us apart and those around us. You all have a long journey ahead, so I think it would be wise to clear the air, on the important stuff at least. Little brother, I think you should go first."

Tuy still looks down, causing her to prompt, "You are the leader, are you not?"

Feeling a pinch to his pride, I guess, he finally raises his head and walks toward a window that overlooks the futuristic skyline. "While King was fighting with Sidney, Luna started to cry on our way to the monorail station, as she had hurt her arm earlier, when you dropped her. I told Sione to go to a stream and fetch some water. By the way the princess held her arm I could tell she hadn't broken it, just pulled the muscle, and some cool spring water would calm it down."

*"Calm down, princess. Once Sione is back we can put a wet
cloth brace around it. I have a unique oil known as spirit oil
with me as well, so it should heal within a couple of hours."*
"Thank you."
Tuy looks in his emergency bag for a thick cloth that can go around her arm.
"I have a wrap in my bag."
"It's okay, your highness. I have one in the medical kit."
A giant smile breaks on her face. "But mine's pink."
*Tuy just chuckles at Luna's unusual cuteness as he opens her
bag. As he searches it, his movements become slower.*
"You know, princess, you have a lot of interesting things in here."
"I figure better safe than sorry."

"She continued to stare at me with glassy-looking eyes—"
"Her eyes were glassy?" I ask.
"Yeah, probably from her crying earlier. Can I finish my story?"
"Sure, sorry," I mutter, knowing her glassiness
had nothing to do with tears.

*"You know, Luna, I realized from the moment you barged into your
father's study that you were a smart girl, so I won't beat around the
bush. Why do you have a fake ID and forged passport documents
with the highest level of clearance in your backpack? And how?"*
"Well, how else do you expect for me to cross the borders?"
"You really planned to tag along, huh?"
"Yep! I knew King would let me come since we share a connection."
"The dream?"
*"Something like that. I made fake IDs for you all as well. I figured once
we get to Antenetta, we can change our identities to match them."*

"At this point, I tried to bait the princess. This little girl is smarter than
we all think. I asked her..."

"Well, won't we be detected at Antenetta?"

"And you won't believe how this peaceful, sheltered child answered me."

"You and I both know that the BPs at the storm entrance of Antenetta wear night vision goggles, so they only see heat signatures, not faces."

"You came up with this plan all by yourself, Princess?" Sione asks, and seems flabbergasted when she responds with a smirk and a nonchalant, "Yeah." He moves closer to me and starts to whisper, but Dr. Lisa swats him in the head with a paper fan and shakes her finger.

"Right now, we are sharing secrets, not creating more."

Sione monitors the room, twiddling his fingers, before blurting out, "What are you?"

Luna's eyes grow large before she gives him the biggest diva hair flip of his life and bursts out laughing. All I can do is put my hand to my head, as the others have started to raise their eyebrows at Luna.

"King, don't you think it is time you share your secrets?" I wonder how Tuy's sister knows. Maybe she can see the burden of not only my secrets but the secrets of others I've forced myself to carry. Sweat breaks out on my forehead. I can't keep going on like this, but at the same time, I couldn't possibly tell them everything.

"Well, I guess I should start with the story about the emperor, don't you think, Tuy?" He nods. "Sione, actually, we lied to you and Sidney."

Sione jerks from his seat and goes to a purple couch. He throws his hands in the air before plopping down and kicking his legs straight out. "Lay it on me, man, but let me get comfortable because I feel like this little session is going to be really interesting."

I smile nervously, not knowing how he will react. Will he feel like he wasn't important enough to know the truth? Most importantly, what will happen to our friendship?

Reluctantly, keeping my gaze at the window, I explain my vision of the island splitting in two, what really happened in the castle, and that the real enemy is this Dark King. I press both my index fingers to my temples. The sweat on my forehead is practically pouring out now. Yet, on the flip side, I finally feel light as a feather after spilling out all of the weight that's been holding me down—well, most of it. Dr. Lisa did say some secrets are meant to be kept. Therefore, I'm taking my visions in the Neuro Center to the grave and protecting the princess's secret as well.

Sione still hasn't said a word and I figure I have to face him. I whisper his name under my breath, only to hear the door slam behind me and angry footsteps going downstairs and out the front door. I exhale deeply and a slender arm comes around my shoulder, along with the tickle of strands of hair on my forearm. "Don't feel bad. You hid those things from him because you thought it was for the best."

"Yeah, but why do I feel so bad?"

Suddenly she is so close I feel the warmth from the jasmine tea lingering on her breath. "Well, at least you got it out in the open. Now you all can work on healing."

I drop my head and try to go after Sione, but Dr. Lisa stops me. "Stay here a while to give him a chance to cool off. Luna, you can come with me if you like, and while we're out we can find you some proper clothes." She chuckles, facing me and Tuy. "All of you."

I blush and politely cross my hands in front of me, remembering we're all still in our skin-tight suits. Dr. Lisa smiles even wider as she throws me a wink and leaves with Luna.

For a moment, Tuy and I remain silent, neither of us having the nerve to speak first. This is the most we've probably kept from each other our entire friendship. I want to muster up the courage to break the silence, seeing as we both were wrong, but unfortunately, that is the one thing I lack: courage.

I inhale the scent of the lavender flowers growing in the room's small gardens. I manage to pull my shoulders back and puff out my chest, but Tuy has left the window and is starting to head out the door. "Wait a minute!" I shout in a harsher tone than I was going for.

"What?" Tuy snaps back. His coldness causes me to hesitate.

Yet, I extend my hand in order to call a truce. "I think we need... Umm... I'm sorry."

Tuy gives me a once-over before scoffing and slapping my hand away. I didn't think a couple white lies—okay, big lies—that I pushed him to expose would tear apart our ten years of friendship. Like the punk I am, I feel tears well up in my eyes, only to be pulled into Tuy's embrace. I am taken aback, for Tuy is the hero type and rarely shows his soft side. I look Tuy straight in his face and he meets my gaze, tilting his head to the side with a smile. Suddenly we burst out in laughter.

"This is awkward," I say.

"I agree."

"Sooo, can we stop having our little bromance right now?" My question causes Tuy to scrunch up his mouth and free me from his embrace. He crosses his arms and tilts his perfectly chiseled jaw in the air, scowling. "Don't talk like that."

I chuckle, knowing he is back into warrior mode. "I don't know why you are so scared to show a softer side of yourself."

"It's not that I'm afraid." He pauses for a second. "It's a weakness."

"We all have some type of weaknesses, that's what makes us human. But believe me, showing compassion is not a weakness, and even if it was, that wouldn't be yours."

Tuy stares at me with confusion.

"It's not important, you'll figure it out eventually."

Not liking my answer, he just rolls his eyes at me. "Did you really tell me all of your secrets?"

"Honestly, no."

"King?" Tuy furrows his brow.

"There are some things I can't tell you—anybody, for that matter."

The room grows silent again, and Tuy doesn't move for a minute until finally telling me that he understands. "But there is one secret I do need to know if we are to continue on this journey together."

I fall back on my heels at his sternness. "What?" I cautiously ask.

"What is going on with the princess?"

I start to mumble and try and come up with an excuse. "What do you mean? She seems perfectly fine to me."

Tuy grabs me by my collar and pulls me so close that our noses touch. I gulp deeply. "Fine, but only if you tell me more about this Dark King."

Tuy scoffs once again as he roughly lets go of me. He begins to pace around the room and grabs his head; then he just stops and his arms fall beside him. "Alright. I guess a secret for a secret. But King, know that after I tell you, you won't be the same."

I probably shouldn't pursue the issue further but I can't help but wonder. "It's fine. My secret will outweigh yours," I say, thinking of the goddess, but Tuy only says, "I sure hope not. Let us sit down. It's a long story."

When he turns to me, his eyes are red, and his face has grown long and lost some of its color. As I sit, Tuy grabs a blanket and hands it to me while patting my shoulder and sinking into the couch next to me, so deep that I can see the weight of the story he is about to tell. Dr. Lisa did say that some secrets are meant to be kept.

— VI —

THE DARK KING

"Okay, King, I know you don't know much about the mainland, but tell me you at least know the regions' and cities' names?" By Tuy's expression, he's hoping I can at least save an ounce of my dignity.

"I know all the regions—Trinity, Antenetta, Road of Bones, St. Royal, our Peace Island, and that one nobody talks about, Ren—but not all the cities."

Tuy's eyes light up. "Well, thank God you know all the regions, and nobody knows all the cities, so we are off to a good start." From there, his story begins:

"You mentioned Ren. No one ever told us why we don't talk about Ren, nor did our teachers go into detail about this region. The reason for this is, Ren is the region the Dark King used to rule over, or still might if he is still alive, which we are hoping he is not."

"Does anyone live there?"

Tuy shakes his head. "Nobody knows because once the region was labeled a dictatorship by the emperor, a giant wall was mysteriously erected, cutting off any contact. But not just any kind of wall—this wall was not made of brick and mortar but spirit energy."

"Spirit energy, really?" I question Tuy with a look of disbelief as he describes things that only appear in children's novels.

"King, I already told you when we started this journey that we are going to encounter some weird phenomena. Peace Island tries to keep the weird out or to a minimum so our people aren't frightened. For example, look at the Fera incident. We were told they were simple honeybees and of course, being simple island folk, we believed it. For the small time during my youth when I was travelling through the regions with my sister, I experienced all types of people, cultures, and the unbelievable. Kasai is so beyond strange, King, that you have no idea. Weren't you shocked about the boats travelling from the sea to underground and through a valve that lets out through the top of a rock wall?"

"The 'Ship Valve' is only a technological advancement. Maybe the royals haven't adopted it yet because they are afraid of the negative change it could bring to Peace Island."

Tuy shakes his head and continues his story. "The fact of the matter is that spirit energy isn't something new; it can be seen everywhere and has been around for millions of years, even on Peace Island. When we saw spirit energy as children, we were told it was nothing more than lightning bugs and to look away, which in turn made us stop believing and unable to see it. In your vison, you said that your body became encased in ligh—"

"Spirit energy?" I exclaim, cutting off Tuy.

"Yes, but not just any spirit energy. The real reason your vision was such a threat was because the energy surrounding you was bright white. Common pure spirit energies are actually dark yellow, like lightning bugs, or pale pink."

"Like the goddess's eyes," I mumble under my breath.

"Who?"

"Uh, nobody for now."

"Anyway, very few people can embody spirit energy, especially pure white spirit energy. Two of those who can are important to our story…" For a moment Tuy pauses, seeming to contemplate something heavy.

"Did you forget who they were?" I laugh.

"Well, the first person is the Dark King."

My eyes grow wide and I sink like him into the sofa, my smile fading. I try to form a word or sentence, but before I can, Tuy puts both his hands on my shoulders and squeezes them tightly. I squeeze my eyes shut, afraid of the secrets he will tell me next. "I'm sorry to say this, but one day I caught the second person using hers. She made me promise to never tell you. It was your mother King."

I slap Tuy's hands from my shoulders and jump up from the couch. "I don't want to hear any more of this story. I never should have asked, heck! I never should have told anyone of my vision. Then I never would have had to go on this journey." I run for the door, but Tuy wraps his arms around me. I try to break free from his embrace but it is no good.

"King, please listen to me. You have to hear this."

I continue to try to break free. I keep my eyes squeezed shut, hoping to black out this world around me. I want to be back on Peace Island!

I think of the day my mother's spirit visited me, the day before our journey started. Then I remember a memory I should have forgotten: the moon and sun emblem necklace she wore in the picture on my bookshelf. The shock of seeing my mother made me forget all about it that day. Now that I think about it, in history class when they taught us the six major regions, Ren was always represented by the moon and sun.

The spinning of my head causes me to stop flailing around, Tuy loosens his grip, and regaining some composure, I turn to him and whisper, "My mother had a necklace with the emblem for Ren. I wonder if her and the king were…"

"King, stop. I understand why you might think that. For many people are more accepting of the other pure energies because those with pure white energy could be seen as in allegiance with the Dark King. That's the whole reason we're on this mission. But, I've always thought differently. Just because your mother had white spirit energy and might be from Ren doesn't mean she was close to the Dark King. Spirit energy is not always a genetic trait, it's a gift from God that has no favorites or hierarchy. Also, you look nothing like him."

"Who? The Dark King, you've seen him? How?"

"Once, when I was a child. As to how and where? Well, let's just say that's my secret to keep." I look at Tuy suspiciously, but he smiles and says, "Nothing bad, just a memory."

I push him to the side with my shoulder and find my way back to the sofa. After a moment. I ask him to start the story again.

"Are you sure?"

"Yes, please. There is no going back now."

"Okay, where was I? This spirit energy that you three have is especially special because you can control it with your will. They say those with white and pink energy have strong hearts. That's what made The Dark King so powerful."

I raise my hand. "Dark King, Dark King, that's all we have been saying this whole journey. Does this Dark King have a name?"

"Oh, guess I should have led with that. It's Ren. The same as the region's, which is why no one mentions the region and we are taught to recognize it only by the emblem of the moon and sun."

"I see," I say, dispirited.

Tuy exhales deeply. "Cheer up, King. Everyone from Ren isn't evil. You know your mother is a good person."

"I guess so. Please continue," I say emotionlessly.

Tuy gives me another look of concern but continues the story. "There may be more people with white spirit energy, but not everybody can control it. Ren was exceptionally great at this, which led to him rising in power, so much that they named the region after him, Ren. The region used to be called Zara, meaning 'queen'."

"Basically, Trinity was the king and Zara was the queen?" I question.

"Very good, young grasshopper. Trinity saw Zara as its right-handed region, literally, being as it sits to its right. So, after the name change Trinity became furious and started to cry about treason and brotherhood, but that comes later."

"There can only be one sun in the sky," I say more melodramatically then I intended, looking out the window at the futuristic skyline.

"What is that supposed to mean?"

"Vaguely, it means there cannot be two ruling kings—which reminds me why I hate my name."

"I thought you got pass that? Just let the past be the past, King." Tuy pats my back, but it still doesn't stop me from thinking about the bullies of my childhood, and then I start to assume the worst.

"But what if Ren really is my father and my mother named me King to infuriate Trinity even more?" I grab my chest.

Tuy shakes his head again and removes his hand from my back. Placing his on mine, he speaks in a low voice. "Maybe. But you're forgetting one important piece of information. Trinity does not have kings because that is where the emperor lives. If she had named you Emperor, maybe. The only person who could have felt some type of way is King Vernon, and he didn't seem too upset when he mentioned it in his study. Nice try, but no. Now, can I please finish this story?"

I smile at Tuy's comforting words and nod for him to continue.

"With no interruptions!" he adds.

"Yeah, yeah, yeah, I understand."

"Thank you," Tuy says as he pulls at the collar of his spandex suit. Mine is also starting to become too close-fitting. A lot of things right now feel like they are wrapping their hands around my neck and squeezing it too tight. "So, when Ren came into power, at first he was a very good king. He was actually in line to become the next emperor, if need be. He was compassionate toward his citizens and gave them all of his time. He rarely wore royal garb. He was always the life of the party when all the regions met annually. But one day in about the eleventh year of his reign, people around him noticed that he had begun to change, and not just mentally but physically."

"Physically?"

"They say he used to walk through the palace, always spreading joy, but abruptly one day he became lifeless and cold. He wouldn't say a word as he walked the palace halls day in and day out. People claimed they could sometimes see a dark aura surrounding him. The king's face started to grow hollow. His bright eyes became encased in large, dark circles and his bright skin had become pale and dull. He no longer smiled or walked among his people. He would lock himself in his study for days. But what people mainly talk about—"

"Boy, these people sure do talk a lot," I say, cutting in with a sarcastic snicker. Tuy replies by raising his eyebrow. Truthfully, his story is starting to get a little frightening, but he continues. "Anyway, the main thing that changed was his eyes. One important thing to note about Ren is that his eyes were a beautiful grey color, a color most people in Kasai don't have. Now, don't freak out, coward, but the legend says that at night they turned red as a blood moon, and before you could scream for help, he would descend from the trees and suck the souls out of his citizens!" Tuy yells the last words in a booming voice, causing me to scream at a high pitch no man should reach.

I jump up and fall behind the couch. I reach back over quickly and grab a blanket to cover my head as I wait for the story to be over, only to hear a loud thud on the other side and Tuy laughing. I peek from under my blanket and over the couch and see that he is laughing so hard that he fell. He pulls himself together and says, "Just kidding," before throwing his head back and laughing some more, like a crazy man.

He always manages to make a fool of me, but not this time. I jump over the couch and put him in a choke hold. "That was not funny!"

"I beg to differ! If you could have only seen your face."

"That's why my father can't live, because people keep making up evil stories about him!"

Tuy becomes still underneath me. "What did you say?"

"I said—" I stop as I have to think upon what I said. Tuy is giving me a look of disapproval. I quickly get off of him and exit the room to run downstairs. But before I can enter the embrace of Antenetta's streets, Tuy catches my arm.

"King."

At the simple utterance of my name, all my words spill out. "I don't even know where that came from. Maybe because I never knew my father. So hearing that he shared the same energy as my mother made me hopeful, no matter how evil he is."

"You know, I never knew my father either. However, this is not a man you want to imagine as your father. Now, promise me that if, on this journey, you find out he is your father, which I highly doubt, you will run far away from that truth. If Ren is your father, bury that truth deep in your heart and let no one know, for your sake and your future's sake."

I nod my head and wipe the tears from my eyes as I realize how foolish I was. I wanted a father so much that I even wished for him to be Kasai's most hated man.

A little while later, the gang all arrive back from the store with some fresh food and clothes. Sione, Tuy, and I go upstairs to change out of our spandex suits, but the awkwardness of spilling our secrets is still in the air, and none of us makes conversation.

"Alright, guys, the food is ready; you can come downstairs!" calls Dr. Lisa.

We run downstairs like wild beasts, being as the last time we ate was about a day ago. At the bottom of the stairs, I stop in my tracks and my mouth drops open. Luna twirls around in a puffy white lace dress with black shoes and a flower crown. She looks up to me and smiles as the whole world around her shines and I smile back at her. "Wow. I guess everyone was right when they said Peace Island had the most beautiful princess in Kasai."

Sione and Tuy let out jolly laughs and nod their heads. "Thank you," says the princess, blushing slightly and bowing her head. The others move toward the food, but I can't take my eyes from the princess. I feel bad, because I know she is not the princess. She raises her head and of course her eyes flicker with a glow of pink.

I kneel down and move closer to her. "Hello, goddess."

She replies to my whisper with "Hello," in a deeper tone, then runs off and cutely asks Dr. Lisa to fix her plate. And that's when I start to wonder: why is it that when the goddess takes over, Luna becomes childlike, but when Luna is herself she is cold and distant? That poor child; I still don't know if I quite trust this goddess. Something just doesn't seem right, and maybe Peace Island isn't the only thing that needs saving.

"Aren't you hungry, King?" asks Dr. Lisa, breaking me from my thoughts.

"Yeah. I was just thinking about something."

"Whether I'm a good cook or not?" Dr. Lisa acts as if she will throw her serving spoon at me and I frantically wave my hands, causing everyone to laugh.

I finally get my food and sit at the table in the dining area, which is also covered with plants and has bright yellow walls and furniture made to look like tree trunks.

"You must really like nature," I state.

"Truthfully, I hate it. It's just that I've lived underground for so long I can't help but collect shrubbery when it becomes available, in fear that I'll forget what the outside world looks like."

"You hate it here?" I ask.

"No. But just sometimes, constantly hearing the turning of gears and looking at artificial sunlight gets old, or should I say, fake," she says with a smile.

"You should join us—" Luna starts.

I quickly pinch her side, as I know it is the goddess talking. She returns my attack with an evil glowing pink stare, and I pinch her again, while adverting the others attention. Thankfully, she cuts the theatrics.

"That's very sweet of you, princess, but I have been on many journeys before. I think I will have to sit this one out."

"Yeah, sis, you might want to sit this one out. It's my time now!" Tuy announces heroically, causing Dr. Lisa to roll her eyes and say, "I really don't know how you two put up with this one." Sione and I laugh and make eye contact for the first time after our fight.

He quickly lowers his head, but instead of cursing me under his breath, he continues to smile. "We just do. These two idiots can be hard to deal with, but they are like my brothers, and no matter what, we are all in this together. To Peace Island!" Sione toasts, and we all repeat back, "May she shine bright as the sun and stay beautiful as golden sunflowers!" laughing and smiling together.

— VII —

THE ROAD OF BONES

"Princess, I have to admit that dress on you is divine. But I don't think it's very practical for this journey," says Sione as he poses like a star tailor of Peace Island, his right hand on his hip and jelly bomb twirling in the place of a tape measure in his left hand.

The princess spins around one last time before saying, "I know. I just wanted to feel like a princess for one more day."

"You will always be the Princess, Luna, no matter what happens on this journey. Just think of us as your humble guards." He removes his hat and tries to bow deeply, but his thick stomach gets in the way, causing the princess to giggle. Sione smiles and moves to the other side of the stairs. "Now, run along and change into the uniform Dr. Lisa has prepared for us. We will be leaving soon."

"You know, you're really good with children," Tuy says from the kitchen.

"Thanks. I thought I was losing my touch because that poor child used to never smile when I made a joke before."

Tuy suddenly runs from the kitchen in such haste that he startles Sione, knocking him on his back. "Ow! What is wrong with you?"

"I forgot," says Tuy to himself, not paying any attention to Sione. "King was supposed to tell me what is really up with the princess."

"What do you mean?"

"You just said it yourself, she is like night and day."

"True. But she's just a kid. They can get like that sometimes."

"No, there is more to it."

"Well, let's go find out before we leave. Your sister did say we have to clear the air—all of it."

"I agree," says Tuy as he and Sione head for where I have been eavesdropping on their conversation. I try to find a place to hide on the terrace, running around frantically until they are right next to the door. I stumble on the edge of the coffee table and fall over. They pull on the glass door, but I lunge for the handle and pull it back closed.

Tuy mouths through the glass, "We had a deal."

I shake my head, "Liar."

"I only lied about the last part!"

Sione looks at Tuy and then to me as he throws his arms up in the air. "Come on, guys, we had a deal. No more secrets!"

I exhale sharply as I loosen my grip on the door, allowing them to come out. I nod my head to Tuy, who nods back at me, and we sit Sione down and tell him the story of the Dark King.

"Wow, what a weird story. How could a person that was so good change so much?" he asks.

"I don't know. Maybe therein lies the answer to King's vision," says Tuy.

"Maybe," I say.

"But wait, Tuy. You never said how powerful he was, far as spirit energy."

"Well, I'm not really sure. But he could wield it to his own devices. They say he could make this strong sword full of spirit energy, so thick that it looked like real metal, and it could split anything in two…" Tuy slowly stops speaking.

We look at each other for a moment, but quickly shake our heads. "Nahhh!" we exclaim in unison.

"There is no way that is what cuts our island in two… right?" Sione gulps.

"Well, I sure hope not," I say.

"If it is true, we will just have to fight spirit energy with spirit energy." Tuy winks at me.

"What?" I cry out.

"Well, you did say you were encased in it."

"But I've never done it before or even seen spirit energy."

"That doesn't mean you can't do it. We just have to find a way to awaken it."

"Do you think that's a good idea?" asks Sione.

"What do you mean by that?" I exclaim, slightly offended.

"Well, Tuy said that white spirit energy is the strongest and only few people control it. What if it brings bad luck or takes over the host? He did say the Dark King started to change."

"I doubt it was because of spirit energy. He already had controlled it for many years before his fall. Truthfully, I just think the guy became corrupt with power. But if white spirit energy does have negative side effects, King has us to keep him straight. And Sione, King has a very strong mind and a good heart. There is no way he would turn his back on us."

"Thank you, Tuy!" I say as I poke out my chest and cut my eyes at Sione, who just gives me a stupid grin. But I also can't help but wonder what if. Since neither of them knows about my second dream, of course they trust my will. Maybe those two different dreams represent two choices. Maybe in the end my newfound power will try to corrupt me and I'll have to make the age-old decision between good and evil. If that be the case, why should I awaken it?

"You know, I don't think we should do this." I blurt out.

"I agree!" Sione shouts quickly.

"Come on, you two cowards. King, you have to trust in yourself more," Tuy says with a serious look on his face.

"I do, but people make mistakes."

"Yes, they do. But people also can do good."

"I'm scared. What if—"

"King, just think on it. I won't make you do anything you don't want to do, but don't you think it is better to be not faced with opposition and ready than to be faced with opposition and not ready at all? Just think upon it, okay?"

"Okay," I whisper unwillingly.

"Good. Now, they say there is a man who lives in a shack on the side of the Road of Bones who is very keen with the spirit energies."

"You know, I really have to meet this 'they' and 'people,'" I say.

"A shack on the side of the road?" Sione blurts out. We look at him judgmentally as he smiles and waves one hand in the air. "Sorry. That's right, treat everyone nicely."

"You forgot what happened with Red?" Tuy teases, raising one eyebrow.

"Oh, please don't remind me about Angela." Sione rolls his eyes.

"Angela?" I ask suspiciously.

"Do you know we ran into her at the market? She laughed at my getup and called it karma as she proceeded to chase me with this strange Antenetta fruit that looked like it had the face of an old man inside of it. You should have seen it. I was humiliated," he says, hiding his face in shame.

Tuy starts to laugh really hard and I know it's my time to escape while they are preoccupied. I start to tip-toe from the terrace back into the house. "Stop!" they yell simultaneously.

I lower my head and shuffle back to plop down on a metal chair. "Fine! I'll tell you what is up with the princess, but know this: it is creepy, spooky, and you might just pee your pants." Making ghost sounds, I flail my arms in the air but stop as Sione and Tuy look at me like I'm crazy. "Whatever, old man fruit," I say, poking Sione's belly.

"Not funny. Now hurry up with the story, man!"

Reluctantly, I begin to tell the truth about the princess. I tell them of how when I went looking for her, we fell into the swamp and I met the 'scantily clad woman.' I then slowly tell them how I learned that this woman was a goddess living inside of Luna. I even tell them about how my mother's spirit visited me and that her visit motivated me to allow Luna on this trip. As I end my story, surprisingly both of them look…normal. "Um, are you two in shock?'

"Nope," they say simultaneously.

"Now how much more can we learn about this scantily clad…goddess?" Tuy asks as he strokes his beard.

I punch his shoulder. "This is serious, because I haven't really decided if the goddess is good or bad. Think about it, when the goddess is in control she is joyful, but when Luna is herself she is cold."

"Well, she is more than likely good. If your mother told you to look for her, then she is probably important for this journey," says Sione.

"But my mother was from Ren. How do we know if this woman is not only from Ren as well, but even worse, a spy?"

"You are forgetting she is not a woman but a goddess. Goddesses do not exist in our world," says Tuy. Both of us once again stare him down.

"This guy really knows too much," Sione says.

"Yeah," I say. "It makes you wonder: how *do* you know so much?"

"Secret!" Tuy winks.

"That's what we are trying to eliminate!" yells Sione.

"My sister said we all could have one, and that's not important for the mission, it really just pertains to how I was brought up! You all still have some of your secrets, don't you?"

Being as we all do still have our personal secrets, we digress, and just in the nick of time as the princess and Dr. Lisa walk out onto the terrace. I quickly whisper to the others not to say a word to Luna about her secret, and they both give me a look back as to say "Obviously."

However, Tuy moves toward me and murmurs in my ear, "But there is one thing you should try to do: find out the goddess's name. Then we will be able to tell if she is good or bad. In Trinity, there is a library with information on goddesses. We'll just keep an eye on her until then." I nod my head so slightly that only Tuy can see, and we wink toward Sione, letting him know we will fill him in later.

"Alright, boys, enough chit-chatting. We need to be at the dock by twelve," says Dr. Lisa. We hurriedly finish getting ready, adjusting our new sleek royal blue uniformed suits. I run my hands over the contrasting gold colored fabric that lays diagonally along my chest and carefully trace my fingers along what appears to be mini circular screens, projecting army medals. I tap one and it starts to change from medal to medal a little quicker. I watch intensively and realize that they match the tangible medals that are on my formal soldier uniform. As I stare at them, I start to feel giddy.

While the others continue to get ready, I decide to look through the backpack Dr. Lisa has prepared for me. The top layer is full of medical supplies and a thermos, probably filled with some of her yummy jasmine tea. I open it to check and the sweet, simple smell of jasmine entices my nostrils. Dr. Lisa comes to me and asks, "Having fun?"

I nod and we both smile at one another.

Dr. Lisa watches, smiling from ear to ear, as I continue to dig into my bag which feels like a bottomless pit, until she takes my hand and tells me that if I go through all the contents it will take all day. She raises me to my feet and taps the first electronic medal on my uniform, causing a list of all the supplies, quantity level, and their functions to appear on my left sleeve. I gasp, as I have never seen anything like this before. I can tell that it's some type of hologram, but I am more fascinated with how. Dr. Lisa, still smiling, just gives me a thumbs-up, which I return with an awkward grin. She pats me on the shoulder before going around the room getting, everyone else situated into their new technology-infused uniforms.

After a few more glances at the strange writings on my sleeve, I just shake my head and tap the top medal, causing the list to disappear as I swing my backpack of goodies over my shoulder. I hook the top of the bag to the golden triangular flap on my shoulders and connect the bottom to the thin gold colored v-shaped belt around my waist, securing it in place.

Once everyone is finally finished getting ready, we all pile into Dr. Lisa's car and head for the docks at the end of town. As we get closer, I can't help but wonder how the "ship thing" works. I mean, it's a ship going up the side of a stone wall into a giant water valve. What is the ship holding on to? Wouldn't it just flip over on its own weight, and how is it able to travel upward at all? I look toward the dock so hard my brows become deeply furrowed. Then Dr. Lisa lets out a low grunt. I see her staring at me in the rearview mirror. "Interesting, isn't it?"

"Yeah..." I pause, afraid of sounding like an idiot in front of her, but my curiosity gets the better of me. "So how does all of it work?"

"Well, King, it's quite simple. About fifteen years ago, the citizens of Antenetta were constantly complaining about the high cost of food and goods. Traders had to travel by Wing Runners and bring back goods in small quantities at a time, laborious and tedious work. Antenetta's growing population was in danger of going hungry. To fix the problem, the city installed electromagnetic plates throughout its walls, which is why you see the yellow caution signs as we get closer to them. Anyway, currents are pumped through those plates using the energy from the storms above. Since the storms are freakishly strong, the metal plates receive a supercharged magnetic ability. The ships themselves also have electromagnetic plates on the bottom, which keeps them from falling over under their own weight. When they reach the entrance, they attach to a track that runs through the valves. At a checkpoint about five minutes in, all the water is drained out, making it more like a ride on a locomotive. Now, for where you all are going; you will be on the second valve track for a good hour and a half. At the end, the ship will be connected to another electromagnetic plate that lifts it like an elevator to the surface dock. The dock is a round metal door that drains out the water and pushing the ship to the surface, and then you are finally above sea and officially sailing on the Western Sea."

After Dr. Lisa's long explanation, we're dumbfounded, except for Tuy. We simple islanders know nothing of electro-mag-whose-a-whatsits. All I see on a usual basis are steam engines and sailboats. One giant ship comes around ever year and practically the whole town comes out to see it in all its wonder. Come to think of it, this car we're riding in is also a wonder. The number of people who own cars on Peace Island can be counted on my hands, and they don't look like this. Shiny chrome outside with giant silver rims and the inside full of flashing lights, numbers, knobs, and even music! The fanciest thing we have are Tubes— and our monorail, but nobody's ever seen it, only heard of it, in my generation at least. Well, until recently.

I realize that nobody has said a word after Dr. Lisa poured her soul out into the explanation of their transit system. I pull my thoughts together and finally say, "You call that simple?" At which Dr. Lisa and everyone bursts out laughing, for a moment leaving our anxiety about this mission behind. I wish we could stay like this forever, peaceful and hidden from the outside world, but I know it doesn't work like that. Even Antenetta broke through the walls just for some contact from the outside world.

At the docks, the electromagnetic ship system is even more amazing than I could have imagined. Sione and I gawk in unison at the grandness of Antenetta as the underground city's lights reflect from the sea and ships falling in this upside-down world. "This is even more amazing than your explanation," Sione says. "So who came up with this?"

"I did," says Dr. Lisa calmly.

"What?" Sione and I exclaim.

"And she said it so nonchalantly," Sione adds, almost falling over.

"I told you all my sister was an amazing woman. Beauty and brains."

"Wow, Dr. Lisa, this is amazing," I say. "One day I hope Peace Island can become this advanced. You should really expand your teachings."

She just places her hand on my shoulder and says, with a smile that warms my soul, "Maybe. But some places deserve to remain peaceful. The simpler things in life are sometimes better than the hustle and bustle of grinding gears. Your homes love for the simple things in life is your little island's charm. You should hold on to that for as long as you can."

The twelve PM ship blows its whistle, signifying its departure. We all wave goodbye to Dr. Lisa, who is blowing kisses at Tuy as he tries to remain masculine, but tears up as he leaves his sister behind. Once the ship fully connects to the railing system, in a sharp motion with the loud clamp of metal plates, we are ordered to go below deck into our personal cabins. In a tight single file, we head down a marble staircase with other patrons into a red velvet hall with gold hanging lamps. I reach for the princess's hood and whisper for her to pull it far over her face. We get to cabin 15, scan our ticket, and enter a medium-sized cabin with four luxurious leather chairs facing each other, a round table holding champagne and hors d'oeuvre, overhead space for our luggage, and a small bunkbed.

"I guess knowing the designer of the transportation system has its perks," says Sione as he looks around the fancy cabin.

"Well, she just designs the systems, not the ships. That's my other sister," Tuy says, causing us to jerk our heads in his direction and give him the evil eye. He laughs out loud. "I'm just kidding. Guess we just got lucky and got a nice room."

"Yeah, I guess so. Hope this luck stays with us for a while," I say.

"Gee, King, way to be melodramatic" the princess surprises me by saying.

"Well, aren't you the pot calling the kettle black?" I tease, at which Luna just smirks and looks out the window. Sione is blinking rapidly, which I guess is his way of asking if she is the goddess, and I shake my head and mouth the words, "she is Luna." Remembering how scared she was in the woods, I'm happy to at least see some emotion on her face that wasn't caused by the goddess.

"Woah!" Tuy cries out as the ship lifts and we are pulled back into our seats.

"Still afraid of heights, Tuy?" Sione asks mockingly.

"Yeah, yeah, whatever. Not afraid, just uneasy."

I motion for Sione to cut it out and leave him alone, but he just shrugs and grabs a blanket to cover himself and Tuy, then looks outside. I too peer through the window, which reflects the city's jagged rock wall. Finally, we return to right-side up and enter a plastic tube. I know Dr. Lisa explained it all, but it's fascinating beyond my imagination. "I feel like Gini," I say. Sione and Tuy agree.

I can tell Luna wants to ask who Gini is, and I lean right next to her ear and whisper, to her surprise, "My pet hamster."

But the little monster only replies, "So what?"

I can't help but scoff to myself, falling back into my chair.

After ten minutes, Sione becomes restless and begins to fidget with the blanket. He eats almost all the hors d'oeuvres and drinks half the bottle of champagne. "Don't you think you should slow down?" I ask him as his eyes start to glaze over.

"Nope. I feel so claustrophobic. I might as well drink myself to sleep or out of my mind so I won't have to keep realizing that we are stuck in an underground tunnel on some type of freaky boat!"

"Alright, calm down, man." I whisper, for Luna is thankfully sleeping, but I have to agree with Sione that looking out the window really does make one claustrophobic. Sione starts to shake and I know he is really about to become drunk and blow our cover if I don't come up with a plan. I search around the cabin for something to cover the window, because Sione is so high off of champagne and honey maple leaves that there's no way he'll just close his eyes and block out its images. In the nick of time, Tuy wakes up and asks me what's going on. I tell him Sione feels claustrophobic and is trying to drink reality away. Tuy grabs the bottle from Sione and taps him on the crown of his head. He sticks his tongue out at him, obviously intoxicated. Tuy fidgets with something on the window, saying, "Over here, King."

He brushes his hand on the sill, and numbers and a plus and minus sign appear, followed by a big red circle with what looks like a dagger in it. Tuy presses the red button and the outside world is finally blocked out, replaced by images of people moving.

"Okay, I know I didn't have that many honey maple leaves," Sione says, making Tuy roar with laughter.

"Alright, guys, tell me you know what this is?" We both give him the evil eye again. "Alright, alright, I just had to make sure," he says as he waves his hands in front of his face.

"Of course we know it's supposed to be like the Tubes we have on the

81

island, but who knew it could appear like that, and without its casing?" I say.

"It's called a holographic tube; it can be projected onto anything. You see, the 'Holopro' over the door is reflecting off the white shade that dropped onto the window frame. It's almost like film in the theaters, but it goes a step further and makes the shows lifelike by creating holographic three-dimensional images," says, Luna who was awakened by the ruckus Sione and I were causing.

I see a cylindrical object emitting light, dust particles dancing as it shines its images upon the white backdrop of what was and still is our window. We look to the princess and tilt our heads to the side together. "What? I have one in my room."

Sione's mouth falls open. "We have this type of technology on Peace Island? Then why haven't we ever heard about this Holopro?" He looks to Tuy and I. "Why aren't you surprised?"

"Well, maybe we are a little desensitized after experiencing the giant Neuro Center beneath the castle, which extracts peoples' memories from their brains," Tuy says calmly.

"Oh yeah, I forgot about that. This is just like the Neuro Center," I say.

"Exactly," chirps Luna.

"You all are so weird."

"You will get used to it, Sione." I say.

I realize I actually had forgotten the technology that Peace Island hides. Who knows, they might have an underground shipping dock as well. I guess that's what Dr. Lisa meant by enjoying our peaceful island while we can. "You know, once people learn about these things, everyone will want one, and King Vernon, being the peaceful man he is, will deliver, probably causing our peaceful island to become cold and sleepless like Antenetta," I add.

"Well, I think we should focus first on the island splitting in two," says Tuy.

"That's not very funny."

"Sorry, just a little dark humor," he snaps back at me.

"But speaking of the Dark King, what happens after we give the message to the emperor?" Sione chimes in, once again hugging the champagne bottle.

"Dark humor, Sione, not Dark King." Tuy snatches the champagne bottle and places it in a safe under the table. "But to answer your question, they come up with a battle plan."

"Trinity has one of the strongest militaries in Kasai! There is no doubt they'll be able to stop the Dark King if he is the one going to harm our island," I say.

"Agreed. But what if they can't stop him?"

"Trinity did it before. When King Ren led his first attack upon them, he was greatly outnumbered. Though Ren was strong his men were not. They said it seemed their eyes were soulless, as if they were in a daze."

"Ren's soldiers were usually good fighters?" asks Sione.

"Yeah. They were originally the strongest military in Kasai, until that day when Trinity stole all their honor."

"I bet Ren was mad."

"Mad is probably an understatement," I say. We all fall back into our chairs and let out a long sigh.

Then in a small voice, Luna asks, "Who is Ren?"

Tuy gently places his palms on her cheeks and shakes his head. "Nobody you want to know, trust me."

"But—"

"Nope. This information is staying classified."

"I already heard you all talking earlier."

"Yeah, but you don't know the whole story." I stick my tongue out at her, which makes us all laugh except Luna.

"Whatever." She rolls her eyes and turns on her side, covering her head with the blanket.

The ship abruptly jerks forward, ending our conversation. Tuy turns off the HoloTube, revealing we have reached a metal cavern. The electromagnetic platforms connect with a loud noise and the ship starts to rise through a metal tunnel to the surface. A voice comes over the intercom informing passengers to fasten their seatbelts. The ship finally reaches the top of the valve, and just like Dr. Lisa said, I can hear the ceiling opening to the Western Sea's surface. The electromagnetic platform spins the ship, perfectly aligning it with the opening. From the window, I can finally see daybreak as the platform turns and unscrews itself from the ships electromagnetic plate. We are set free and finally able to sail on the blue ocean waves.

"Finally, fresh air!" Sione yells on the deck, still slightly intoxicated, causing the other passengers to look at him strangely. I run to him and try to cover his mouth, but he breaks loose and bounces from corner to corner. I give up once Tuy tells me to just let him go, and catching my breath, I have a chance to take in the ship's massiveness.

I never thought I would be on one of these giant metal ships. I chuckle to myself as I think about the time I almost joined the Peace Island Sails Corps. Life out at sea seemed fun. Just you and the open water, away from the hustle and bustle of the world. I would only have to worry about the ship's well-being and making my commanding officer happy. But of course, I would also have to worry about going to battle if we crossed a gang of pirates.

"King..." Luna says as she pulls on the sleeve of my uniform.

"What is it, princess?"

She points toward the helm of the ship. "Doesn't that blue smoke remind you of—?"

My chest tightens, and before Luna can finish her sentence, I cut her off. "Peace Island Sails Corps. Luna, we have to go!"

I know that this is not the regular sails corps, but the royal one, which emits a dark, almost crimson-blue smoke from its ships' stacks. I look around while holding Luna's hand tightly. The deck spins in circles as we move closer and I try to think of something. There is no way we're going to be caught this early in the game.

So many questions still need to be answered. Tuy comes toward us, obviously wondering why I am distressed, and then he sees the smoke. He runs to Sione grabbing his hand, pulling him behind him, to the left-hand side of the ship's stern, and there they are: lifeboats. I run toward them and motion for Tuy to look down. And without even acknowledging me, he calmly picks up the intoxicated Sione in all of his greatness and jumps off the side of the boat. I peer over the side and Tuy is motioning for me to drop Luna down. When I pick her up, she's surprisingly cooperative, without putting up a fuss. I give her a look of reassurance as I slowly let go, dropping her into his arms. As she gracefully descends through the air like an angel, I remember when we found her behind the bushes, how Tuy carried her back from oblivion—but here I am throwing her into oblivion. However, now there are capable hands on the other side, and she lands light as a feather into Tuy's arms.

Now it's my turn. I look behind me before I go and see the front of a dark red ship with a golden phoenix on the bow. A young woman with brown hair woven in multiple locks requests permission to board. The captain of our ship comes down and grants it. A long metal bridge connects the two ships and she crosses it. By her attire, a long green coat with pauldrons that curve at the ends, I know she is the ship's captain.

"King, what are you doing?" Tuy demands, but before I jump, my curiosity gets the better of me and I wait for a moment to hear what she has to say.

"Good afternoon, captain. I do apologize for this, but I am with the Royal Sails Corps of Peace Island. We are in search of wanted criminals from our homeland."

The captain rubs his hands through his beard and says with surprise in his voice, "Peace Island? Criminals? I didn't think you all had too many of those, especially ones who had the means to escape such a distance from your island."

"Yes, it is a very rare occasion. But this bunch is quite special and I'm afraid any further information is classified."

"Understandable, but at least tell me something about these criminals so my crew can help you look for them."

"All I can tell you is that they are three men travelling with a small child."

"Bingo," I whisper, but maybe a little too loud, as the young woman, without changing stance, looks over the captains' shoulder and stares directly into my eyes. Shivers shoot down my spine. With a yell, I totter over the side of the ship and fall onto the lifeboat. I bump into the others as I kick and flail my arms.

"There they are, the lifeboats!" the Royal Sails Corps captain shouts.

"Cut the ropes!" I scream.

Sione jumps up, swaying a little, but I catch him as he taps the bottom electronic medal on his uniform, causing two curved swords, which he cutely calls 'heart', to materialize out of thin air. He sways a little from the alcohol, but with precision he crosses the swords in front of him, cutting the two ropes holding up the lifeboat. We can't help but yell as we plummet down the side of the ship. We hit the water so hard that the boat almost flips over, but Sione manages to balance it by grabbing both sides and holding them down with raw power.

Above me, I see the ends of the captain's brown twists fly through the air over the side of the ship and trail behind her until they are out of view. "They are getting back on *The Phoenix*! Hurry up and turn the motor on." Tuy kicks the motor in high gear and we speed off, past the Antenetta ship, but before we go a mile *The Phoenix* appears behind us out of thin air.

"Where the heck did they come from?" Sione yells.

"That's why they call it *The Phoenix*. When I was thinking about joining the Corps., they told us, as a phoenix rises from the ashes, this phoenix rises above its prey from the mist of the sea," I say.

"Well, we have to lose them somehow!" yells Tuy.

But before we know it, *The Phoenix* is right beside us and turning its cannons on us. Tuy tells me to grab the princess.

"Sorry," I whisper to her.

"Hurry up," she says, seeming unworried.

I move behind the princess and put her in a choke hold, and Luna, being the smart girl she is, even squirms around as if she is in real danger. The captain stands at the railing of the ship. I face her and snatch off Luna's hood. The commander once again looks directly into my eyes. Her posture is still stiff and she doesn't even bat an eyelash or tell the cannons to stand down.

"Are we really going to be like that, Adira?" Tuy yells to my surprise.

I whisper to him, "You know her?"

Tuy smirks and without even changing his line of sight, says, "She used to be my commanding officer, before she switched to the Corps."

Now I see why he is so strong; with a commanding officer who seems like a mountain, how could you not be?

"Just doing business, Tuy. Now, I think you know better than any of us that it would be in your best interests to come quietly, and we can sort this whole thing out at home."

"I'm sorry, but we can't do that." The air grows cold, the sky grows dark, and thunder rumbles in the distance. Adira finally loosens her back muscles as she leans on the ships railing and gives a smirk identical to Tuy's. "Well, I guess we'll have to do this the hard way."

"Are you so consumed with pride that you would risk the princess's life?" yells Tuy.

"My, my, it's funny hearing that from you. You and I both know that I don't return home until I have caught my prey, and unfortunately for you, you have fallen into my web."

As the thunder booms, rain clouds finally show their faces and pouring water makes visibility low. Lightning accompanies the thunder and rain in their symphony.

"Adira, you really have changed." Tuy lowers his head, wearing a sorrowful expression that I have never seen on his face before.

Adira looks at me one more time before turning on her coat tails and sending an order for our deaths. The cannons point toward us and, one by one, are loaded with gunpowder and the fuses lit. Everything from that moment goes in slow motion. I can't believe that a Peace Island soldier would actually order a hit while the princess, a child, is being held captive. It goes against everything a Peace Island soldier should be.

The first cannon is fired, and even as it cuts through the ocean's surface, shooting up a giant geyser almost turning over our boat, I still don't register what is happening. Luna has freed herself from my grasp and is pushing me. Suddenly, she starts to rock the boat rapidly, sending me overboard along with the others. As we fall into the water, the cannons are still blaring around us. I can't hear anything over the ringing in my ears, and my blood boils that someone would be so cruel. I feel no fear in this moment, just anger, to the point that dark wisps of matter swirl around my hands.

"King!" Tuy shouts. The world still moving slowly as I see him waving his hands. It is heading straight for me, a cannonball, but more importantly, the princess is still holding on to me for dear life.

"Don't be afraid. You are strong, you are great, and you are a King," I hear a voice whisper.

And before I even know it, I place my hand straight out in front of me toward the cannonball. It becomes entangled in the black matter that circle around my whole body. "Now," whispers the voice, and I clench my fist, causing the cannonball to disappear. Then I fix my eyes on the general and the world speeds up, coming back to life, as the projectile I vanished reappears and crashes into the side of *The Phoenix*. I can hear it all: The screams, Sione freaking out, and the grand thunder and crackling lightning. I look to the ship, which is now in flames. Adira still stares at me, and before I can process her next move, she pulls out a silver 45 caliber pistol and shoots me in the chest.

The bullet, hitting hard, seems to sit at the bottom of my stomach and weigh me down. I try to breathe, but the air shoots through my body like daggers as the waves crash around me. My eyes grow hazy and the lightning bolts above my head start to spin like beautiful ballerinas, dancing and twirling above my head. I suck in what feels like my last breath, but before I close my eyes, before the ballerinas make their adieu, Luna's tiny hands cup my cheeks, her pink glowing eyes gaze into mine. She cries out my name as the water around us becomes crimson. She places her hand on my chest and I scream in pain as the bullet is slowly screwed out of my body until it floats in front of me.

Luna turns her focus to Adira, who for the first time actually moves with haste, though not quickly enough. Just like I did, Luna closes her fist, and the same bullet the captain shot through my chest goes through hers. She falls off the side of the ship and is swallowed whole by the ocean below.

Luna places hands that glow with a light pink spirit energy on my chest, and I can feel my breath returning to me and my blood starting to warm. The hole in my chest closes and tears well up in my eyes as I whisper Luna's name under my breath, holding on to her tight as *The Phoenix* thankfully retreats. However, when one is in the storm, the first sign of the valley is usually an illusion to trick believer's hearts.

Lightning cracks all around us until one bolt hits right in front of me, striking Luna. Pink spirit energy and my dark spirit energy combine as I am torn from her and thrown back, crashing into the waves around me.

The pink spirit energy shoots into the sky, where it swirls around like a baby tornado. I call out Luna's name. Deep down, I know King Vernon would understand us letting his daughter join our journey, but if anything happened to her, I would willingly walk to the execution chamber myself. I swim toward the light, thinking that if I can reach her it will be like the time in the forest when I met the goddess. Although as I get closer to the pink spirit energy the water becomes hotter, even to the point of boiling,

I can't stop. I keep swimming, but before I can reach her, Tuy grabs me, and tries to keep me from going any farther.

"King, your skin!"

I hadn't even noticed, but in places it is starting to peel off.

"King, we have to leave her."

"No, Tuy, we can't. We are responsible for her."

"Don't worry, I'm sure the goddess is protecting her."

"The goddess, how could I forget..."I start to frantically call out for the goddess. I scream at the top of my lungs, so loud that I can be heard over the thunder. Tuy joins in, as does Sione. We call for her, praying that she will hear our cries; then everything stops and the lightning becomes blindingly bright.

The waves calm and the sun breaks free from behind the clouds. A beautiful summer breeze tickles my face, and before us is a beautiful woman with blue hair like the blue waves.

"Is that her?" Sione stutters.

"Yes, she is the goddess." As we swim closer to her, she greets us with a signature bubbly smile. "Don't worry, the princess is fine, but I will have to stay in this form for a while in order for her to heal."

"Who are you?" Sione stutters again.

"You can call be Rania," she says, still smiling. "Now follow me; I will lead you to safety." Rania throws her hands into the air and creates a small ship out of spirit energy. "Go ahead, get on board."

"Is this the pink spirit energy you spoke of, Tuy?" Sione asks as we settle inside it.

"Yeah. I never thought I would see it in my lifetime, since not many humans are blessed with it. Mainly goddesses and guardians."

"Very true, but I once met a human with pink spirit energy—just once," boasts Rania.

"Really...who?" we ask, leaning with fascination toward the goddess.

Rania smirks and looks off into the distance. "Nobody you all know, just a very sad woman. They say those with this energy are very compassionate and giving but have very fragile hearts."

We shrug our shoulders at each other, as we finally see the shoreline.

As the spirit boat hits the golden coastline of Antenetta's outskirts and the entrance to the Road of Bones, it disappears right from under us. We land on the shore with a loud thud. Rania apologizes for forgetting we were mere mortals and could not land gracefully as her.

Once I finally compose myself from all that happened out at sea, and the fact that a goddess is standing before us, I look up to Rania. Her blue hair has now faded and turned into long brown and blonde curls. She stuffs them into a black sunflower patterned scarf that covers most of it, only leaving out a few curls at the top. She is no longer dressed like Luna or like the first time I saw her, thankfully. She wears a pair of loose fitting wide legged black pants that has two mini gold sunflower pins along the right and left hem. Her loose burnt orange top leaves her right arm exposed. The long scarf, which almost reaches her knees, sways in the wind and fully reveals her right arm. I wince. Upon her arm is a wrapped bangle, a beautiful jewel, but the same opal color as the necklace Luna gave me. I'm not really sure how I feel about this woman. However, I shake it off—she is not my focus, but the unknown road ahead.

Past the coastline, I see a lush green field filled with sunflowers taller than me. Tuy tells us we must keep moving in case there were more ships behind us or the captain tries to track us on foot. He mumbles that last part, and I look at him strangely. I'm sure that he saw Adira fall from the ship with a bullet hole through her chest; why in the world would he think she is still alive? But I just shake it off. We did just come from a hard battle, and we all are likely to say and do some strange things.

We walk through the green pastures, heading for the giant wall of sunflowers. Once there, Tuy runs his hands along the stems, touching each one at a time. I look to Sione, who wonders aloud if he might have hit his head on something out at sea. Rania snickers and tells us that he is looking for the entrance to the Road of Bones.

Tuy finally waves his hands in the air, slips his arms in between two thick sunflower stems, and falls into their embrace, disappearing from our sight. Rania, of course, having no fear and knowing more than we could possibly hope to learn in our lifetimes, quickly follows him and disappears as well. Sione and I hug each other in misery and yell out loud before running between the two sunflower stems, still holding each other. Once inside, we are surrounded by sunflowers. The path is narrow and can only be travelled by walking sideways. The ground beneath me is covered in thick vines oozing bright green sap. I stick my tongue out in disgust as I try to hurry through this path. Seeing Rania up ahead, I speed up even more. We walk through the maze of sunflowers for what feels like hours, and then I finally see it in the distance: the edge of glory, the exit.

I shuffle my feet so quickly that I keep tripping on the vines beneath me. Behind me, Sione shouts to wait for him but I become selfish, ignoring him. One thing I can't stand is tight spaces. I've broken out in a heavy sweat and I feel my breath becoming shallow. *Just a little while longer, King,* I tell myself.

I continue my fast-paced shuffle, but I no longer am tripping on vines. Instead, the ground has turned an ash grey and I am kicking up dead vines and moss. The once bright sunflowers have withered and lost their color. Instead of solar rays above me, they give me a menacing stare of pitch black night.

The last patch of sunflower vines are wrapped intricately together at the end of the maze creating a gate made of vines. I push my way past the dead flower gate and fall into an even deader land, falling on the dry bones of an unidentifiable beast. The ground beneath me is no longer full of lush green grass but of dirt, rocks, and animal carcasses already rotted to bones like the one underneath my fingertips. For miles in front of me, all I can see is barren nothingness.

"I'm guessing we are now on the Road of Bones?" I say.

"Yep, but this is just the start. It seems like a vast sea of nothingness. However, its terrain changes so much that many go crazy before they get to the end," says Rania.

"Well, why the heck are we going this way?" Sione cries out behind us as he finally escapes from the sunflowers.

"Because the Road of Bones is the only way on foot around Ren," says Tuy. At the name of Ren we all become quiet, even Rania. "I'll admit this path is definitely dangerous. Most people travel by boat all the way to Oak City, which is the only city with direct transit to Trinity."

"So how long is it going to take us to get to Oak City?"

"That I don't know." Tuy gives us all a stupid grin.

"Gee, you know a lot of things but you tend to miss the important details," says Sione.

"It will probably take us 3 weeks to get there by foot," Rania says.

Sione lets out a giant exclamation of excitement as he runs to her side and hugs her. "I forgot you were travelling with us. Please stay in this form for the rest of the trip," he says, snuggling closer to Rania, who is so surprised that her eyes have opened wider than the barren field in front of us.

She says nothing, but her mouth does not close, her jaw hanging so far that I think it might touch her toes. Tuy and I hurry to grab Sione off of her and lightly knock him over the head, causing him to fall on his butt. "Ow! What you do that for?"

"Dude. You can't just go up and hug her like that, I mean she's not... real," I say awkwardly.

"I beg your pardon, King. Just because I'm a little different from you all doesn't mean I'm not real. You shouldn't hold being divine against me. And just so you all know, I actually like hugs. I was just shocked, that's all." Rania flicks the tail of her scarf at me and opens her arms wide, giving permission for Sione to continue his snuggle fest.

Tuy shakes his head at the both of them, who have clearly lost their minds to hug in the middle of this dead land. "You can keep lollygagging around, but I'm going to keep moving."

I run behind him and leave Rania and Sione to their stupid game. Tuy and I walk a good five miles through the barren land, but Rania and Sione still haven't caught up. I tell Tuy that we should wait for them as we have put some distance between us. Tuy just scoffs and says Rania can handle herself and Sione is probably safest next to her. We continue, walking in silence, until I see a little farther up the road what looks like a grassy path. I shout to Tuy that we should go this way and he agrees.

Once we reach the grassy path, we see before us no longer miles of dusty plains but instead grand mountains. The road soon turns rocky, and we find ourselves climbing up the side of a mountain with great twists and turns. At one point, I look to my left and we have travelled so high that I cannot see anything beneath me, only fog. In the distance, huge mountains that are all different colors, probably from blooming flowers, cradle small villages in between them.

"Now I see what Rania was talking about!" I yell up to Tuy, who turns around and answers, "Yes this changing terrain is very amusing. This is a grand adventure, isn't it?"

I think back again to when we found Luna and he asked me if I did not see the adventure that could come from a missing princess. "To this extent, is this the adventure you were talking about when we found the princess that day?"

"I don't know, do you believe it to be so?"

"Please, Tuy, you know I hate when you speak in riddles!"

"Well, of course I couldn't foresee all this. Her sharing a body with a goddess and us heading to Trinity. But I knew that day something special was going to come from finding her, especially when she gave you that necklace. You still have it, right?"

"Yeah, I can't take it off...literally."

I catch up to Tuy as we reach a stretch of flat ground and can finally rest. Tuy takes out some of his sister's electrolyte-infused water, meant to quench your thirst and give you an energy boost too. He passes me a cup as he asks, "how much you want to bet that that necklace is cursed?"

I want to knock the stupid look he is giving me off his face. His favorite sport is soccer, but his favorite pastime is trying to scare the living daylights out of me. I throw my head back and say, "Tuy you're not going to scare me with that, especially since Rania saved our lives. Why would she tell Luna to give me a cursed necklace?"

"Just because she saved us doesn't mean that she is a good person, or whatever she is. I mean, it's weird. You can't take it off, and if someone tries touch it, it burns them. It's almost like it's holding some type of energy. Hey! Maybe the curse of the necklace has something to do with your spirit energy, especially since yours is black and not white."

"What?"

"When you were fighting, the energy you used to stop the cannonball was black."

"Well, maybe that time, but my vision showed white spirit energy."

"There is another rumor that says at the end of Ren's life, well on the battlefield, they started to see him use black spirit energy...maybe you're about to die."

"Tuy!" I stand up and throw my cup of water at him, only causing him to fall over with laughter and say he is sorry.

"And Ren has nothing to do with me!"

"I know, I just wanted to lighten the mood," says Tuy, smiling, "but

I guess we can find out more when we find the old man in the shack, especially now that we really do know you have spirit energy."

All I can do is nod, blatantly frustrated with him joking at my unknown powers and afraid of the idea I might have a connection with Ren. Sometimes he really does take it too far. It's like he doesn't even realize we killed a woman. The air suddenly grows stale and awkward between us, and neither of us says a word until Tuy finally breaks the ice.

"You know, you were pretty cool the way you saved the princess."

I look up at him in amazement, for he is never one to give compliments, and especially not to me. Something is definitely wrong with him. "I just did what I had to do. Even though I didn't know I could do what I did."

"Poor Luna." Tuy lowers his eyes to the ground and I realize he is talking about the captain.

"Yeah, but it wasn't like she was the one who hurt Adira. That was Rania."

"Well, to be fair, she did shoot you in the chest."

Tuy's words make me laugh out loud and place my hand on my heart, as I had forgotten all about it, but the red bloodstain on my uniform had not. Even though Luna closed my wound, I still see a small cut and I know the scar of near-death will always remain with me. "Yeah. I couldn't imagine having her as a commanding officer. But I guess I see why you are so tough."

"She was a tough one, but she made me a better solider and most importantly, a better man."

"What do you mean?"

"She was my first love," Tuy says with so much heartache in his voice that when the wind picks up and blows rainbows of flowers from the neighboring mountains before us, it seems they're sending their condolences. Once again, neither of us says a word. We killed his first love.

—VIII—

The Academy

In my selfishness, I didn't even realize how much my friend was hurting. I always wondered why Tuy was so cocky and selfish and unaware of others, yet I too missed the pain that I caused my friend. A pain I cannot take back. I consider how I could have assessed the situation differently. If only I had noticed the connection between them, I could have stopped Rania from hurting Adira.

I mean, I was safe after she removed the bullet; why did she have to strike her down in such a manner? Couldn't she have just knocked her overboard? A bullet to the chest seems a little too harsh. Though she shot me first, she was only doing her civil duty to the crown. She might have went about it an unconventional way, but she was fulfilling her mission; she truly believed us to be criminals. We took out one of our own who was only trying to do well. We killed my best friend's first love.

First love... First love... I repeated it over and over again. The feeling of falling from heaven to earth and back again with no air. Your chest can't help but tighten and immobilize all your reason. Love is a dangerous thing, especially when shared between a dangerous man and woman.

I try to think of words to say to comfort my friend, but nothing comes to mind except a cliché, "I'm sorry."

"It's okay. All is fair in love and war, especially when it's actual war," Tuy manages to choke out.

"Why didn't you stop her? You could have said something, yelled, screamed, anything!"

"Well, she was no angel either, King. She did actually shoot you first."

"But she was just doing what she thought was right as a solider."

"No. She had changed. I could see it in her eyes. You can run to battle and try to justify your means by hiding behind pride for one's country, but that doesn't always make the choices you make in battle right. We all have to make choices in life and sometimes they turn out good or bad, and we all must be prepared to face the consequences. Adira had become blinded with power, making her less compassionate and only concerned with her success rate. She was no longer a commanding officer, just an assassin. She made her choice, and Rania made hers." Tuy tilts his head back and sucks in the electrolyte water he probably wishes was a lot stronger.

"So, were you two actually an item?"

"Officially, no. Just when she called, I would come," says Tuy, throwing his head back again.

"Oh, I see." I decide not to push the matter any further, being as it seems to be a tragic love story. "Those villages on the distant mountain across from us, what land do you think they are a part of?"

"Probably Ren."

"What?"

"Like I told you, the Road of Bones is a way around Ren. It's a massive region that holds many villages and one main central city. Those are the southernmost villages of Ren."

"People still live there?"

"Of course. Ren led his coup d'état farther inward, at the border of his region and Trinity's. Most of these folks wouldn't have experienced the full fallout from their king's betrayal. I'm sure there are many who still live peaceful lives behind the wall."

"There is no way they could be peaceful. Those poor people are stuck in a cage, unable to see the world. Don't they realize they could just scale down the back side of the mountain and escape over here to free land?"

"They probably do, but at the same time they might be staying because they're happy. Think about it. We Peace Island folk are also not really concerned with the outside world. Why? Because we take everything we are taught at face value. We just fall in line and think that this is as good as life is going to get. They are probably common folk who are happy as long as they have their families, which I don't think is a bad thing at all."

"Even if freedom is right in their backyard?"

"Well, I'm sure there are those who have tried, but I'm also sure when they got to the bottom of that mountain and tried to cross the lake, banging for days on an impenetrable spirit barrier, they finally understood what fear and pain really are."

"How could a country be so cruel?" I say coldly.

"Well, the people don't hate Ren. The country is not the one holding them there, but the rest of the world has abandoned them and locked them away and vowed to never mention their name. They are the lost people. In this way, all they know are the ways of Ren. To them, their region is God and the rest of Kasai must seem like the devil."

"They certainly are lost," says a haggard voice behind us.

Tuy and I turn around to see a plump woman with black hair in the shape of a beehive dressed in a hot pink hiking outfit. She is breathing heavily as she walks up to us and motions for water. I hurriedly grab a cup from my bag, as it looks like she will faint at any moment. After she finishes guzzling down the water, she pulls out a lace handkerchief and wipes the corners of her lips; once done, she folds it back into a perfect triangle and places it in her pocket. The woman then removes an embroidered velvet cushion from her bag, places it before her, and gracefully sits down, leaning on one side. "I do apologize. That was very rude of me, but hiking this mountain is certainly starting to get to me as I get older."

"Don't be silly, you don't look a day over twenty," says Tuy, causing the woman to let out a boisterous laugh. I am glad that he is back to himself, at least in this moment. He really is a strong solider.

"Well, thank you, young man. You're too kind. But please let me introduce myself. I am Ms. B. I run a dance academy just up the road."

"Oh no! Not more bees!" I throw my hands to my mouth, realizing what I accidently blurted out. Tuy just laughs at me and apologizes, saying it is a long story. But Ms. B doesn't get mad; she just gives me a motherly pat on the head and tells me that I am a cute little fellow.

She then asks us what brings us two up here, because most outsiders don't travel on the Road of Bones, only those who live in the nearby cities and villages. Tuy and I pause for a moment, obviously trying to come up with an excuse. Still worn out from our last battle, we both draw blanks. Ms. B surprises us by letting out another boisterous laugh and pinching both our cheeks. "It's alright, you don't have to think of any fables to tell me. As long as you are not strange men, which I can tell you are not. Since you two seem to be from a distant land, I suppose you need a place to stay for the night? Especially with those nasty wounds you have acquired from somewhere."

I quickly cover my chest while Tuy shyly puts a hand over his own injury. A cut on the arm is easier to explain, however, than a slightly open gunshot wound that doesn't bleed. We look back at Ms. B, who is smiling at us with rosy cheeks, and shake our heads like little children to say yes to her offer of accommodations. "Alright! Well, let's be going soon, for you don't want to be on this road at night." She has already packed up her cushion, wiped her cup clean and returned it to my bag, and started back along the road. Tuy quickly gets his stuff together and we follow her.

We no longer have to scale the mountain. Now the road ahead of us contains many turns and some narrow pathways, none of which stop Ms. B, who walks like a pro, knowing every sharp corner. We walk for another thirty minutes and come to a fork in the road. To the right, I can see multiple villages in the distance, and the other way is covered in fog. Of course we go to the left. I turn around, and peering back at the quaint villages on the other side of the fork, I can't help but pout.

We descend farther into the foggy road. The fog is so thick I can't even see Tuy or Ms. B in front of me. However, being the pro that she is, Ms. B calls behind her and tells us to hold hands. I feel around in the fog for Tuy's hand, but once I find it, I really start to miss the villages I never knew on the other side.

My feet break free from the ground and I find myself shooting up in mid-air. I hear Ms. B up ahead shouting in joy, and Tuy as well, but I know he is only acting macho for he is afraid of heights. We fly through the fog, but I have no idea how. I just hold on to Tuy's hand for dear life.

"Make sure you keep holding on tight, boys!" Ms. B yells from the fog; she doesn't have to worry about that, for there is no way I'm letting go of anything, or even opening my eyes, for that matter.

"Wow, King, you have to see this!" Tuy calls, but I shake my head as the wind hits me so hard it feels like it will cut my skin. Tuy continues to yell at the top of his lungs and that old curiosity calls me again. I take a deep breath and slowly open one eye. The earth below me is no longer able to be seen. All around me are floating rocks and beneath me, thick fog. I look up and see Tuy smiling at me. I squeeze his hand so tight, but then I start to wonder, if I am holding on to Tuy and he is holding on to Ms. B, then what is she holding on to?

As the fog around us clears, it reveals the stars in the sky and lakes beneath us. I take this opportunity to finally look at Ms. B, who I now can see is holding on to a giant green vine and swinging us through the air as if we are riding on a tire swing. "I thought we were going to your academy, Ms. B!" I yell.

"We are, young King. Stop worrying so much and just enjoy the ride." She curves the giant vine, making us sway and swirl in the air. I think I am going to be sick.

I shut my eyes tight and pray for this ride to be over soon. And thankfully, Ms. B finally calls out that we are almost there. I open my eyes and see a giant grey stone mansion on an enormous giant brown iceberg-shaped rock. The rock holds not only the mansion, but a small lake and a tiny valley which wild doe run through. Ms. B whips the vine once more, swinging us sharply to the left and breaking free from it. We fly through the air, still conjoined by the hands, to land on a small, flat rock beneath the giant landmass. Without breaking a sweat, Ms. B nonchalantly calls out for us to keep following her as she leaps from the flat rock to a smaller rock and then to another. They act as stairs to the floating mansion.

"Well, there is no turning back now," says Tuy. Left alone on the flat rock, I contemplate just throwing myself over the edge. I don't know how much more my heart can take of this. Poor thing has already been pierced, literally. I exhale deeply and think to myself, *you are a soldier, King, let's start acting like one.* I swing my arms back and leap with great gusto from rock to rock, up the stony stairway to Ms. B's academy.

Made it, I congratulate myself as I finally reach the valley beneath the academy. "Come on, King!" calls out Tuy, who is already on the other side of the valley. I take off happily, glad to be back on solid ground, even if that ground is floating in mid-air. As I run through the valley, doe run alongside me. I do a slight twirl and smile up to the starry night sky. I can't help but show my excitement for this moment of peace. I feel that nothing can touch me. It's just like the day we all had dinner at Dr. Lisa's, free of worry.

At the end of the valley, long stone stairs lead up to the academy. Finally excited with the adventure before me, I run up them in a hurry, unaware that Tuy has stopped in his tracks at the top. Bumping into him makes me almost fall down the flight of stairs, but I manage to catch myself. I regain my composure and ask Tuy, "What is it?"

I can't quite decode the expression on his face. I move my hands as I get ready to call forth my sword but Tuy just smiles and shakes his hands.

"Well then, what is it?" I ask again, agitated that he is tainting my peaceful moment.

"Something that is really going to piss you off." Tuy sucks his front teeth. I push my way past him, only to find myself mimicking Tuy's expression. No doubt, the academy in front of me is insanely grand, almost like a small castle. Stunning stained-glass windows at every side reflect a beautiful rainbow on the lake. The courtyard houses many flowers that share the beauty of the little students I see dancing in the windows. All of this is so beautiful, but none of it compares to the two people who stand in front of us under the emerald archway into the courtyard: Sione and Rania.

"By the looks of it, they seem like friends of yours. But why does it seem you two aren't happy to see them?" asks Ms. B, placing her finger to her chin.

"We are happy to see them, just surprised," I say.

"Well, honestly, me too. The only people allowed here or who know the way are the staff and those admitted to my lovely dance academy."

"Hey, you guys made it!" Sione says cheerfully as he runs to us.

"No, young one, the real question is: how did you make it? I mean, of course, you are welcome if you are friends of my guest, but how?" Ms. B raises one eyebrow and leans close to Sione. Behind her, Tuy and I wave our hands for him not to say anything that has to do with Rania being a goddess.

"Well, it's fairly simple. As we travelled along the road, we stopped in the village to the right of the fork. We told the people there that we were looking for our friends and we happened to meet one of your students who said that they might be here. She told us we had to wait in the courtyard for you, out of respect, of course." Sione gives the hugest grin that screams he is lying straight through his teeth.

"I see," says Ms. B, backing off a little. "Well, what is your name, son?"

"I'm Sione and she is Rania." Sione points, at Rania who waves at Ms. B from a distance.

"Very well. You all seem innocent enough. Come on in so you can at least get out of those damp and dirty clothes and have a hot meal. You will like that, won't you, Sione?" Ms. B teases as she pinches Sione's cheeks. He gets so excited that he pulls her to lead the way, both of them laughing joyfully as they race to the kitchen, looking like mother and son.

Once Ms. B is inside, Tuy and I quickly shuffle over to Rania and ask her how the heck she got here so fast. Rania gives us a wink before throwing one finger to her lips and saying, "It's a secret," as she runs into the academy. Tuy and I stare at each other for a moment.

"Next time I'm staying with them," I say, holding my stomach as the nauseating memories of flying through the air come back to be.

"I agree," says Tuy, holding his stomach as well.

"I thought you enjoyed the ride?" I taunt as we walk up another set of stairs, but when I place my hand on Tuy's shoulder, I can see that his face is very pale.

"King, you know I hate heights," he says as he pushes past me and enters the academy. I laugh to myself, slowly learning my friend might not be all that brave either, just a really good bluffer. Maybe that is what bravery really is, just a bluff and hoping for the best outcome.

I enter the dance academy, which is swarming with young girls in pink tights and black leotards, as well as some boys. The entranceway has two parallel, curving grand staircases. I look up and see children peeking over the banister and popping their heads out of rooms along the adjacent hallway.

However, they all run back as quickly as they came once a tall, slender woman with a crooked nose and giant mole taps her ruler on the wall. The very stern-looking woman doesn't even glance our way, but from her silent presence, I just know I wouldn't want her for a dance teacher. I guess it doesn't matter anyway since I have two left feet, I think while trying to move them to the smooth traditional music I hear through the halls.

"Young King, would you be interested in taking a class?" enquires Ms. B from behind me, laughing.

I turn around and shake my head frantically. "Oh no! Definitely not. I am one of the worst dancers on my island. But I do enjoy swaying to music in private."

"Yes, it is a great escape and one you don't necessarily have to be good at, especially when you are alone and it's just you and the melody."

I smile at the woman who once again is warming my soul. "By the way, Ms. B, I thought you went to the kitchen with Sione?"

"I did. I just came to find you. Upstairs you will only find living quarters, but down the hall to the right is the teachers' lounge. Shall we?"

"Of course. You have been leading me to amazing places all day, so what's a little more?" I say with the huge smile still on my face.

As Tuy, Ms. B, and I walk down the corridor, which is a lot quieter than the left wing, she looks like she is lost in thought. I ask if she feels well. "I am quite all right, young King. Thank you for your concern."

"It's just you look like you have a lot on your mind. Forgive me for prying, I know we just met."

"That is true, but why do I feel like I have met you before?" says Ms. B, stopping in her tracks.

"I don't think that's possible. This is the first time I have left my island."

"Oh, I see," says Ms. B, regaining some color in her jolly cheeks as she continues walking. "I guess you just remind me of one of my previous students."

"Probably," I say, still slightly concerned.

"Well, here we are." She motions Tuy and I toward the entrance of the teachers' lounge.

Sione and Rainia are sitting at a round wooden table with a grand feast in front of them: roast chicken, fish, all types of vegetables, pies, and cakes! I only usually see this much food during the Salt Festival.

"Ms. B, this is way too much food!" Tuy exclaims.

"Maybe. But the table has already been set, so sit and eat."

We thank Ms. B and sit with the others. Before taking a seat, she heads to a corner of the bright orange and rust-accented teachers' lounge. From a rectangular box, she pulls out a horn-shaped object that seems to be made of gold. It sort of looks like the Gramas attached to our parents' music boxes, except this horn is attached to a black cord connected to a box on the wall. Also, instead of playing music, Ms. B holds the horn's opening to her mouth and begins to speak. "All staff, please come to the teachers' lounge after class to greet our special visitors. All staff, after class, please come down to the lounge to greet our visitors. Thank you all."

"I hope you don't mind entertaining my staff," she says to us. "We don't have many older visitors up here."

"No, we don't mind at all," says Tuy, who has already started to dig into the food.

"And if they are as nice as you, of course we would love to meet them," adds Sione, who is already on his second plate.

"Lovely." Ms. B clasps her hands together and finally takes a seat to eat.

I dig in as well. Delicious Brussels sprouts, leeks, and cabbages fill my plate. I don't realize how hungry I am until I start to chow down, and then I eat voraciously, until I feel Rania's slender fingers in my hair pulling out a stray cabbage leaf. Holding it in front of her, she opens her mouth wide and laughs out loud, and I can't help but join her. "I guess I didn't realize how hungry I was."

"Me too," she replies, but when I look at her plate it's mostly full. I wonder if goddesses don't have to eat much.

Rania catches me staring at her plate and tells me, "Speak for yourself, rabbit."

"Hey, I am a proud vegetarian!"

She laughs again. "Very well, but I am a carnivore." She pulls out the knife from the side of the roasted chicken on the table and cuts a piece, which she swings in front of my face before swallowing it whole. This performance is followed by a menacing laugh. And all I can do is stare at her blankly. "I was just thinking, you don't have much on your plate."

"Oh, I see…" says Rania, blushing.

"I was going to tell you not to forget that a young girl is trying to heal inside of you," I whisper as I slip a few Brussels sprouts on her plate. "She is a growing girl who needs her vegetables."

Rania sighs and reluctantly starts to chew the veggies I placed before her.

I think about Luna and what happened. I lean back toward Rania and whisper to her, "The princess will be okay, right?"

Rania turns to me and for the first time is gentle and serious. "Of course, King. I'm taking very good care of her. She is important to my well-being, too."

"Thank you. I hope she will be able to return soon."

"Gee, I didn't think that you wanted to get rid of me that quickly."

As I jump up and hit my knee on the table, the others stop eating and look at me strangely. "I thought I saw a bug," I say, putting Ms. B in a tizzy. She skips out of the room mumbling, something about needing to place more po berries around the school and how embarrassed she is that I had seen a bug. I sit back down slowly and look to Rania. "No, of course not. I enjoy your company, but I'm just unsure why my mother told me to seek your guidance."

"Want to go out on the balcony?" she asks. I nod and we tell the others we're going out for fresh air on the balcony at the back of the teachers' lounge.

I look over the giant lakes and valleys in the academy's backyard, a little nervous at what Rania will say to me. Then slender hands touch my cheeks as she turns my face to her. Her hands are ice cold. I look into her amber eyes, and for some reason tears form in my own.

"On this journey, your life will change. I am not allowed to tell you exactly how or even if you will like me and your friends in the end."

"What do you mean?"

"I don't know how to tell you, but your life is not what it really seems. The moment you were born, your life was twisted by many lies. A lot of people's lives were affected by your birth."

"My birth? But I'm just a simple island boy."

"Do you really believe that, King?"

I want to respond "Of course," but for some reason I can't. I think about General Claude and the scene between him and my mother that I've only recently remembered. I even think about my mother's soul visiting me and my ability to see visions and now the ability to harness spirit energy. I guess I am more than I expected. "Rania, I just don't understand any of this."

"And for right now you won't. But you have to find those answers in order to take your rightful place in this land and to stop the destruction of your island."

"Rightful place? You talk as if I am a king."

Rania chuckles and pulls at my cheeks as she returns to her jovial self. "Well, you never know. You might be."

I throw my hands up and stomp around like a child, then lean half my body on the balcony. "But you do know, don't you, Rania? Please tell me!"

"King, you and I both know life doesn't work like that. If you really want to find out who you are, you have to go through this journey to see how strong you truly can be. Learn what makes you angry, what makes you cry, and how you treat others in different situations. A perfect life complete with a road map cannot be handed to you on a silver platter."

"Well, if you are not here to give me a map, why did my mother lead me to you?"

"Just because I can't show you the whole way doesn't mean I can't give you a few hints. We're in this together, though, you have to put in some work as well. I'm just here to make sure you don't die, which I think I'm doing a good job at, seeing as I saved your life already. One point to team Rania!" she says, throwing her hands in the air like a cheerleader.

I just exhale and set my face on the balcony's railing. "Well, nothing about me has really changed since we started this journey. I don't think it would really matter if I die or live."

At my words Rania's eyes glow, not her usual light pink but a strange dark pink. She creates a whip of spirit energy and throws it around my waist, then reels me in closer to her. As I look into her eyes, the world around us stops. We are back in the strange upside-down world where I first met her, and she is back in her full form: blue hair and skin covered in specks of gold and bare at the chest. She then begins to speak in a very low and serious tone. "King, I would say go ahead and die if that is what you want, but unfortunately your life is not your own. I told you it is connected to many others' lives as well. How could you be so selfish?"

"Well, maybe I am selfish. They're obviously getting by just fine, I mean, they are living."

"You can be alive but dead. Dead on the inside, and that is not living."

Thinking on Rania's words, I look down to her island in the sky and above me to the real world. "Like the people in the villages across the stream," I say under my breath. Rania tilts her head to the side, and before

I know it the world above us no longer shows the balcony of Ms. B's Dance Academy but the villages in the mountains Tuy and I saw earlier.

"Exactly, King. Somebody's life in there might need you and they don't even know it because they are trapped behind an invisible wall."

"I see. But why me?"

"Why any of us, King? This is what we call destiny. You can either rot away, never living, or find your God-given destiny and maybe help change the world. Don't be afraid, King. That is your only flaw, fear."

I rub the back of my head as Rania reads me like a book. At first I am surprised, but then I remember she is a spiritual being. Everything is just becoming too much for me, but in the end, if this is my destiny, I guess I must face it. I always did want to be seen as a brave hero. Rania is now smiling as if she could hear my thoughts. She mouths something, but the waterfall beneath us crashes into the rocks around it, making it hard to hear her. She falls backwards as her spirit whip releases me, and we both fall through time and space.

I am back once again on the balcony. Doubting I will ever get used to the strange realm Rania resides in, I grab my stomach, wishing I hadn't filled up on veggies earlier. "Couldn't you have made a smoother landing?" I croak, making Rania laugh even as she apologizes. "Is that how you and Sione got here so quick?"

"Very good, King. See, I told you, you have very keen senses, and you have to keep living to find your true abilities."

I tilt my head to the side as I feel she is stretching it a bit. Anyone who travels through time and space, rushing from one dimension into another, would suspect she has some type of teleportation power. Gosh, I must be going crazy. Teleportation power! "I miss Peace Island!" I cry out as I grab my head and drop to the balcony. Rania leans over me and shakes her head in disappointment as she asks, "Weren't you listening to anything I just said? It will only get tougher from here on out, so you better find a way to use that fear to your advantage."

She begins to head back inside, but I remember one more thing. "Rania, wait! What about this spirit energy? I mean, I caught a cannonball with my bare hands and just with the clench of a fist, I shot it back in the direction it came. Well, actually more like teleported it." Still on the ground, I furrow my brow and look at Rania intensely.

"King, I told you I can't tell you everything!" She yells for the first time as her eyes glow and her hair stands straight up.

"Rania, you really shouldn't make that face. It is not becoming of you," I say causing her to throw her hands in the air and exit the balcony, slamming the door behind her. I too throw my hands in the air and sprawl out on the cold cobblestones. Above me, the sky has lost many of its stars as I sit in darkness, the schools lights my only friends. "I at least should have asked her about this necklace," I say to myself as I turn on my side, revealing the broken-winged butterfly necklace.

Funnily enough, it is a light pink color and the metal feels cool as I run the silver chain through my fingertips. I look back up to the night sky and let out a long yawn. I feel like I haven't slept in days. The few stars above me start to sprinkle down on my eyelids, making them heavy as I drift off to sleep.

"King…King…" a voice whispers to me in my dreams. I see nothing but all I can hear is the man calling out my name. I feel myself walking farther, but know not where I am going. "King… King… I am here."

"Where are you? Do you need help?" I ask as I go to press the electronic medal that would call forth my sword, only to find that I am not wearing my uniform but a pair of silk pajamas and a heavy robe. It is a royal robe and even worse, it is covered in blood. I throw the royal garb far from me and it falls into the surrounding abyss. I hear my name again, but this time it is called by multiple voices in small, maniacal whispers. I grab my head, and as the voices get louder, my chest feels tighter, almost like a hole is being burnt into it. I grab the place where I was shot, but it is not there, it is in the center above my heart.

My eyes shoot open as I wake from the horrible nightmare. I grab for my chest and pull my hands back in shock, as the necklace is hot as a volcano! I jump up and lean forward to move it away from my chest, which is now blistered. The orb encased by the broken butterfly wings is no longer a pale pink but a strange coppery orange. The color swirls around in the orb, moving like lava; it's thick and pulsating and I think the orb might explode. I try to pull the necklace off of me, but it won't budge. I keep jerking my hands back, as the necklace seems to get hotter every time I try to yank it from my neck.

Stay calm, King, I tell myself. I take in deep breaths, but to no avail, as the necklace chain continues to burn the back of my neck.

"Young King, are you alright?" Ms. B asks from behind me.

The necklace cools and goes back to its regular opal color. Covered in sweat, I push it back under my shirt and lean to the side as if nothing is wrong. "Yeah, everything is fine. I was just resting out here and a bug fell on me."

"Ugh! Those pesky little critters! They even find their way all the way out here."

"Yeah, annoying little guys," I say as I jump up shuffling from side to side.

"Well, I was just wondering where you were. All the teachers met with your friends and took them to meet the girls, but I noticed you weren't there."

"Yeah, I guess I was more tired than I thought. It's so peaceful up here."

"It quite is. In my younger years, I fell asleep many a times wrapped in the stars' embrace," says Ms. B eloquently, but her smile slowly fades as it is hard for me to smile back at her.

She places her hands on my shoulders and asks, "Would you like to join me for a nighttime cup of tea? Cosmic Lotus Tea is the best for an uneasy mind."

I look up at her with wide eyes, surprised she could tell right away what is wrong with me. She extends her hand and I place mine in it, letting her lead me to her nighttime study.

Once inside, I sit on a long pink velvet chair. Ms. B moves to the small stove and puts on the teapot. I look around the antique, heavily draped room and see that many of the walls are covered in pictures, mostly of what must be her past students. I ask Ms. B if it is okay for me to take a closer look and she says of course. I scan the walls, looking at the young, talented dancers, some smiling with friends, some practicing, and others posing with Ms. B.

Farther down the wall, the pictures change from students into what seems like her family pictures. I find myself pausing, as much of the background looks familiar—too familiar, almost like Peace Island. Wait, it is Peace Island in these pictures! Ms. B is wearing a long white coat and posing on a beach, the hidden beach I saw while I was in the Neuro Center. But how?

"By the look on your face, it seems that I am exposed," she says from her chair. I turn around and she waves her hand for me sit down. She places a pot of Cosmic Lotus Tea in the middle of the marbled-wood table in front of her. I slowly return to the long pink chaise, trying to find the words. Ms. B looks at me. I guess she wants me to say something first, just in case. I move from side to side on the chaise, then awkwardly lean forward and pour myself and Ms. B cups of tea with shaking hands. The whole time I am unable to look at her. I don't want to lose another warm person, as everyone around me is starting to become something they are not. Then I remember how Rania told me when I was born, my life was surrounded by lies. I exhale deeply and finally look up at Ms. B, who still has the warmest smile you have ever seen. Maybe her lie won't be so bad.

I clear my throat and gulp down the tea, forgetting how hot it is. I throw the cup from my mouth and grab my lips, causing Ms. B to cover her own mouth trying not to laugh. Now I'm trying to hold in my laughter too. As the positive atmosphere is restored, I manage to ask her what is up with the pictures on her wall. "Ms. B, that picture looks like it was taken on Peace Island. Was it? Are you from there?"

She answers yes to both of my questions, so quick and unruffled that my mouth falls open. She goes on to say that she was a scientist on Peace Island and it was nothing to be ashamed of.

"Did you happen to work in the Neuro Center?" I slightly cross-examine her, hoping for more.

"Well, I did work beneath the castle. How do you know of the Neuros?"

"It's a long story…" I start off slowly, but for some reason I don't want to lie to Ms. B anymore. She has treated us with nothing but care and all our team has done is lie. I know I can't tell her the whole truth, but no more blatant dishonesty. And she worked under the castle, so I am sure she has encountered plenty of the strange ins and outs of Peace Island. "I know it's going to sound weird, but I sometimes can see visions, so I had to go down there so they could look into it."

"Oh my, how interesting." Ms. B pokes my cheeks, taking me by surprise. I chuckle it off as I draw away from her.

"Golly me. Sorry, young King. How rude. It's the scientist in me."

"I understand. By the way, King Vernon calls me that."

"I know, and your mother."

At the word "mother," I feel tears build up in my eyes. "You knew my mother?" I knock my knee into the coffee table, almost toppling over the late-night tea. Ms. B flails her hands in front of her and motions for me to sit again, telling me to calm down. Embarrassed, I look to the floor, clutching my hands together as I sit back in my seat. I ask her the same question, but softer this time.

Ms. B answers, to my greater surprise, that she actually knows all of our parents and the Dance Academy used to be on Peace Island. Students used to travel from all across Kasai to be trained by her. She tells me the academy is where Sione's parents fell in love and that Tuy's parents never could see eye to eye. Tuy's father always acted like he was the leader of the group. She goes on to tell of how they were some of Peace Island's greatest dancers, how she watched them progress from middle school children into well-rounded adults. She even tells me about Sidney's parents and that she was surprised Sidney isn't included in our group. I just smile at her, as there's no way I could tell her about that story. I vow to not even think about what I did to Sidney.

As she continues speaking about our parents and how the island was when she was a little girl, I start to wonder how old she really is, but I figure I would be way out of line if I tried to cross those waters.

"So, what happened?"

"What do you mean, young King?"

"Well, I thought you said you were a scientist—"

"One can have two jobs, one for monetary gain and the other for passion. I just decided as I got older to go full-on with my passion, and thankfully the monetary gain followed as well. Also, the whole Fera incident didn't sit well with me."

"You know about the Feras?"

"Unfortunately, because I was one of the ones that helped create them."

I lean back and gasp in my chair like a woman on Sunday morning hearing the latest gossip at the Sandy Beach hair salon on Peace Island. "Ms. B!" I exclaim.

"I know, young King. I am not proud of it either. But it really did start out as a simple experiment to multiply the rate at which bees produced honey. As you know, honey is the highest grossing trade good from our island. But that is why now I always make sure I seek out the whole truth, and always try to be one step ahead. Everything is not as it seems, like you and your friends." Ms. B takes a long sip of her tea, making her cheeks flush rosy red. My head spins a little bit as I realize she knows a lot more then she is letting on. I look over to the corner of the room where she prepared the tea and notice an open bottle of Floral Liquor, the perfect combination with hot tea. No wonder I feel so easy.

Ms. B is still smiling at me and I feel a lump in my throat. Sweating profusely, I feel myself stuttering, "Ms. B, are you trying to seduce me?"

At my words, she almost drops her teacup and saucer as she chokes back a parade of giggles. She throws her hands to her mouth, probably in fear of waking her sleeping students. Ms. B shakes her head from side to side, looking off into the distance with her eyes glazing over. "My, my, my, I never thought I would hear that again. Your father asked me the same thing."

I feel my world stop. "My father?" I choke out.

Ms. B looks at me and taps herself in the head. "This stupid mouth of mine. King, please do not ask me further about him. I will answer any other questions you have, but not about him."

"But Ms. B—"

"King, no," she says, giving me a stern look. We enter a staring contest and I can feel my blood boiling. Rania was right, there are so many lies around me, and lives that I have affected, it seems. I continue to stare at Ms. B, not giving in. I just need to know something.

I become unable to hold it in any longer as I think of my suffering mother. Being a single mother on Peace Island was no easy task. Many look down upon you and jobs are hard to find.

Finally, all the emotions from my past come over me full force. I hunch over and sob and shake uncontrollably.

As I continue to cry, I feel a light hand upon my back and hear Ms. B breathing heavily. She tells me not to cry and how hard it must have been for my mother. Ms. B once again taps herself in the head at the mess she has made by her slip of the tongue. "Okay, young King, if you would just stop I will tell you this one thing."

I slowly look up and she tells me, "No matter what anyone says, your father was a very special child. An amazing dancer, of course, obviously because he had a great teacher—"

I stare in confusion as she goes off track. Clearing her throat, she apologizes and continues. "Leaving you was one of his greatest sins, but in his lifetime, your father accomplished something very great. Poor child, that is all I really can tell you. You must learn who he is on your own. It seems you are on a very special journey, not only to find yourself but to set right the mistakes your parents have made, so you all might be able to live in true peace. But also know this, King, no matter what anyone tells you—" Suddenly Ms. B pauses and moves very close, causing me to think my theory about seduction was right. I quickly shake off my foolishness, though, and focus fully on her words: "Your father did not leave you willingly; he left you, in order for you to live."

I quickly pull back from Ms. B, waiting for her to tell me she is lying, but I fear I am now in the realm of the truth. I lunge forward and take her by the arms. "What do you mean?"

Yet she does not answer; she only lowers her head, and for the first time her smile fades and a tear falls. "Young King, I cannot answer that. Just remember this, no matter how strange it might sound: in this story, somewhere out there is a broken clock stuck in time, waiting for someone to move its hands, shine it back up, and start it anew. Don't get caught up in the reality. You must go beyond this world to set it back right and move the hands of time." Ms. B brushes my hands from her arms and leaves the room with me still in the same position, holding on to nothing.

Unable to bear the weight of the truth, I fall to my knees. I think the floral liquor is finally getting the best of me, as my head is so heavy I can barely keep it from tilting over. In the end, I just give in. A little sleep never hurt anyone. Well, at least when your dreams aren't out to get you. My head tips back and I settle onto the plush white shag carpet, descending into a deep sleep.

— IX —

THE MAN IN THE SHACK

The sun kisses my cheeks as I twirl in a cocoon of silk. A soft nest of feathers hides my face from the new day. I plant my face even deeper into the pillow on the bed, which I guess someone moved me to after they found me in Ms. B's study. I begin to drift back into sleep, not allowing myself to remember the stories of last night. A sharp pain suddenly hits my side and it won't let up.

I jump up and come face to face with Sione. I hit him on top of his head and he starts to fake cry. I roll my eyes, not in the mood for playing games. Sione notices my aura and calms down enough to ask me what is wrong. I just shake it off and tell him I am tired. In the end, Sione shrugs it off too, though I'm sure he is not completely convinced.

Sione rolls off the side of the bed and says that the academy students have made us a big breakfast and I should come downstairs soon. I nod, left behind with the weight of my thoughts as he goes to the door. But I don't want to be anymore. I call Sione's name and he turns to me. Before I know it, everything from last night comes spilling out. After I finish my long rant, Sione's face looks the same as he cockily shrugs his shoulders.

"Ms. B told us all about our parents last night, while you were sleeping on the balcony. But the information about your father is surprising."

I hit my head the same way Ms. B did because I probably should have left the part about my father out. Sione bursts into laughter and tells me I am turning into Ms. B. He closes the door and comes back to sit on the side of the bed.

"So, what do you think the whole 'setting the hands of time back' clock story was all about?"

I exhale deeply, taking a moment to answer. The same question has been haunting me all night. "I'm not sure. Maybe it has something to do with my father."

"Who, the Dark King?"

I jump at Sione's words and give him the evilest look he has probably seen in his whole life. "He is not my father. Why do you and Tuy insist on joking with me about that?" I say through gritted teeth.

Sione face turns sour as he avoids eye contact with me. "Sorry, King. I mean, at first, I was thinking he was, but now I know he is not. Last night we sort of told Ms. B about our real mission, and she said she had crossed paths with the Dark King before. But the good news is, she said he has grey eyes."

"I already know that, but that doesn't mean anything."

"Let me finish, King. The most important thing she said was, that he has a son, but he has grey eyes, and well, man," says Sione as he moves to close for comfort, "you just have plain old boring brown eyes, and dark brown at that."

I push Sione's face away from mine as I try to grasp the importance of the conversation. Where has this son been this whole time? Does he still live in Ren? Or is he beyond the wall… waiting!? Then it hits me and I grab Sione's arm. "Do you know what this means?"

"Yeah, that it's probably the son who is trying to get revenge for the way Kasai treated his father. So, why not start a war by attacking the most peaceful land in Kasai? We came to that conclusion after Ms. B told us many of the elders believe Ren is dead, but they know for a fact his son is still alive. That's why the spirit wall is still blocking Ren off from the rest of the world."

I stare blankly at Sione, feeling my blood boil. My arms take on a life of their own, gravitating to Sione's neck, and before I know it, I'm putting him in a choke hold.

"And at no point did you all think that 'maybe we should wake up King and brief him on this information'?"

Sione taps my arm, trying to get out of my grip. "What the heck do you believe I'm doing right now?"

Frustrated, I release my hold and throw him to the side. "Well, who figured all this out?"

"Tuy, with the help of information from Ms. B."

I scoff. "Figures. But there are one or two things that don't make sense. In my vision, something destroys our island. If his son still lives in Ren, how would he destroy our land from behind the wall? And two, Ms. B says that the elders know what his son looks like, so, wouldn't that mean he *is* beyond the spirit wall? And if the son is no longer behind that wall, we are in greater danger than we could have imagined."

"The elders probably saw him as a child, before the fall of Ren. But if somebody saw him after, why wasn't he stopped? In the whole nation very few people have grey eyes."

I take a moment before answering Sione. "Truthfully, I don't know. Maybe he covers them. But the good thing is, at least we finally have a target. The Dark King's son."

"I bet that's one strong bloke."

"No, Sione! That's even better, he probably isn't as powerful as his father."

"But he splits the island in two!"

"True, but how old did Ms. B say she thinks his son is?"

"Probably between the ages of eighteen and twenty-one. She told us that Ren supposedly died when his son was still young."

I snap my fingers, jump out of bed, and start to pace back and forth, Sione following me with his eyes.

"Exactly," I say, stopping in place. "There's no way he could have been taught how to wield spirit energy like his father. Somehow he awakens his father's powers, but recently, because if he already had them, he could have carried out his plans at sixteen. For example, look at Luna: she's only ten years old but understands so much!"

Sione jumps up and joins me in my theories. "Wait, King! Maybe the thing you are supposed to set right is a person, and that person is the Dark King's son. He might be in a place where his heart is consumed with revenge. But you are meant to show him that he is not his father. That with positivity, he could bring Ren back to its glory days and rejoin Kasai."

I jump on Sione, hugging him and slapping his back, telling him he is brilliant. We smile at each other in admiration of our own detective work.

"But wait. Why me?" I ask, causing Sione to scratch his head.

"Well, you did say that you believed your mom was a citizen of Ren. And last night Ms. B told you that your father had accomplished something great but lost you in the process. Maybe your parents were of high-status with a lot of influence, and knew the son. But honestly, you might be a coward but you definitely have your mother's strong positivity. Truthfully, King, positivity and love could change the world, or dare I say warm the heart of a bitter prince?"

"Maybe. Well, we must find him before he learns how to use his father's powers to their full extent and becomes consumed by them."

"Poor guy. He has probably lived so long with so much hate in his heart. It's not easy for a kid when the whole nation hates your father," Sione says as he pulls out a handkerchief and wipes away fake tears.

I snatch the handkerchief from him and tell him, "That is not nice."

Sione shrugs his shoulders and says, "At this moment he's still the enemy and already has in his head the thought to destroy our island and the rest of Kasai. Therefore, until we meet him and change him, he is public enemy number one."

All I can do is agree.

After breakfast, the whole team regroups in the courtyard of the academy in the sky. The girls and all the teachers stand at the top of the stairs holding their ballet slippers and tapping them together, their way of saying goodbye. The girls begin to part like waves, and Ms. B comes out from in between them and tells us to stand in a line and hold out our hands. She starts with Rania, placing a small lotus flower in her hand and kissing her forehead. She makes her way down the line and does the same for each of us, but stops at my forehead and adds something. She sets an olive branch in my hair before winking at me and placing a kiss upon my forehead. She then pulls back and says "Not to worry, King—I'm not trying to seduce you."

The others' heads snap in our direction as my cheeks become warm. But Ms. B doesn't flinch as she just claps her hands in the air. She tells us to get going, as it is dangerous on the Road of Bones at night. We all salute Ms. B as she calls us precious gems, but once we turn to leave, I feel empty. It's wonderful for a Peace Island citizen to be living a great life off the island. Yet, even though we are high in the air, I can still see the mountains of the backside of Ren to my right, and I realize I'm no different than them. They might have a physical wall locking them in, but it seems Peace Island has a mental wall locking us in.

"Finally made it!" We all squeal leaping free from the schools giant swinging vines, finally back on solid ground—well, ground attached to the mainland. We head off once more down the Road of Bones. We walk for what feels like hours in quiet. Then Sione suddenly leans over to me and asks if we really need to go see the man in the shack. As I am still unsure about this spirit energy thing, I shake my head yes. I tell him there is no guarantee that after we find the prince he will willingly change his ways. Sometimes you have to fight power with power. It's better to be prepared and not called than to be called and not prepared. Sione leans back and gives me a look of approval, saying he didn't realize I was wise. I stick my tongue out at him as we continue down the road silently.

The road starts to become shadowed with trees and bushes until we are in a full forest. I hear many animals around us in what now is playing out to be an eerie scene. I start to have a bad feeling. Tuy looks back at us and we all call forth our weapons, putting on our highest guard, but not high enough.

From the dense forest, a giant elk stampedes through the trees. He reaches the road and crashes what look like twelve-inch-thick antlers into Tuy, lifting him 10 ft. in the air. I look at Rania, who has already set out to catch him before he crashes back to the earth. I plant my feet firmly in the dirt road as I grip my sword tightly, taking a strong stance and so does the elk. He poses with his front hoof perched before Sione and I, as if to show off all of his majesty. This beast is no regular elk. It has to stand at least thirteen feet high, with thick brown hair and a strong build. His antlers,

L. STITT

four of them, look sharp as swords at the edges. Each is a different color. I look more closely and a wave of fear comes rushing over me.

"Sione," I mutter, gripping his shoulder. "Remember the story about the different spirit energies?" He nods. "Look at the colors on this beast's antlers. What do they remind you of?"

Sione looks at me, and I see rather than hear him mutter, "Crap." The elk rears, standing straight up and throwing a ray of green spirit energy from his left back antler. Sione and I dodge it in time, falling to the opposite sides of the road.

The elk cries out and swirls his head in circles, he picks up so much velocity, he creates a wind storm mixed with spirit energy. His great show of power starts to drag our bodies through the rocky forest, separating us even farther. Sione and I reach out for thick branches, clawing at the ground, trying to find stability as rocks, twigs, and trees play ball with our bodies, but to no avail. We are pushed farther into the forest. In the distance, I still hear the elk groaning.

I pull myself together and grab my sword. The pain shooting up my back, from being blown through the forest, is unbearable. I try to roll to give myself momentum enough to get on my feet. Except, after pushing myself through small bushes, I come face to face with a cliff.

I shoot up and cry out in pain. Grabbing my back, I walk to the edge of the cliff and look over it once more. I recognize the cliff from my dream in the Neuro Center. What meaning could this possibly have? I feel a cool breeze and wonder what strange thing will happen next, but this is no time to be worried about myself. I turn to run back to battle, but the battle has come to me. Golden eyes appear behind the trees, and before I can lift my sword, the grand elk runs toward me like he did to Tuy. But instead of catching me on his antlers, with great agility, at the last moment he turns and kicks, pushing me off the cliff.

Bouncing off branches that cut and gnash my skin, I cry out with every impact. I look up and see the elk peer over the side of the cliff, almost like he's making sure he got the job done, before he turns to walk away.

This cannot be my end. I can't die. For if I die, so does Kasai. I still must get to the emperor and find the prince. "The clock has to be set back right," I whisper as I extend my hand and grab a thick branch growing from the face of the cliff. I yell out in pain, attempting to pull myself back up to a ledge on the side of the jagged mountain. I use all of the strength inside of me, screaming for dear life, pulling myself up branch by branch.

Making it to the ledge, I fall over into its safe embrace, lying like an unborn child. I lean my head on the wall and try to catch my breath. Once I do, I scream out for Sione, Tuy, Rania, and even Luna, but no one answers. My cheeks grow warm, but I push emotion to the side and grab my sword, which I use as a cane to lift myself.

I fell what looks like at least 30 feet from the side of the cliff, I call out for the others, but still no one answers. I try to reach one of the branches, thinking I could climb back up the mountain, but my arms are too weak. I yell once again, this time only for Rania. Of all people I expect her to be okay—she is a divine being, after all—but she does not answer my call.

At least I no longer hear the elk. But I start to panic, as I am not sure what is going on. I grab my chest as I feel a sharp pain. I remove the black chest plate from under my uniform and look under it to see blood spreading over my left breast, where I was shot a few days ago. Reaching for the cliff wall, I cannot grasp it because I'm coughing uncontrollably. Blood begins to pour from my lips. Still trying to find something to hold myself up on, I fall back and my head crashes into rock. I have to be the weakest soldier there ever was.

I look over to the mountains of Ren, which are farther off than before, though the peaks are still in my sight. All of this because of Ren, because one man became consumed with power. His past sins are turning so many lives upside down. I hate this journey, I hate that our princess killed someone with her bare hands, I hate that Peace Island's dirty secrets are seeping out! I even hate this damn grey-eyed son that nobody has ever seen. All of this because of bottled-up hate. How cruel is this country before my eyes?

My blood boils and with my last strength I yell at the top of my lungs, full of hate for Ren. I scream over and over again. As I cry out for the last time, the mountains of Ren let loose a loud rumble, as if they are volcanos about to erupt. White spirit energy, so powerful and even more amazing than Rania's pink, shoots up in the air, twirling and swirling. It turns toward me. I try to dodge it, but my pain has become too great to move well. Before it strikes me, though, it stops inches from my face, dancing before my eyes before wrapping around me. I grab for my neck as my necklace grows hot; I look down and see it is the same color it was the night it burned me on the balcony. The white spirit energy twirls one last time before erupting in the air again, but this time it enters the forest. I hear a great roar as the giant elk that tortured me and my friends is pushed over the cliff by the white spirit energy, passing me, as he falls to what I assume to be his death. With that, the spirit energy returns to the distant mountains.

I feel paralyzed, trying to figure out what I just witnessed. And why did it come from the direction of Ren, of all places? I finally gasp for air, just realizing I'd been holding my breath. I clutch my chest, which is no longer bleeding. Shaking, I wipe the blood from my mouth and once again reach for my sword. I am afraid but I must keep moving for my comrades. I lean again on my sword, standing, I want to cry out once more for somebody, but I'm scared of what I will hear in return.

I look up with tears in my eyes, knowing my worst fears must have come true. But then a long, thick rope falls from the edge of the cliff. A dapper man with a long white beard peeks his head over and gives me a reassuring smile. He scales down the mountain, in one swift motion grabbing me from the side, and pulls his way back up with me in his arms. Once we reach the top of the cliff, he places me down and stretches out his back before standing up straight. I find myself in awe, as this man who has just saved my life looks at least seventy years old. And though he wears a dandy suit, a very odd choice for the middle of the forest, I might add, I can tell he has the body of a twenty-year-old.

I try to speak, but it feels like blood is still in my throat, making it hard not to cough. The old man shakes his head and props me up to lean on him, though I still use my sword as a cane. He leads me back through the woods, which are now full of broken branches, most likely caused by the elk and the spirit beam I witnessed earlier.

When we get back to the main road, I see the others all laid out on a giant metal cart. I weasel out of the old man's embrace to run to my friends. For a moment, I stop and look at myself, covered in blood, cuts, and bruises, and wonder how I am no longer in the excruciating pain I was in a few minutes ago. I shake off this phenomenon and move closer to the cart. Sione, Tuy, and surprisingly Luna have all been beat up pretty badly. I tilt my head to the side, wondering what could have happened with Rania to make her lose control.

Once again, I try to speak but I am unable to. I look at myself frantically, then over to the old man, who just pats me on the head and motions for me to get onto the cart. At first I don't lie down, unsure of who this man is. Just because he saved me doesn't mean anything. As Ms. B says, the truth isn't always the whole truth. I call forth my sword, but before I can make a move the old man knocks it from my hands with his foot and catches it. He swings it around him and taps the hilt on my head, causing me to stumble and lose my balance.

As I'm on the ground, he says in a strong voice, "Don't worry, I am a friend. I live in a shack down the road. I will care for your friends and that little nasty problem you have with your throat."

The man in the shack. I stand and bow my head, apologizing. The old man waves it off and helps me onto the metal cart. He goes to the front of the cart and picks it up with great strength, not even putting a crease in his brown dress shoes. I look at him in concern for how he is going to pull this cart with four people on it; this is a task that would even be hard for Sione. The old man blinks both eyes at me, an oddly cute expression, as if to say he will be okay. I lie down completely next to the others as the old man starts off down the road with great gusto.

While I look up, trees are speeding past me, but soon we break from the forest's embrace and the sky can fully be seen once again. I take a closer look at Luna. Thankfully, she isn't hurt as badly as the others, just a few cuts and bruises. I look past her to Tuy and notice beyond him that we are going up the side of the mountain on a narrow road. I grow queasy. Unable to shout even if I wanted to, I just lie back down. Surprisingly, I make eye contact with an awake Sione.

I lean up and look at him as if to ask what happened. He just shakes his head and closes his eyes. It is some type of relief to know that Sione has regained consciousness. Tuy looks like the most injured out of all of us. He is out cold, bruised, and has not just cuts, but gashes all over his body. I wince as I see a long cut going down from the side of his neck to his chest, most likely caused by the elk's first attack. How in the world is he alive? I peer at his chest, praying for any type of movement, and yes, my prayer is answered.

I grab my throat, still trying to find a way to speak, but to no avail. I just fall back onto the cold metal cart. We finally come to a stop and I jump up, leaning over Sione, and throw up over the side from the bumpy ride. I feel Sione hitting my back. I wipe my mouth and nod at him while raising my hand and placing it on his shoulder. Sione makes an ugly face. "Are you crazy?"

I try to speak, but even after throwing up I still am unable too. Sione sits up, pushing me off of him, and asks what's wrong, but even I don't know the answer to his question.

The old man comes around to the side of the cart, surprising Sione. "Your friend has dried up blood in his throat. So he is having trouble talking.

My eyes grow large as I point to the ground where I vomited.

"Calm down, young man. You see, that blood in your throat isn't your only problem. With just that, though uncomfortable, you still would be able to speak a little. Something else must have caused you to lose your voice. Nevertheless, it will take time to heal." Sione shrugs his shoulders and I become very confused, yet almost as if he can read my mind, the old man adds, "But it is very strange that everything else about you is okay, especially being covered in cuts and bruises. I guess somebody wanted you to be quiet for a while." He laughs.

"I'm sorry, but who are you?" asks Sione, leaning over the side of the cart. The old man too leans back, kind of shocked at Sione's rude tongue. I pop my friend on the shoulder, making him holler in pain. I freak out, having forgotten he was injured, and start to apologize with my amazing body language skills. Sione continues yelling at me and the old man begins to laugh uncontrollably.

"You two are very funny. Now look, I could spend all night out here, but it is getting cold. You, the one that can't speak, help me grab your friends and come on inside," he says. I nod my head and gently pick up Tuy as he fetches Luna.

"Well, what about me?" yells Sione. I roll my eyes as I go back to give him a shoulder to lean on, all the while holding Tuy. As Sione gets off the cart, he looks up and yells in my ear, "Hey, it's the shack!" Sione points at it, then looks to the old man and says, "and the old man! It's the shack and the old man. The man in the shack!"

I pause for a moment, looking Sione dead in his face, judging him harshly. I wonder if he hit his head in the last battle, but then I remember he is just being himself.

I shake my head and drag him along, past a wooden fence with yellow lanterns attached at each post. The shack in front of me looks old and small. It reminds me of a picture a child would draw when trying to draw a house. The shack is a simple rectangle with a triangle roof and two windows in the front.

The old man gently holds Luna in his arms as he fumbles with his keys. He lets out a squeal of joy as he gets the key into the hole on the first try, then says something about how dark it gets at night out on the Road of Bones.

As we enter the shack, our mouths drop open. One would expect no more than a bed, kitchen, and couch all stuffed in one small room, but that is not the case. The front of this perfectly drawn child's-house is only the foyer to a much bigger floor plan.

Sione and I stand in the middle of a marble floor with a crystal chandelier above our heads. In front of us, steps lead down to a huge living room filled with expensive furniture, all types of trinkets, and even a HoloTube. The old man tells us not to be shy and to follow him, as we need to take our friends to their rooms—especially Tuy, who he says needs to be treated immediately.

"Who is going to do this treatment?" Sione asks as we head down a long hall farther in the back of the shack.

"Me, obviously." The old man smiles as Sione and I look at him in surprise. But then I swat Sione away, realizing that this old man is more than he seems. How else could he hide a mansion on the side of the road by constructing it to look like a shack on the outside? His strength brings up another question as well, and all while dressed like the gentlemen in the southern tailor shops on Peace Island. I know that Tuy and Luna are in good hands.

Sione and I wait in the room the old man prepared for us while he tends to Tuy and Luna first. The double bedroom has simple white décor, small greenery, and strange abstract golden vases and art forms. I squeeze in between a giant purple and gold twisted vase in the corner and look out the window that was hiding behind it. Thankfully, I can't see the mountains of Ren in the distance. Their menacing presence isn't something I need think about at the moment, but having no self-control, I do. I bring my hands around my neck and try to speak, but only painful screeches escape my vocal cords. I exhale heavily as I throw my body onto the windowsill, which is large enough for me to take a seat and even has a small cushion. I look out at the fog-covered valley. Looking farther down, I screech in wonder. I pull some of the plant leaves from the vase and throw it at Sione, who jumps up, frightened, probably dreaming that The Elk had returned.

He sees the leaves at the bottom of his bed and looks over at me. I wave for him to come to the window and point below at the pool. Just like at Ms. B's, Sione doesn't show any excitement. "Most inns have pools, King."

I furrow my brow as if to ask, what does he mean by inn?

Sione tells me that the old man had told him that this place is actually an inn for weary travelers on the Road of Bones. Though he doesn't get many customers anymore because most people travel to Oak City by ship. I tilt my head again, but being a weary traveler myself, I just nod and look back out the window. Sione places a firm hand on my shoulder.

We both look out, slipping off into a daydream; then there is a knock at the door. We turn around and Sione tells them to come in. The door creaks open slowly and the old man slips into our room. Without wasting time on small talk, he tells us to lie down.

We lie side by side as the old man rummages through a big black box. It looks less like a doctor's bag than like a big toolbox with multiple shelves. He pulls out all sort of strange-looking tools as he mumbles to himself. I gulp at the sight of an actual drill, then wince, for my throat is still in pain. The old man turns to me first.

"Sorry, young man, I can't really do anything for you. You have to let that heal on its own. But!" he takes out a strange, light green oval fruit and shakes it from side to side, while I can hear liquid swishing around. "I have a ko fruit. This little guy will ease some of your pain and hopefully have you talking in a few days." The old man pulls out a long knife, cuts off the top of the fruit, and grabs a straw from his toolbox, placing it in the fruit in one single motion. He hands me the fruit and I smile to say thank you.

Truthfully, I'm quite parched. I wrap my dry lips around the straw, only to spit the juice back as quickly as it came. The old man lets out a typical old geezer laugh, slapping his knee. "Oops. Forgot to mention, it's unbearably sour." He winks at me and pushes his hands under the fruit, telling me to drink up and to not leave a drop.

I throw my head back in disgust, but the old man gives me the look of a thousand grandfathers, and I give in. Then he turns to Sione, who starts to roll off the bed in an attempt to escape. The old man grabs him by his utility belt. "Not so fast, piggy."

"Hey," says Sione with a sad look on his face. The old man just shrugs and says he calls them as he sees them. He motions for Sione to take off his uniform and under armor, revealing his rock-hard abs and lean muscles.

"Well, seems I was mistaken," says the old man in awe. Sione just nods arrogantly, reminding me why we never go to the beach together anymore. All the ladies would be looking my way, but then Sione takes of his armor, which includes extra padding, and reveals his true self. I secretly roll my eyes and purse up my lips while sucking on my sour juice, and unfortunately Sione catches me. He starts to flex his muscles and I want to vomit. Such a show-off.

"Would you hold still?" says the old man, hitting the flexing Sione. "What in tarnation are you two doing? It's not good to pick on your weak friends, young man, because one day they might become strong and then you will want to be on their good foot."

At his words, I return the same arrogant look Sione gave me. Yet I too am wacked on the head as the old man gives both of us his famous look, causing us to lower our heads.

While he continues to see about Sione's wounds, I look down at my body and wonder again, how was I covered in so much blood but I'm already recovering? Even stranger, my chest doesn't even show a scratch. How could a closed wound suddenly open? I know I didn't hit it as I was falling as I mainly fell straight back. Blood just started pouring out, as if my death was only on hold.

The old man looks over to me, and it seems that he too is wondering how I am covered in so much blood while no longer having any wounds. "It seems that you found favor from afar," he says. I tilt my head to the side as a way to ask what he means. "I can tell your wounds were healed with some type of spirit energy… pure spirit energy."

"Maybe you healed yourself, King!" exclaims Sione. I turn to him and turn back just as quickly to my finished ko fruit on the nightstand, taking the straw out of it and throwing it at him. I swear my best friend can't hold water.

"Your friend here can wield spirit energy?"

Sione starts out speaking slowly. "Yes, that is actually why we are here. We were looking for you, hoping you could explain more about spirit energy. Truthfully—" Sione sees me cut my eyes at him and stops in mid-sentence.

The old man looks at me, but instead of the look of a thousand grandpas, he simply gives me a warm smile, the same way Ms. B did. He places his hand into mine. "I know we just met, but you can trust me. However, I won't force you to tell me anything you are uncomfortable with."

He turns back to Sione and finishes the final touches on his arm before packing up his stuff and heading to the door. He opens it, but stops and turns back to us. "I mean, we don't even know each other's names. So, I understand. However, it seems that you all will need my help. If you desire the truth in this world of lies, come to the common area around twelve at night on the day the weak one finds his voice. Also, be sure to bring your other male friend—he will be well by then—but leave the child. For we have many things to discuss, and it will be past her bedtime."

Sione finds the strength to stand and manages to extend his back some as he walks to the old man and shakes his hand. "We will be there."

"Very well. But until then, please make yourself at home. There is plenty of food in the refrigerator in the common area. Oh, and there are some fresh clothes and comforters in the armoire. I am sure you want to get out of those messy clothes and change those bloody comforters. Let's not act too much like men now," the old man says while giving a wink and closing the door behind him.

As the door shuts, Sione falls straight back on the bed, but jumps up in abruptly remembered pain. "Did I say too much?" he asks as he turns to me. I whip my hand in the air as if to say, it doesn't really even matter. I head for the armoire, pull out the fresh clothes, and make my way to the shower. As the water runs over me, washing off the blood that covered almost half my body, I finally let it all free.

One tear escapes my eyes, soon joined by its friends. I crouch in the shower and let the warm water tear at my back. I start to cry even harder.

I try to scream but I can't even do that. Unable to burn off stress with my voice, I punch at the tiled shower wall. Truth be told, I don't want to speak with the old man in a few days, nor do I even want to know his name. He might have saved me from that cliff, but what he will tell me about this spirit energy scares me. As I think further on the matter, I clutch at the broken butterfly necklace, which at the moment has no life within the gem. Even the burn mark from it has healed. I feel like a freak.

I'm turning into exactly what the kids used to call me. I was so happy to tell them that I could sometimes see in the future. I just wanted them all to know that I had a dream that the teacher was going to bring in raz cakes next month for some of my classmates' birthdays. I thought everyone would be happy, but when my dream actually came true, it was a whole different story. Everyone looked at me as if I was some sort of monster. They would stick gum in my hair, trip me, and one day I was even stoned.

I smile slightly, remembering that was the day I met Sione. He was large, round, and in charge. Once Sione was on my side, the other kids dared not bother me. He said that he felt sympathy for me; being bigger than all the other kids, he was also picked on. He told me that day that I shouldn't let what makes me different be a hindrance to me, but instead I should use it to my advantage.

That stupid grin he had on his face. I don't believe that I have made my differences into my strengths. I just hid them in fear of being labeled a freak. But I guess those differences are mad at me for locking them away for so long. Now they are practically bursting out from inside of me, letting the whole world know the freak has arrived. I don't want these powers; I have a sword and that is all I need to fight my battles. I don't want to be the freak; I just want to be normal.

Knock knock. "You okay in there?" asks Sione from the other side of the door. Quickly I wipe the tears from my face, even though they wouldn't have been seen. I grab a towel and wrap it around my waist. Peeking my head out the door, I come face to face with Sione. I nod, pretending to be happy, but to no avail. "Why are your eyes red?" he asks. I wave my hand in front of my mouth and use the fact that I can't talk to avoid his question, but that doesn't work on him. "Something's wrong, and just because you can't speak doesn't mean you can't write. There's some paper in the top drawer of the nightstand. Get changed and get to writing. I'll be out of the shower soon." Sione pushes past me into the steamy bathroom throwing my clothes at me as he slams the door dramatically.

I change reluctantly, as I go to the nightstand and pull out a small black leather-bound notebook with lilac lined paper, which is a strange and expensive accommodation for an inn, but it's whatever. I make my way back to the windowsill and sit lovingly in its embrace. It has begun to rain, and for some reason I feel more melodramatic than usual.

As I write the first word, on what feels like freshly pressed paper and smells like flowers, I lose myself. Soon I'm writing uncontrollably. I let out all that I have been keeping in since the beginning of the journey. My memories of General Claude, the meeting with my mother, how I still don't trust Rania, but most importantly that I don't even trust myself.

I am so afraid to learn about this energy inside of me because I am not completely sure, one, that I can live up to its power, and two, what if I go mad with it like King Ren? My mind is not always the safest place and sometimes I have no control. I see things I don't want to see, and now these foreign powers are manifesting themselves into the real world from within me.

Do you know what it's like to not be in control? Especially of your own life?

My hand shakes as I continue writing under the moonlit, rainy night. I wipe my tears roughly as I bleed my soul onto the pages of the black leather notebook. I finally pause.

I find myself in a place I am in often. Afraid that if I share everything, I will lose everything, that Sione will also think of me as a freak. That one of few people who loves me for who I am, will turn on me. My mother is already gone; I don't want to lose my friend that is like my brother. The pen shakes uncontrollably in my hand as I start to curve out the first letter of the darkest of my inner thoughts.

"Woah! Are you writing a book?" Sione places a heavy hand on my shoulder. I jump up and close the book as my deepest fear hides deep in my heart once again. Sione swiftly grabs the notebook from my hands and sits down on a chair in the corner, turning on the gold lamp beside it.

"Why were you writing over there, dude?" He asks, pulling out a pair of tiny black wire glasses from his bathrobe and looking up at me. I just stare back at him. "Ah! I forgot you can't talk. But from the looks of it, you were having one of your melodramatic moments." Unable to deny the truth, I do my best impression of Ms. B, by thumping my head, causing us both to laugh. Well, at least I try to laugh, but only end up hurting my throat. "Take it slow, King. You have to heal soon so we can talk with the old man. We need to get to Oak City sooner than later. Also, don't worry about Tuy and Luna. I'll go check on them later." Sione finally flips open the notebook that contains all of me and dives in.

After what feels like hours of me biting my nails and breaking out into a cold sweat, Sione shuts the leather-bound notebook with one hand and lets out a heavy sigh. He doesn't look up at me, instead staring at the closed notebook with a concerned face. I can tell he is trying to think of the words to say. He finally composes himself and lifts his head, but he only whispers, "Wow."

I quickly look back out the window, afraid what more he will say. Afraid that he will finally realize the freak that I am. But instead of greeting me with judgmental words, he whispers my name gently. I slowly turn my head back toward him. He smiles at me and I slowly do the same.

"I'm sorry we didn't realize the effect this whole trip would have on you. We all just sort of rushed in...well, to be fair, Tuy did, as I didn't know of this trip's true intentions until later. However, I knew the journey began from a vision, and I know how sensitive you are when it comes to that. Every step we take, you must fear that it will lead us all closer to the end, the bitter end. But know this, King, I already told you, the things that make you different don't make you a freak or a bad person. Because of your uniqueness, we have the opportunity to save our island. You are strong and once you learn about these powers, I know without a doubt you will have complete control. Look at the way you stopped the cannonball and saved the princess, and how you managed to walk away from The Elk attack without a scratch on your body. You freakin' fell of the side of a cliff, but managed to not fall to your death.

"I didn't tell you but when that light, spirit beam, or whatever it was came and killed The Elk, he had me pinned down and was ready to attack. I had none of my weapons and he had both of my arms pinned under his massive hooves. But you know what? At that moment, I could hear you screaming, not out of fear but a battle cry. You were determined to make something happen even though you were at your breaking point, and what did you do? You made the impossible happen. The faith that you had was strong enough to call energy from the side of a mountain, killing the elk and ultimately saving us. That type of faith, hope, and strength can only come from a man with a strong mind. King, I'm begging you not to fear the unknown, but trust yourself. You know who you are and you know, deep down inside, you can handle this. I believe there is too much love in your heart for you to end up like the Dark King."

I wish I could say I'm one who doesn't show emotions a lot, but I would be lying to myself. After Sione finishes speaking, I can't help but jump up and hug him. I can feel that he is taken aback at first, but he quickly gives in to my show of affection. I finally pull from him and bashfully look away, embarrassed at the unmanliness I showed, but Sione just brushes it off. "There's no reason for you to be embarrassed. We men have to let out our emotions sometimes, or it will all just build up and eat away at our insides."

For the next couple of days, I take time to recover in the comfort of the inn. I rest, eat a little, rest some more; Sione and I even go to the pool. All the while we're waiting for Tuy and Luna to wake up. "I'm starting to worry about them," Sione says, turning from the HoloTube in the common area and looking at me on the other end of the couch, "and you as well. It's been four days and you still can't talk. It's obvious that ko fruit is no good!"

I agree with Sione, but as I am powerless I slouch back into the couch and return my focus to the drama on the HoloTube. Sione whacks my arm, unfortunately taking my attention from the addictive acting of Trinity's star actors. "King! This is serious! This is no time to be worried about Lyon's parents faking Moon's death, in order for him to marry the woman they chose to be queen. I mean, you can't speak, aren't you worried? I'm going to figure this out. Where did that old man go?"

I point to the front door, indicating that the old man went out for the afternoon. Sione grumbles and plops back down on the couch, folding his arms in front of him. "Well, let's not sit here all day. I'm going to visit Tuy and Luna's room, you coming?"

I shake my head and jump up off the couch with Sione. We make our way down from the common area and around the corner, entering Tuy and Luna's room at the end of the hall. I wince a little, as it still pains me to see both of them hooked up to oxygen tanks along with needles and fluids being pumped into them. Their room looks just like ours, but feels like a hospital, which I hate.

Sione sits next to Luna and begins reading a book to her that he found in the library at the opposite end of the residence halls. When I sit down by Tuy, I feel bad that I cannot comfort him with words. In the corner, there is a small porcelain pitcher filled with water, a porcelain basin, and a white towel. I pour the cool water from the pitcher into the basin, get the towel just damp enough, and begin dabbing Tuy's forehead. This is all I have to give him. I am wary of the cuts and bruises on his face; not wanting to infect any of them, I pat around them slowly.

A good hour passes, and after getting to the end of the chapter, Sione says that we should fix something to eat. I nod in agreement as we haven't eaten since breakfast.

"By the way, did you know that there is a giant elk leg in the freezer outside?"

Shocked at Sione's words, I imagine the old man going back and searching for fresh meat from the dead elk. I jerk back, accidently rubbing the towel roughly over the gash on the side of Tuy's head, making him jerk as well.

"Tuy!" exclaims Sione. Tuy grabs my hand, which is still lying on his gash. He opens his eyes slowly and moves my hand and towel from his forehead. I nod to say sorry, but do not break our shared gaze.

Words cannot describe how happy I am to see him coming back to. Now I understand why in the old stories of war, they tried to take out the leader first, hoping to cause the whole army to crumble. Without Tuy, Sione and I have felt lost for the past couple of days.

"Why are you two staring at me like that?" Tuy whispers, obviously in pain. At his words, Sione and I foolishly fall upon him with hugs. He winces, but he is the soldier of soldiers, so we know he can take it. Plus, we know he likes the attention. Tuy lightly pats our backs and we finally let up off of him. He tries to lift himself up in a sitting position, but is still weak. Sione helps prop him up.

"What the heck happened?" Tuy asks, focusing on the image in the mirror behind me of his bruised and beaten self.

"We were ambushed by a giant elk. It took you out first, by ramming you from the side."

"Oh, that's right. Foul beast! Didn't even hear him coming, but I felt him." Tuy manages to let out a laugh of dark humor.

"Yeah, he definitely showed you. Rania saved you, though. I believe she caught you before you fell, but we're not entirely sure. Right after he attacked you, he didn't waste any time turning his focus on us."

"I see. I do remember being in Rania's arms, but something strange happened"—Tuy exhales sharply and grabs his head— "but I just can't remember."

"Don't strain yourself, man."

"Well, what about you?"

"Stupid thing pinned me down and tried to give me a shot of spirit energy straight through the chest."

"Spirit energy?"

"Yep. The Elk had four antlers, each one contained a different spirit energy. He held all of them at the crown of his head."

"Strange. It doesn't seem like a creature like that would be roaming around on the Road of Bones. Most of the Majestics, which is what the elders called enchanted or magical beasts, live near a village at the northernmost point of Kasai, at the tip, behind Trinity."

"Okay then, what are you suggesting?"

"Well, I assume this is the old man's shack."

"Correct. It's actually an inn, though."

"Inn, shack, whatever you want to call it, it's all the same. Anyway, that village is a good thousand miles away from here. What would a grand beast like that be doing so far from home?"

"It almost makes you feel like someone planted him there, just for us."

"Yep. And get this, most of the Majestics are peaceful, especially Elk."

"Well, well, well, looks like somebody has finally caught on to our secret mission," Sione says, rubbing his hands through his hair.

"Seems that way." Tuy leans back on the headboard and turns his face to me with a strange look. "What's the matter, cat got your tongue?"

Sione busts out laughing, almost falling off the side of the bed. I grab the towel in the basin and throw it at him. "Sorry, man. Sorry. But yeah, the cat actually does have his tongue. Actually more like The Elk." Sione busts out in laughter again. This time I pick up the basin and act like I'm going to throw it at him. Sione just sticks out his tongue.

"It ate your tongue?" Tuy leans forward as he tries to look in my mouth. I hit myself in the face and just keep my hand planted for a minute as Sione continues to laugh. Tuy is still staring at me, mortified. I open my mouth slowly and he squeals, scared of what lies or doesn't lie behind my teeth.

I stick out my tongue and even put on a show, twirling it around. I snap my fingers at Sione and nod for him to tell Tuy. Sione finally stops laughing, tears in his eyes. "That was pretty funny. But no, the elk didn't eat his tongue. He somehow lost his voice. We thought it was dried blood in his throat, but the old man said even with that, he would still be able to talk a little. So our conclusion was, somebody was just trying to shut King up, and whatever the problem, medical or supernatural, has to heal on its own."

"I see," Tuy says, giving me a good once-over. "But, uh, let me ask you another question. Why don't you have any battle scars?"

Sione and I look at each other and then back at Tuy. Sione moves closer to him and places a firm hand on his shoulder. "It's a long story, and you're going to want to get comfortable."

After Sione finishes the story, Tuy sinks farther in the bed and seems puzzled for some reason. I tilt my head to the side to ask him what's wrong. He shakes his head before saying, "Very interesting."

Just then the door swings open and the old man stands there tall, dressed in an all linen, loose blue sweatsuit. "I see that you are finally awake." He moves to Tuy's side and begins to check his vitals. "Well, I would say that your friend here will be fine. I would even say he can go for a walk, at least around the lobby, maybe a little after twelve." The old man winks and leaves as quickly as he came. I try to yell after him to ask about Luna, forgetting that I have no voice. I tap Sione and point toward the princess, hoping he'll go after the old man and figure out when she will be recovering. But Sione, who is probably annoyed with my continuous slaps on his arm, misses the timing and the door closes.

I'm frustrated that he can find time to read to Luna, but does not even think to ask about her situation. I jut out my chin toward Sione and roll my eyes before exclaiming, "Luna! You forgot to ask about the princess!"

I quickly bring my hands to my mouth, coughing uncontrollably. Once it passes, pain still tickles my throat, but I can now speak. I look at Sione and Tuy and smile.

Sione smiles back and says, "Well, I guess we're all ready to go."

Lies

We fill Tuy in about meeting the old man at the lobby around midnight, and arrive at that time looking like a band of patients. We've pushed Tuy in a wheelchair, while Sione holds his bandaged arms close to himself, trying not to hit them on anything. But there I am, no scratches and a voice that finally sounds like an angel.

"Must be nice," Tuy says, looking up at me from his wheelchair. I give him an awkward smile as he clicks his tongue and turns around.

"Yippee! All of you are here; glad you could make it." We turn around to find the old man dressed in silk pajamas and carrying a pot of Cosmic Lotus Tea. "Well, time is of the essence. Follow me." He heads down the hallway opposite the residence rooms.

Before I can start off behind him, Sione leans in and whispers, "Gee, these Road of Bones village people sure do love their Cosmic Lotus Tea and pajamas."

"I heard that!" the old man exclaims from down the hall. Sione and I look at each other, shocked, and say not another word. The old man pops his head out of a room about seven doors down. "And if you are talking about Ms. B, she got her love for Cosmic Lotus Tea from me, being as she is my ex-wife. Humph." He waves his hand into the room sharply as he disappears.

Tuy looks up at Sione and grits his teeth. "I don't even have the energy to say anything."

"Sorry…" says Sione.

"How many more times am I going to have to hear that?"

"A lot," I simply say, making us all bust out into laughter.

We enter a room that looks like all the others, way to plain to be the old man's room. Tuy points to the far corner, where the bathroom should be behind a cut-out, but in this room the bathroom wall has been pushed to the side to reveal a hidden passage with a long flight of wooden stairs. Tuy gets on my back, being as I am the healthiest of us all, and we make our way down. At the end of the stairs, we come to a study room and the wall shuts behind us. Lanterns around the room light up the stone walls. It contains miles of books, a desk in the far corner, a small stove, and four large velvet chairs that curve at the ends and are placed around a large square coffee table. The old man places the tea on the coffee table and tells us to sit down.

That day was the start of my new life. The start of the new
me and understanding all that I am and could be.

"Alright, spirit boy! What can I do for you?" The old man offers me a cup of tea and leans far back in his chair.

I take a sip, getting ready to speak. But before I can, Tuy cuts me off. "I don't mean to be rude, but if we are going to share our purpose with you, don't you think we should at least know your name?"

The old man gives Tuy his famous evil eye of a thousand grandpas. "After all I have done for you youngsters these past two days, you didn't even tell your friend my name? I understand the mute, but what about you, Piggy?" Both Tuy and I snort a little as Sione chokes on his tea and spills some on his shirt. He clears his throat as he tries to flex his muscles. "Oh, stop that foolishness! I know what you look like under there, but you'll always be Piggy; I think it's cute. Now, that don't get you off the hook."

"Well, to be fair, sir, you never told us your name," says Sione.

The old man pulls back and makes the most hilarious dumbfounded face I have ever seen. We all are quiet for a moment before, abruptly, the room erupts with laughter.

"Well, aren't I a terrible host?" says the old man, running his fingers through his beard. "My name is Phoenix."

"Phoenix?" we exclaim somewhat rudely.

The old man gives us another look before he shakes his head and chuckles to himself. "Yes, you could say my parents were a tad eccentric. Well, most parents of Ren give their children what seem like uncommon names to you normal folk."

"You're from Ren?" we all exclaim once again.

"Yes! Now stop yelling!" yells the old man himself. We apologize and lean back in our chairs, taking sips of our tea.

The old man, or Phoenix, asks once more what he can do for us. However, knowing now that he is from Ren, I'm not sure if I should share our desires with him. Then again, my mother was from Ren and he was once Ms. B's husband, so he can't be that bad. I look to the others and give a nod of approval.

Tuy sits up in his chair and begins to tell Phoenix the events that have led us to where we are now, of course leaving out minor details. Tuy goes on to say how we want to learn more about spirit energy in case we come in contact with the Dark King.

When he finishes, Phoenix's face has grown very long, showing his wrinkles, the same face King Vernon showed the second time we went to the castle. We wait in anticipation for what he will say. "Well, if you want to learn about these special powers in order to be prepared, you must first understand your adversary, the Dark King. Shall we?" asks the old man, getting up, and for the first time, I see him with shaky hands.

He pulls down an old leather-bound notebook, which looks like the one from the nightstand in our room. Phoenix sits again, licks his finger, and smoothly turns the pages, stopping at page forty-five. With a big breath, he blows away the dust that has hidden in the book's crevices, revealing words that actually glow a dark opal. The same shade as my necklace. While the others cough and swat away dust particles, I quickly place my necklace in my shirt in case it decides to show out.

"Now, where shall I begin?" The old man scans the page before he throws his finger to a single paragraph, and wisely utters, "Ah-ha."

He starts out by telling us that the true story of the Dark King is a tragic one. He says Tuy was partially correct about the glory days of King Ren, but the story of his fall is one that many misinterpret. Ren was a great King. He treated all of his people with love and kindness. Therefore, he was granted a pure spirit energy in order to better serve his people. God must have given him the ability to wield spirit energy. For in a few years he would have to face an army from a faraway land that did not belong to Kasai. The foreign army would come from the north and try to seize everything he had worked for as their own. These poor souls did not realize they would be fighting more than a mere man.

Though Ren was human, he had a strong spirit and divine favor, giving him greater strength than most and the ability to do miraculous deeds. After the army was brutally defeated, the victory of King Ren was sung throughout Kasai. He was praised so much that the emperor decided to make the region of Ren his most trusted ally. For years, they served side by side. During the good days of Kasai, our world was very fruitful. We reaped great harvests, money, and most importantly, happiness.

However, as it is in this world, good things don't last for long. The good years only spanned a decade, until a trickster found her way into the midst of Ren. The old man stops for a moment and takes a sip of his tea, then turns his attention to Tuy.

"You were right, young man, about King Ren becoming cold and distant. How his eyes turned hollow. However, that was not because he was feeding on blood, as you told your friend to scare him." Phoenix laughs. "He started to look hollow because the trickster was draining him of his spirit energy. Essentially, she broke his heart and then his spirit.

"I told you earlier that King Ren had a strong spirit, but he had an even stronger heart. One needs both to wield such energy. No one knows where the trickster came from. But what we do know is that she was disguised as a protector. She told him that she was sent to protect him, that in a couple of months Trinity would turn its back on Ren, out of fear that he would become more powerful than the emperor. They say for forty days and nights she fed these lies to the king, so much he stopped eating, became irrational, and spent days upon days in his study. They say it seemed he was searching for something. Hundreds of books were sprawled out on the floor, and he always had one in his hand. That's probably where the story of his eyes turning red came from. He just needed sleep." The old man chuckles again.

Phoenix continues his story, telling of how he felt so sorry for his king. In the end, he was only human and Phoenix could understand him being deceived, especially since the trickster was a woman. King Ren was particularly weak when it came to women.

"I'm confused. If King Ren was losing his spirit energy and becoming belligerent, how did he find the rationality to plan an attack against Trinity?" I ask.

"Very bright man you are. He did not. It was all a lie. The trickster was the one that lead an attack on Trinity disguised as the king. She was so smart; she did it a month after King Ren changed the name of the country to his own. Poor man, he didn't even ask for that. She was the one who sent in the decree. Anyway, after the attack and name change, Trinity came to Ren's borders with a full army. So of course, King Ren, not knowing what was happening behind his back, believed what the trickster had been telling him. It was a bloody battle."

"You were there?" asks Tuy.

"Yes, I was. Do not be alarmed, but I was one of Ren's right-hand men."

We try to hide our shock, but must be unsuccessful, as the old man just smiles at our judgmental stares. "Don't worry. He basically locked us all out once the trickster took over his mind. We didn't know what went on behind closed doors until days later, when the maids would come and tell us the things they saw. I still feel horrible till this day. I just wish we could have done something. I saw that young man grow from a boy into a man, but in the end, I failed him. Such a pure soul became lost."

Sione, who is sitting closest to the old man, leans over and rubs his shoulder to comfort him. "Thank you," says Phoenix before clearing his throat and continuing the story. "In our bitter defeat, many had died or been severely injured. We fought out there non-stop for three whole days and nights. In the end, we were pushed back and Ren, who I assume came back to his senses for a moment, erected the giant spirit barrier around our land that remains till this day."

"Why a barrier?" I question softly.

"To protect his people. However, after the wall was created, we all became distraught. Our capital had almost been burned to the ground and now people were cut off from seeing their loved ones in other regions."

"Why didn't anyone revolt?" asks Sione.

"How could we? After that day, the king was never seen again, and we heard nothing more about the trickster."

"So how did you escape?" Tuy asks.

"Simple. I too can wield spirit energy," says the old man as he makes a ring of pure white spirit energy.

We all stand up in unison, and he just laughs again. He motions for us to sit down and tells us we should have guessed that, being as we came to see him for training. Phoenix then makes us even more uncomfortable as he tells us he was King Ren's trainer. I think and think of something to say, but no words come to mind. Once again I really start to feel that learning about this energy is a bad idea.

The room has become unbearably silent, but I must speak up. "This spirit energy seems as if it brings bad luck."

"Not necessarily. But when one gains power, others want to go the easy route and take it. The higher you go, the more problems you encounter. The spirit energy had nothing to do with his corruption; it was his own personal flaws that did that. Don't be afraid of this, young King. What you have is a beautiful thing. You will be alright. I mean, look at me! I'm as normal as they come," says the old man, kicking his leg in the air and crossing it in front of him with a wide grin. I just nod my head, taking in everything.

Sione raises his hand, but looks at me before speaking. I figure he will mention Ren's son. I nod for him to go ahead. I'm actually curious how Phoenix will respond. Sione tells him our theory of the Dark King's son. For a moment, the old man pauses, thinking. He looks up and tells us it is true that King Ren has a son. But he would not be the one to destroy our island; more than likely the trickster will be.

"She has already drained his father's energy. But when one reproduces, one sometimes passes a genetic inheritance to their child. More than likely, the prince would take some of Ren's power. She is probably waiting for him to discover his true self so she can finally control all of Ren's powers and become the supreme ruler of Kasai. You all are right that our young prince needs your help, but not because of a personal inner turmoil for revenge. Protect our prince from this woman. Do not let another great man fall to her lies and corruption. Also," says Phoenix as he leaves his chair and goes down on one knee, "I do not know if my lord is still alive. Many believe he has died. If you find him on this journey, please save him, and tell him I am sorry."

I feel so bad for this old man with tears in his eyes, for those people, a great nation taken down by one corrupt woman, all for power. But I can't help but feel like there is more to this story.

As Phoenix raises his head and stands tall, he leaves us with his last few words for the night. "But I bid you all, no matter how strong you are, be wary of those who call themselves goddesses and guardians; for not all those who guard are trying to protect you. Sometimes they are guarding you from your inner self, hindering your ability to see them for who they really are. While you are trapped by them, thinking you are protected, they steal and kill all around you.

Please, young ones, do not fall in this dangerous web. Guard your minds, for the mind speaks to the heart and the heart nurtures the soul." The old man walks to me, grabs my hand, and looks at me solemnly. "Now, since you know what is required of you, let us begin our spirit training."

For a whole week, Phoenix trains me. First, we start with the mind. Every day, I'm expected to read at least five books completely in five hours. If I'm not able to do so, I have to do five hundred push-ups, jumping jacks, and squats all while lifting Phoenix. While I'm reading, he walks around me with a long stick, with which he whacks me in the head if I start nodding off. After the mental training is over, we move on to the heart, doing so many cardio exercises that my heart will never stop racing. And then after the heart comes the most important part, the soul.

I make my way down another secret passageway in the inn. This time the stairs lead me to an underwater hot spring. The water is strikingly blue and reflects off of the grey rocks, which seem naturally lit. As I get closer I see that diamonds are embedded in them. The water's reflection bounces off them and creates a small universe of sparkling stars around me. I run toward Phoenix, who is in deep thought with his eyes closed in the spring.

"Master! Do you see this?" I exclaim a little too loudly, making him open one eye and reach for his stick behind him. "Ow!" I exclaim as he whacks me in the head.

"There is no time for you to be mesmerized; just get in."

I push my lower lip out. I mean, we're surrounded by diamonds; even the smallest explanation would help, but in the end, I guess it doesn't matter. I slowly dip myself in the hot spring. The water's scalding. I slide over to Phoenix, who opens both eyes in shock and shoos me to the opposite side of the small pool. "Uh, what are we doing here?"

"Finding our center." I scoff a little at the cheesiness of Phoenix's statement. "Young King, this is very important. You must put all your focus into this. How strong your spirit is determines the amount of control you will have over your spirit energy."

Understanding, I close my eyes and begin to take deep breaths. Phoenix tells me to think on positive images, happy moments, and the people I love. "Now, I would tell you to imagine a world filled with negativity and your loved ones dead, but you have already experienced pain. I apologize, but Sione filled me in on your childhood. How they treated your mother, and how they treated you, just for being yourself. That is a type of pain you do not want to return to.

"Your life might not be perfect, but it is a lot better than what it was. You do not want to lose the positive aspects of it or those you love. Your spirit must be a hundred times stronger than pain if you are to win against the powers of the trickster. You have the power to save your island, your friends and family, and even yourself, with the raw energy of your spirit. You can and you will turn that rawness into something tangible. Turn the fear of losing into spirit energy, as you have done before with The Elk. If you give in to pain and fear, you will fail. Hold fast to positivity and hope! Now release it!" Phoenix yells as he places a firm hand on my heart.

I try to feel something boiling up from inside. I think about being greater than my pain. I try to call forth the energy, but alas, nothing happens. I take a peek at Phoenix and see him shaking his head as he gets up from the water. He pats me on the back and tells me to stay in meditation until I get it right. I sit in the same position for hours before exhausting all my strength. I fall back into the water and spread my limbs out.

I open my eyes and look at the diamond-filled ceiling above me. If I could just grab one...like I did that cannonball. I extend my hand and tense my fingers, trying to make something happen. I stretch my arm so far that I feel like my shoulder will pop out of its socket. *Almost got it*, I think to myself. Positive, think positive, above pain. *Pain is me not having this diamond*, I think, and then it happens. The white specks of lights start to encase my hand. I grin and extend my arm to its limit. I open and shut my hand tightly, and before I know it, there it is in my fingers, a huge, perfectly cut diamond.

I laugh in excitement at figuring out how to control my inner energy, but even more at the fact that I'm holding an actual diamond. I twirl around in the water and start kissing the diamond, but as I do, I notice darks specks start to eat the white specks of light. "Shoo, go away! Go away!" I swat at the black specks, but just like the cannonball had, the diamond disappears. A minute later I hear the secret entrance reopen and slam shut. Phoenix comes back downstairs with his wooden stick in one hand and a diamond in the other—apparently, my diamond.

I bury my head underwater, trying to avoid a beating. Phoenix calls out for me above the surface, but there is no way I am answering. I will just drown. But that is not an option, as Phoenix starts to hit me with the wooden stick through the water. I yell as I jump up out from the hot spring. He jumps in wearing his fresh blue linen suit, and grabs me by the arm, and shakes the diamond in my face as he clicks his tongue.

"Young King, you know better. You saw dark energy, did you not?"

"Yes," I whimper.

"You do not want to see that ever again. That means you are relying on negative energy or ill intentions. We want to train you in the ways of using your spirit energy positively. You don't want to become like the Dark King, do you?" Phoenix whacks me with his stick one more time and I yelp out, "No."

"Very well. Don't let it happen again. However, I am glad to see you have some remorse. The reason I ended up holding this diamond is because you used a highly skilled technique that transports your energy through space and time, usually attempting to reach a faraway enemy with a long-range attack with spirit energy or a weapon. Your thoughts determine where this object will end up. Guess you had me on the brain, hmm? However, I will let you have it," Phoenix says mockingly as he tosses the diamond in the air.

I jump up from the water and catch it with both hands, confused.

"After all, you did finally tap into your powers by your own will. You deserve it. But next time, no negative energy, only positive. And only pure intentions. You understand?" threatens Phoenix, and all I can do is bow my head and say, "Yes, master."

As the week continues, I slowly become able to make my spirit energy appear at will. Truthfully, it's a lot of fun. The little specks feel like small fairies dancing along my palms. I find myself shooting beams here and there and teleporting objects just for fun, and before I know it, it is my last day of training.

I go out to the valley behind the inn, alone. There, I unleash all that I have learned, pushing myself to my limits. *I must be prepared*, I keep thinking. Once finished, I find myself exhausted and breathing heavily. I wipe the sweat from my forehead and plop down and snuggle in the high blades of grass, letting the solar rays warm my face. As I sit in the sun's embrace and work on restoring my energy and calming my mind, I hear a voice say, *"Wonderful."* I open my eyes, but I see no one. I don't panic, as I have become accustomed to it. However, for some reason I can't help but stretch out my arm above my head and reach with all my might for the sun.

A single tear rolls down my cheek. How could a voice be filled with so much pain? "Who are you?" I yell out loud, but of course the voice doesn't answer. I squeeze my eyes shut. I am able to understand so much now, but I still know nothing about this voice in my head. I throw my outstretched arm down next to me, frustrated, and a sharp pain shoots through my limb. I open my eyes and turn to my side, only to see that I am holding a giant sword. It looks like steel, but is made completely of pure white spirit energy, just like the one from the story about the Dark King. Then, suddenly, from the distance I hear footsteps coming toward me. When they're closer, I see Phoenix and the others, even Luna, who finally woke up a few days ago.

"What is this?" I whisper to myself. I let go of the sword but it does not disappear; it just lies in the valley, in all its greatness. This sword has to be at least five feet long and fifteen inches wide. How could anyone wield such a thing? And why is it here before me?

I start to freak out. I pat at the sword, trying to dissolve it, but some type of barrier surrounds it. I remember that the mind controls the heart and the heart nurtures the soul. I sit down crossed-legged in the valley and mediate, whispering under my breath, sweating uncontrollably at each impeding step from the others. I ease my mind and slow my words and thoughts. I have better control when I am not anxious.

"You look really cool like that, King." My eyes fly open. Luna is right in front of me, holding out a flower she picked on the walk here. I awkwardly accept it as I peek toward where the sword had been. Thankfully, it has disappeared.

"Enough training for today, young King. You have done enough. Even warriors know the importance of rest. Come on inside, I have prepared a special meal for you and your friends." Phoenix turns on his heels and the others follow. I get up quickly and try to follow them, but double over and grab my chest, which feels like something is burning a hole into it. I pull the cursed necklace from under my shirt and it is just as I thought: the gem has turned the orange color that burns my skin. I clutch the pendant tightly even though it's still hot as fire.

When I finally think that I am in control, somehow I lose it all.

Once our bellies are full, we all stand in front of the shack. The old shack that hides so many wonders and so much information inside. Phoenix comes out from the front door with four black cloaks. He walks slowly in front of each of us, just as Ms. B did, but instead of handing us olive branches, he adorns our backs with the cloaks. Holding our shoulders tight, laying his final touch of knowledge upon us. Once he gets to me, he smiles and kisses both of my cheeks. Shocked, I blush and the old man gives me one more laugh. He tells us to be on our way and that it gets very cold the closer you get to Oak City. We all bow and turn to head back up the road, but I stop for a moment and turn around to call after the old man.

"Master!"

"What is it, King?"

I walk back to Phoenix, digging in the only normal pocket on my Antenetta uniform. I pull out the olive branch Ms. B placed in my hair. "This is for you," I say, putting it in his hands. Phoenix looks at the branch and tears fill his eyes. Astonished, I ask, "How did you know it was from her?"

"This isn't a normal olive branch. It is a golden olive branch from a holy tree some far ways from here. The same tree we first fell in love at." Phoenix looks up and pulls me into a hug. "Thank you, King. You truly are a wonderful human being, one whom I believe could one day actually become a king. A noble, peaceful, and righteous king."

"Thank you," I reply as we leave each other's embrace and wave goodbye.

"What were you doing?" asks Sione.

"Nothing. I just had to give something to Phoenix for all that he has done for me."

"I told you the man in the shack would be amazing," says Tuy, smirking at me.

"Well, right you were. I never knew I could learn so much."

"I didn't get to learn anything," says Luna, crossing her arms and pouting, causing us all to laugh.

"Yeah. We almost forgot what your voice sounded like." Sione laughs harder than he should. Luna kicks him in the shin and says, "Not funny," as she storms off ahead to walk next to Tuy. "Great, the brat is back." Says Sione grabbing his ankle and hoping on one foot.

"Well, you did ask for it," I say, shaking my head and leaving Sione behind to wallow in his pain.

— XI —

⊕AK CITY

Phoenix told us that the train to the outer villages of Trinity leaves every three days from Oak City, and that we must make haste. We decide to rest for just two hours, the setting of the sun now looking like a ticking time bomb. I look at the others; their faces have grown dark and their movements weary, but they keep going, so I do as well.

On the morning of the third day, we come to a crossroads with a wooden sign that has five different arrows engraved with city names, next to the miles it will take to get to them. Our sweaty and tired quartet huddles together and, like meerkats, move our heads in unison searching for Oak City. "There!" Luna calls out. We look at the sign pointing north that says Oak City and has the number *30* next to it. We throw up our hands in joy, knowing that we will make it to our destination in time to catch the train. So, we press on.

However, as we get closer to Oak City, it becomes colder just as Phoenix had warned. I pull my cloak in tight, hoping to stop the lashes of chill wind. Luna is shivering intensely. "You guys, let's stop for a moment," I say. I expect our team to tell me that we do not have time and to stop being so weak, but instead in grand unison they all exhale and fall flat on the ground, groaning and sending up complaints.

Sione asks once again why he has to carry so much stuff. Tuy tries to hold it in and look cool; all the while his neck is bright red and he is rubbing his legs aggressively. Then there is the princess, asking in a soft voice why it is so cold in a valley under a bright sun. I tell her I was wondering the same thing. I open up my backpack and pull out a warm, fluffy pink scarf that I wrap around Luna. She gives no response, but instead turns her back to me. That response doesn't last long, as Luna comes face to face with a faun.

Her scream is so loud that it sends a stampede of faun straight for Sione, who dodges them in the nick of time by rolling on his belly. He grabs his heart, holding on for dear life. When he looks at Luna, he seems ready to finally blow his top, but he calms down as he sees that the poor child has landed into my arms and is holding on to me tight. I pat her head and whisper in her ear, "It's alright. It's just a baby deer."

Luna shakes her head and nestles against my chest, which becomes warm with her tears. Unable to find the words to say to this poor child who has been through so much, I just hold her close. Yet I'm strangely glad that she is back to her ten-year-old self with ten-year-old emotions.

"Luna, are you crying?" asks Sione as he leans in to see Luna's face. As she looks up, she breaks free from me and turns her back.

"No!" she shouts. I nudge Sione and Tuy shakes his head.

"What? I was just checking on her," whispers Sione.

"You know she doesn't show many emotions. You should have just let her be," I say to him.

"Poor thing was probably crying for more than a stupid deer. Who knows the last time she got to have a good cry without worrying about what people will say?" says Tuy, looking off into the distance.

Sione just rolls his eyes as he throws up his hands, stomps to his bag, and angrily pulls out his scarf and gloves.

"Alright," Tuy says, "let's rest here for twenty minutes and then we have to get moving."

I lie down in the cold valley and can finally rest peacefully. I look up to the blue sky and then to my side, taking in the valley between mountains full of faun, butterflies, frogs, rabbits, and all types of wild life. They all migrate toward the stream flowing alongside the road. I take in a breath of fresh air.

"I wonder," I say softly. I outstretch my arm and make sure no one is around before I try to make the giant spirit sword appear again. I stretch and stretch for a good ten minutes, but nothing happens. I just waste my break. I roll back over, this time on my right side, and I see Luna by the river feeding a faun.

I sit up and chuckle proudly to myself. Slowly, I sneak behind her before grabbing both her shoulders and playfully roaring like a monster, making the animals run away. However, she only jumps slightly and gives me an evil glare. "Sorry," I say, scratching the back of my head.

"It's okay," Luna says as she bends down and places her hands in the river.

"Luna, it's too cold." I pull the child's hands back from the water. "You just got better, you don't want to get sick again."

Luna stares at me blankly, wiping her hands on her pants and placing them back in her gloves to warm them up. I figure I'm getting on her nerves, so I start to walk away.

"Was Tru nice?" Luna asks in stronger voice than usual.

"Tru?" I raise an eyebrow.

"Yes, Tru the goddess."

"I thought her name was Rania?"

"No, I am positive that when we first met she told me her name was Tru." Luna suddenly clasps her hands to her mouth and slouches over. I run to her and place a hand on her back.

"What's wrong?" Luna looks up at me, almost on the verge of tears.

"I forgot it was supposed to be a secret," she says and hangs her head.

"It's alright. I promise I won't tell anyone," I say, patting her on the back. Luna places her two tiny hands on my cheeks and squeezes them tight. She looks me dead in my eyes, not with the childish innocence of sharing something that really is no big deal, but with fear. Raw, unadulterated fear that she had just said the unthinkable.

"You promise? You *promise*?" Luna asks over and over again, squeezing my cheeks tighter. However, I stay calm, placing my hands over her small ones and pulling them from my face.

"It's alright. Names aren't a big deal, but soldier's honor"—I put my forearm across my heart—"I won't tell a soul. As far as I'm concerned, this conversation never happened," I say, smiling at Luna, and finally the child wipes her tears and smiles back.

"Let's move out!" Tuy calls. I pat Luna on the head and we flip up our hoods and head out.

We continue up the road, and it begins to snow, slowing our steps. Tuy, who is in front, waves his hand frantically and runs ahead, only to fall flat on his bottom and disappear from our line of sight. I pull Luna behind me and call forth my weapon, as does Sione. We run to where Tuy fell, and plop, we also fall on our backs on the icy road. Luna stands above us and all we see is her mouthing, "Whoa!"

I follow her gaze and can't believe my eyes. In front of us is a city completely covered in ice beneath the sky's unrelenting snow. We all get up, rubbing various aching parts of our bodies.

"What the heck is this place? And why the heck is it so cold?" Sione pulls his clock tighter around him and shivers, doing a happy dance in a place that's not so happy. *Bonk bonk!* We all jump into fighting stances and turn to what sounds like an alarm going off behind us. Instead, we are blinded by headlights from an old red pickup truck. I put my hand over my eyes, trying to see who is in the truck.

"Calm yourself, boys. This is a peaceful city, and you all really shouldn't be walking in the middle of the street," a young woman says, leaning her head out the window. We shyly put our weapons away, walk to the side of the truck, and apologize.

"It's quite alright, most outsiders are shocked when they come to our city. But let me be the first to welcome you to Oak City."

"Thanks. Is it like this all year round?" Tuy asks suddenly in a deep voice, causing all of us to snap our eyes at him, even Luna. The thin young woman, who is covered in a finely contoured black padded jacket and pants, matched with a puffy white fur hat, scarf, and white fur boots, giggles and smiles with her only feature that can be seen, large hazel eyes.

"Afraid so. And you guys are way underdressed for this weather. I mean those thin uniforms, probably very practical, under those medium thick cloaks, ain't gonna cut it," she teases. But on a serious note, the little one you have with you doesn't look so good. Come with me and I'll get you all the proper outerwear."

"Oh, we wouldn't want to impose."

"Don't worry, it's alright. I run a clothing store in the neighborhood."

"Oh, I see," says Tuy. The young lady waves her hand for us to get in. Tuy appears frozen, being as his smooth voice and awkward eye twitches didn't do him any good. However, we all push past him and jump in the red truck, as the cold is beyond bearable.

We finally come to the end of the Road of Bones and cross into the frozen city over a tiny bridge that is encased completely in ice and snow. The car becomes awkwardly quiet as we all try to warm up. I look out the window and rub my hands together, in awe again at this strange city. I look at the other cars travelling through the streets, which number only four, including us, and notice that the cold air even freezes their exhaust, creating an eerie fog. One would think a place like this would only have a few people or none at all, but surprisingly, the town center is full with people out and about. They're covered from head to toe in fur or thickly padded clothing, revealing only their beautifully colored eyes to the world, and some not even that.

We continue farther into Oak City as we cross through the square with its ice-covered buildings and statues. The locals are so used to the weather that women even sell food and accessories on the street. I turn to Sione and smile, prompting him to smile back at me. We both have to turn away before the lumps in our throats grow bigger. This small town, cold as it may be, is still so warm, full of people, families, fun, and culture. It might be secluded and the weather less than ideal, but it seems alright. It seems peaceful, just like Peace Island, if a lot colder.

"Alright, here we are," says the young woman as she gets out the truck. "Move quickly, you guys, you don't want to freeze to death now." We all scramble out of the truck and run into the boutique store, a thick cloud of freezing mist following us.

"How do you all do it?" Sione asks, leaning on a body form.

"Simple. We just do. This is home," says the young woman as she finally takes off her hood and face scarf to reveal long, brown hair, pale skin, and freckled cheeks. She is beautiful, and Tuy is visibly in love.

I clear my throat and look around the boutique, where every surface is covered in fur coats and fancy thick dresses. "Nice shop you have here."

"Thank you."

"It doesn't look like you have any men's clothes, though," I say, looking from side to side and only seeing piles of dresses.

"I don't," says the young woman, smiling innocently at me. I slightly tense up as I jerk a little too the side throwing my hand to my head as I rub my hair awkwardly and we enter a staring contest.

"I'm sorry, what was your name again?"

"I didn't tell you," she says carelessly.

Becoming a little annoyed, I roll my eyes. "Well, would you mind—"

"Alright, King, calm down." Tuy places his hand on my shoulder, cutting me off, and turns his face to me so that the woman cannot see. "Remember, nice," He says, tilting his head to the side and giving me a sadistic smile. Tuy turns from me and once again his deep voice is back. "Sorry about my friend. I just think the cold is getting to us. Our home is a lot warmer than this."

"Yeah, it can do that. My name is Olena," she says, extending her hand to Tuy, who shyly shakes it. I feel like I will puke.

Sione taps me on the back of the head. "Don't be such a sourpuss. Love is a beautiful thing." He winks, making me want to throw up even more.

"Excuse me, do you have anything to drink?" asks Luna from a fancy brown couch she has found in the corner, as she covers herself with the blanket from the armrest elegantly.

"Why yes, sweetheart, I do. Just wait one moment." Olena runs to the back and brings out a cup of hot tea. She places a hand on Luna's cheek and says, "You know, one would think that you were a princess and these three blokes are your bodyguards. You are very graceful."

We all stop in our tracks and start to send crazy signals to Luna not to say anything, as we know how she likes to play games and sometimes lacks a filter. But thankfully Luna just smiles and says, "I wish. We live in Trinity and are just trying to get home."

"I see. Well, why didn't you travel by ship? The Road of Bones is very dangerous, especially with a young child."

"I'm not that young. But we were doing research. The man you were fussing with is my father. His name is King, and the other two, Sione and Tuy, are his partners. I begged to come along this time for research and he finally allowed me to."

"Well, isn't that very exciting," says Olena, not suspecting a thing. We throw some thumbs-ups behind her head.

"Oh, by the way, what time does the train leave?" asks Luna.

"In three hours. But since you are so sweet, you can wait here until it's time for you to leave"—Olena turns and looks at us— "and I guess I will let your father stay."

"Well, he does like the cold, so he will be okay either way," says Luna causing Olena to laugh as well as Tuy and Sione, but I find nothing funny. However, I do feel happiness that Luna is happy, even if it's from telling a lie.

"Alright, here you are, boys." Olena drops three thick fur coats and hats in front of us. "These should keep you warm on your way to the train station."

"Thank you," says Sione as we all dress into our new coats and drop our cloaks in our bottomless backpacks. Olena walks over to Luna and pulls out a small pink fur coat with a matching hat and gloves. "There you are," she says as she adjusts the garment perfectly. "Clothes fit for a princess."

"Thank you," Luna replies as she begins to pet her coat like it's a soft bunny.

"Well, you boys should be hurrying. I really wish I could take you all, but I have to make these deliveries. The train station is a short distance from here, so you should be fine."

Tuy moves closer to Olena, takes off his hat, and gives her the bow of a soldier. "Thank you so much. We don't know how we could ever repay you."

"Don't mention it. Just trying to spread a little compassion in this selfish world. But Tuy, dare I say that the manners you have seem more like a soldier's than a researcher's?"

Tuy just smiles at Olena before putting his cap back on. "Well, we must be going now. If you are ever in the area, I pray our paths will cross again."

"And will that area be Trinity or maybe…an island?" Olena asks softly. Sione and I look at her in shock, afraid that our identities have been revealed, but Tuy doesn't bat an eyelash.

"Who's to say? Things aren't always as they seem." He turns around and heads out the door. I hurry Luna along, linking arms with Sione, as I turn and wave goodbye to Olena and follow Tuy before our cover is blown. I turn back to close the door only to hear Olena whispering, "No, no they are not." And I shut the door on their short but sad love story.

We arrive after a good fifteen-minute walk to a building that does not belong. This black cobblestone edifice with gold trim looks like it has never been touched by snow or ice. It's is so enormous that its three steeples hide in the clouds. As we walk into the station, it bustles with people from all different regions, going from here to there. Past the people, a grand staircase welcomes us. It leads to the center of the station, where a giant clock sits in the middle. On the main platform, ten tunnels all lead to different regions.

"Look, you guys, there's one for Peace Island!" Sione shouts.

"Whoa, but where does it let out?" Tuy and I ask.

"Simple. Remember the town we saw in the distance on the beach? It goes there, to St. Royal, and then from St. Royal you have to catch a ship which lets off at the docks behind the castle," says the princess. We turn and look at her, but all she does is shrug. "I don't know why Daddy doesn't tell others about it. I guess you all could just think of it as the royals' private charter."

We click our tongues at her pompous attitude. "Well, guess Peace Island isn't really all about equality and peacefulness after all," says Sione.

"No place really is," Tuy chimes in.

"Just survival of the fittest," I say as we all shake our heads in agreement, except Luna.

She stomps her foot on the marble floor. "How dare you! My father has given Peace Island everything! He might keep certain information from people, but it is for their own good. So what if the royals and influencers have more than others? Don't be mad at them because they succeeded in life. Trust me, in order for them to get to where they are, it took a lot of hard work and effort."

"Maybe for a few, but I'm sure most of them got ahead by slipping money under the table," snaps Sione. Luna kicks her tiny leg down again, folds her arms, and stomps off. I try to go after her but Tuy just says to let her go.

"Does she really expect us to take her seriously when she's walking around looking like a big fluff of cotton candy?" Sione asks. I try not to laugh, but give in as I watch the princess march away and part the sea of people in her bright pink getup.

"But guys, we were a little too harsh. She is young and just full of positivity. All she knows is the inside walls of the castle. Formal this, formal that. Money here, money there. So let's cut her some slack," I say.

I head out to look for Luna as Tuy and Sione go to purchase our tickets to Rise, one of the outlying districts of Trinity. I finally spot a cute pink fluff curled up on the wall next to the gift shop with its head between its knees. "This is an odd place to take a nap," I say, sitting down next to the princess. She turns her back to me and doesn't say a word.

"Look, I know what we said was pretty harsh. But life is different for us. I admit, we might have been hating on those in Royal Town, but that hate is only on the surface. Truthfully, it's not hate but dissatisfaction. We know your father is a great king. Though we have different statuses, which affect where we live and other things, at the same time, we all are one and can come and go anytime we please. Why is that? It's because your father thinks of all citizens as his children. Some might do better than others, but he gives us all equal opportunities to succeed. I have to admit that as we continued on this journey, I was a little upset to find out everything that was kept from us. I think your father's only flaw is that he sometimes can love us too much. He hides the rest of the world from us, without even asking if we want to be hidden. Nobody is perfect, Luna, but we do respect your father and your family. I apologize if we overstepped our boundaries, but the world is not always black and white."

After I finish my speech, Luna looks up at me with red eyes. I feel horrible. "I know. I just hate when I hear it from other people."

"And you should. He is your father. That's the funny thing about family, no matter what, we have to stick together through and through."

"Thanks, King." Luna gives me a hug.

Sione and Tuy rejoin us, bow their heads, and say, "Sorry, Luna."

"It's okay," she says while wiping her tears. "Well, let's get going."

"Alright, you all! This is it, we're almost to Trinity. We just have to push on a few more steps. Everyone, put your hands in the circle," Tuy says, changing the atmosphere as we get in a huddle and place our hands on top of each other. "For Peace Island!" We give a battle cry and throw our hands up in the air, screaming, "Bright and ferocious as the sun!" Causing us to receive strange looks from those around us.

We step onto the platform and board a train that doesn't match the station which holds it. Sleek and shaped like a bullet, this train doesn't sit on a track but floats above it. Luna says it can travel up to a thousand miles per hour, and I think I am going to be nauseous.

The train takes off slowly but soon picks up speed. Trees and buildings pass by us in a twinkling of an eye. Poor Oak City is now lightyears away and we have only been on the train for a minute. I sink down in my seat, curling to the left so I won't have to look out the window. I come face to face with Sione, who has his eyes shut tight. Luna and Tuy are sitting in front of us, and just like on the magnetic boat ride, they shake their heads at me and Sione. Tuy tells Luna that some things never change and he wonders if we will ever feel the spirit of adventure. We both shake our heads in protest.

"Well, you better find it soon. Because once we cross over into Trinity it's not going to be pretty," says Tuy.

"Why?"

"Well, if Peace Island has this train service that can reach speeds of a thousand miles per hour, news about the princess and Adira has probably already been relayed to the emperor."

"Oh yeah. I forgot for a moment that we're actually fugitives." I wince, thinking of all we have done so far and fearing that it will all be in vain.

"Don't worry. I will think of something. Remember, I'm a great liar." The princess smiles.

"Well, we'll cross that bridge once we get there. We know our true intentions. Also, lying's good for when we're in a sticky situation, but let's not make that a habit now, princess." Tuy returns her smile sarcastically.

I shut my eyes as he adds even more stress on my already nauseated stomach.

"We will be arriving at the Trinity district of Rise in fifteen minutes. Please make sure you have all of your belongings."

Sione and I jump up, grab our bags from the overhead bins, and fall back into our seats, holding them tight. When I sit, I mistakenly look out the window and can't believe my eyes. We're crossing a sky-high bridge and it looks like we are floating on clouds. There is only fog beneath us that hides a world unknown. Ahead, there is the biggest city I have ever seen in my life. On top of all of its lights, which I assume to be outlying districts, sits the city center, Trinity, and the castle of the grand ruler of Kasai. The distant castle reflects the city lights below, which glimmer off of its crystal walls. The palace though intimidating, reminds me of an octopus, though the head is shaped like a spear, the rest of the palace spreads out in eight different directions like octopus's legs, and each leg is gold. But the most spectacular thing about the emperor's crystal home is that at the top of it sits a burning flame.

"The Inner Flame," says Tuy.

"What?" I ask, not breaking my trance.

"The fire that sits upon the castle is called the Inner Flame. It represents our continent's name, Kasai, a fire that cannot be controlled."

"Well, that makes no sense because it looks pretty tamed up there," says Sione.

"Always so literal. The fire is to represent the people of our nation. We are strong and unbreakable as a whole. We will not be controlled. When Kasai was first founded, we were under the rule of a country called Kane. Kane was a cruel ruler, abusive and corrupt. A typical dictatorship. But then one day the people couldn't take it anymore. They had built this country up from nothing, yet they did not have riches, good health, or even freedom.

"So, one day all the people of Kasai got together and rebelled. You see, there's strength in numbers, but more importantly there is strength in being in one accord. They wanted their freedom, but most importantly they wanted to enjoy the nation they help build. They say that once the angry mob got to the leader of Kane's doorstep, he fled with his tail in between his legs, and he and his men sailed away.

"You all know the first emperor of Kasai, Vince Zyel? Well, on the day of the revolt he stood on a rock by the sea, above those who he didn't know at the time would become his people, and shouted, 'I heard the enemy cry out as he ran away that these people have fire in their eyes! An inner fire that cannot be controlled, a fire that will not be tamed, a fire that will set this world aflame. Today and together we shall call this land that we built Kasai! And we will be the people who will not be controlled, the people who burn like an eternal flame. But we dare not repeat the sins of our enemies. Instead of burning with hate and evil, we will burn with passion and love, and share with this world knowledge and peace!'"

Thank you all for choosing Muz Transcontinental. We look forward to seeing you again, and welcome to the Trinity district of Rise.

The train comes to a halt and suddenly cheers are heard from behind us. The other passengers had been listening in on Tuy's history lesson, as he was pretty loud. People clap and Tuy, who loves being the center of attention, waves his hand in the air and bows. "So much for blending in," says Sione. I throw my hand to my head, already nauseous and unsure of what lies ahead. Reconnecting my backpack to my Antenetta suit, I stand and push past Tuy's fans to get off the train.

— XII —

TRINITY

"Thank you. Thank you. Thank you," Tuy says as he finally jumps off the train and joins us on the platform.

"Ew," I say, pointing to the kiss mark on his cheek.

"What?" He rubs off the red lipstick. "Oh yeah, she was a little enthusiastic." Tuy laughs heroically with his hands on his hips.

"Cover your ears, Luna, you don't have to witness this." I put my own hands over her ears and we both walk away, heads in the air.

"Don't be so jealous, King. I'm sure you will find love one day!" Tuy yells behind me, and I want to kick him as hard as I can in his shin.

We leave the train station and enter Rise, a district of old brick and mortar buildings. Small shops line the fancy and quaint streets that overflow with arts and culture. People are singing and painting portraits for a couple dollars at every corner. However, Rise is very modern at the same time. Earlier, from the train, I could see that the different districts each cater to a different theme or culture. Once inside, I really feel how grand these districts are; they might as well be considered cities. The district we are in goes on for miles. I look up, hoping to get a closer glimpse of the castle, but I can no longer see it.

"Alright everyone, cloaks up," Tuy says as he throws off his fur coat and changes back into his cloak. I do the same, but I neatly fold my fur coat, placing it in my bag. I fold Tuy's as well before handing it back to him and saying it might come in handy, so he should still carry it. He scoffs at me

158

but takes the folded fur in his arms and holds it close, almost as if it were a woman. "Let's find shelter for the night," he says as he leads the way.

We walk down an alleyway that is narrow, dark, and a little eerie. Strange men and women converse among each other while checking us out at the same time. I grab Luna's hand and pull her close to me, and for once she doesn't swat my hand away. However, she does whisper under her breath, "Thank you, sir coward."

"Ha-ha, very funny," I whisper back to her.

Once we are out of the alley, we come to a harbor on the outside of the city. We walk along the water until we reach a place called Château Jolie, a petite building with a sign on the outside: *Travelers Welcomed. Only $50 a Night!*

"Perfect." Tuy turns to us, smiling, and motions for us to follow him. Sione leans toward me and questions if he has just been making this whole thing up as he goes along. I nod. "Probably."

We enter the petite château and are greeted by a skinny young man with fluffy hair and tattoos. He swirls around in his chair with his feet kicked up on some sort of box. He twirls the toothpick in his mouth, leaning back and looking us up and down. I hurry to Tuy's side and say, "Um, I think you chose the wrong place."

"Nonsense. This will do, well, just for the night at least. And haven't I always told you not to judge a book by its cover?" Tuy whispers back to me before he practically skips to the desk where the displeasing young man waits.

"Hello, sir," says Tuy as he throws his hand to the counter and leans in.

The young man blatantly rolls his eyes as he continues to twirl the toothpick in his mouth round and round. "We only have one room left, and it only has one bed," he says as he finally stops rolling his eyes at Tuy and turns his attention back to the HoloTube.

"We'll take it!" Tuy says way too loudly as he slams his hands once again on the counter.

The young man, flustered at Tuy's happiness and loudness, shakes his head and slowly gets up. He goes into a room behind the counter and comes back with a key attached to a small wooden flame keychain. "Alright, that's going to be one thousand dollars."

This time Sione yells. "For one night?"

"Sorry, rates go up when the festival is in town."

"Festival?"

"Yeah, it's Independence Day," says the young man as he gives us all a strange look. We pause for a moment, first in disbelief that a hotel of this caliber would cost a thousand dollars, even during a holiday, and secondly at the realization of how long we have been travelling.

Kasai's Independence Day is on the twentieth day of the fifth month of the year of our Emperor, and we left on the first day of the fourth month. I shake my head, as we are now at a standstill, knowing we don't have a thousand dollars. But then I remember. "Oh yeah," I say under my breath, taking my backpack off, flipping it upside down. I rub my hands over the bottom of the backpack, revealing a hidden virtual keypad display. I tap in 165-083, a password I've used since I was a kid, opening a hidden pocket on the bottom just wide enough to pull out a gold bar.

The hotel clerk almost chokes on his toothpick as I place it on the counter, lean in coolly, and cheekily ask, "Will this cover it?" I'm a little heartbroken that I must part with one of my secret treasures, but I figure pulling out a gold bar for an obvious price gouging scammer will lead to less questions, then if I dropped my gold bar at a Peace Island market. I will just keep the other one on display, I guess.

"Uh, yeah," stammers the clerk. He hands me the keys to the room and runs off into the back, most likely to slip the gold bar into his personal bag, but that has nothing to do with me. "Alright. Shall we?" I motion for us to go up the old wooden stairs that lead to the room.

The room is just like the wooden stairs: old. But it does have a nice bed, clean sheets, towels, a HoloTube, and a window that overlooks the city. It's standard but will do for the night. We all drop our heavy backpacks on the floor, as Tuy tells the princess the bed is hers and to go ahead and make herself comfortable. I find a small chair in the corner and take a brief rest there, but it doesn't last long as the moment I have been waiting for arrives.

Three bobbing heads surround me, and even before they can ask, I say, "I found the gold bar in the manager's room at the fish market when I was moving Sidney to safety. Because…you know, you never know when a gold bar will come in handy."

"Sure, dude. We all know that you carried that around for this very moment." Smirking, Sione shakes his head and stares out the window at the night's festivities.

"Well, no matter the original intent, it sure did come in handy." Tuy turns on his heels but suddenly stops. "You did only find one, right?"

I gulp but am able to smoothly say, "Yeah, only one."

"I see. But I guess it doesn't really matter. Finders keepers, losers weepers. Right?"

"Yep," I say, and Tuy returns my smirk.

The festivities are ongoing late into the night. I lie on the cot that the tattooed dude downstairs provided us with and pull the damp blanket over me, and I start to think to myself how far I have come. Even though we haven't made it to the center of Trinity yet, truthfully, I didn't think I would make it this far. As far as I'm concerned, I should have died out at sea or even when we travelled through the Plains of Thunder, but here I am, about to deliver a message to the emperor. Hopefully we can relay that message before they punish us for kidnapping the princess. If I can see his face, I will finally feel like I have made something of myself, I think as I drift off into sleep.

"King, wake up!" Tuy yells as he shakes me and slaps me lightly in the face.

I knock his hand away and sit straight up. "What the heck, man?"

"The princess, she's gone!"

"What?" I throw the blanket off of me and toss on my clothes and shoes before we make a beeline out the door. We push past the new hotel clerk—the old one probably ran off at night. "Where could she have gone?" I exclaim, standing in the town square. Over a thousand people are moving so quickly that I feel like my head will spin off. However, I look around frantically for her. Tuy suggests we all break up and search some of the shops and parks.

I run around this unfamiliar land for what feels like hours, but there is no princess to be found. I spot many young girls that look like her, but none are her. I start to panic. King Vernon will kill us if we've lost his daughter. I look up at a sign on the side of an excursion office that reads: *This Way to Trinity* and wonder if they took her in the night. I furrow my brows and take a deep breath as I set off for the emperor.

I run and run until I reach the edge of Rise, I expect to be faced with some type of grand wall or gate, but instead I find that after I run up a long stairway, as If I was ascending into heaven, I am smack dab in the middle of the palace—the courtyard, to be exact. There are guards all over the well-designed space, which is filled with tons of plants and bushes and a white marble fountain. I see them and they see me. I squeeze my eyes shut, realizing I made a stupid decision. Maybe I should have gathered the others before going to the emperor's home.

"Excuse me," says a voice behind me. I spin around, expecting an immediate blow to the head, but instead a soldier is bowing. "Um, thank you," I say, scratching my head.

"Right this way, young King," says another voice.

I snap my head back to its original direction. "How do you know my name?"

"We will go over all that in detail when we get inside," says the second speaker, who by his outfit is most likely some type of butler in the castle. As I follow him through the courtyard, the crystal walls of the castle come closer and closer to me, and the Inner Flame disappears.

Once it is fully vanished from my sight, I stand before crimson red double doors. The butler knocks three times, then twists a doorknob and pushes it open. Everything on the other side is dazzling. The main hall of the castle is bright, and the outside world can be seen through the crystal glass, so it seems distorted, but beautiful; the reflection is mesmerizing. Above my head hangs an enormous chandelier. The grey marble floors are engraved with gold flames throughout. The entrance hall narrows off into eight different directions, just as it appears on the outside, each with a door and hallway leading to another part of the castle.

"Your presence is needed in the eighth leg of the castle," says the butler.

I chuckle a little at the fact that he didn't call it a hall or side, but an actual leg. "Like an octopus leg?"

He winks at me. "Exactly."

"Really?"

"Yes. The emperor designed this castle after his favorite food. He is quite playful, so don't be too alarmed when you meet him."

I clam up once I hear the words *meet him*. If the emperor really is behind the eighth door, what will I say? I am so not the prim and proper type. I find myself frozen until I hear a little girl's voice coming from the door, and before I can stop my feet, I practically skip over to the mysterious eighth tentacle.

I tap on the gold-plated door three times, and on the third I hear a small voice say, "Come in." Timidly I push open the door, revealing a long red carpet that travels down the pillared room to the emperor's throne. I stop dead in my tracks as I come face to face with the emperor himself.

Compared to the time when we first met King Vernon, this moment is more nerve-racking. This is the man in charge of all of Kasai. I never thought he would be right here in front of me. I've only ever seen him in newspapers and through the Tube, but at this moment he is here in front of me, in living color.

The emperor is a tall, skinny man around the age of sixty. He has decorated his long, curly black beard with flowers and wears a gold headdress in the shape of a flame on his bald head.

"I told you to come, child," he says in a small but strong voice. I jump from the position I've been standing in for a good while. The emperor smirks slightly. "Or should I come to you?" He pushes himself off his gold and crimson throne and begins to make his way down the stairs in front of him, his long gold robe following.

I pull myself together. The guards' faces in the room hold the same look the Peace Island guards had when King Vernon bowed to us. I jog in order to meet the emperor halfway. How incredibly rude of me, to make Kasai's most powerful man leave his seat for a low-ranking soldier. As I run, the emperor doesn't slow down; it almost seems as if he is speeding up until he too breaks out into a sprint and we meet smack dab in the middle of the throne room.

"I'm sorry, your majesty. I wasn't thinking clearly. You didn't have to leave your throne for someone like me," I say, panting as I look to the ground and shuffle my feet.

"My dear child." The emperor places a gentle hand on my chin and pulls my head up to meet him eye to eye. His are beautiful, shining almost as bright as the flame on top of the castle. "Do you see it?"

"I am afraid I don't know what you mean, grand ruler."

"The Inner Flame."

"Yes," I say, slightly shaking.

"I see it in you too, young King—"

"How do you know my name?" I throw my hand to my head, realizing how rude I am being to interrupt the emperor.

"A little butterfly told me." His smirk breaks into a light chuckle.

"The princess?" I exclaim.

"Yes. Don't worry, she is safe. She is with her father."

I tense up once again as I look around the room, trying to assess the situation. I want to move my hand to call forth my sword but I am afraid, afraid of what the emperor will think of me. Instead all I can do is look up at his burning eyes and squeak out like a small child, "Are we in trouble?"

"Far from it!" says a booming voice from behind me. I turn and see the one face I was too ashamed to face, King Vernon. A lump forms in my throat and before I know, it tears start to flow. I feel weak and ashamed. "Your majesty," I squeak again but to my even greater surprise, the king rushes to my side and holds me close as if I were his son. Unsure of how to react, I just stand still in his embrace. "It is quite alright. Luna told me everything. Thank you for protecting my daughter. Thank you."

Though I can hear the king thanking me, I can't process it in my mind. Since the day I betrayed my country by attacking my fellow soldier and running away with the princess, I've prepared myself for living life on the run. I figured Antenetta would be a good fit for me. Why am I being accepted back with open arms? When everything I did calls for execution? "I am willing to accept any punishment you have for me. Please don't punish the others; it was I who allowed Luna to go on this journey with us."

The emperor laughs behind me, squeezing my shoulders, and says, "This is a great soldier you have here, but young King, lighten up."

"Yes, I agree. King, you are not in trouble. There are much greater things at stake than a runaway princess. I knew from the beginning none of you kidnapped her—as I told you, she has been quite different lately. But now I know why. She has informed me of the goddess. Also, let me apologize about Adira, as it was the council who sent her after you all. I was so furious once I found out. I was afraid that something would happen to my precious Peace Island children.

"I know you all are upset with me, as you have learned that I've been keeping great things from you. But I did it only to protect you. For my whole reign as King of Peace Island, I have wrestled with the idea of sharing the true outside world with my citizens. But for some reason, every time I just don't believe I should. Our little island is so peaceful and I wouldn't dare jeopardize it. However, I knew some of you would want to experience the outside world, which is why I have always left the door wide open for those who wanted more."

The king places his hands on my cheeks. "And I am so proud of you for wanting more. King, you were never meant to be ordinary. None of you are. You all are destined for something great, no matter how big or small. You just have to find it, and once you, do don't back down, but reach as high as you can and take it!"

I no longer can contain my tears nor hide behind the false idea that I would be okay with never returning to Peace Island. I feel horrible for doubting the king and his intentions. This whole journey I only thought about going home and going back to my normal life, a life of comfort. I never stopped and realized, until this moment, that this past month and a half was one of the best times of my life. Others considered me important and I felt important. I learned new things, good and bad, and those bits of knowledge started to change me. I experienced new cultures and people and even strange beasts, and it didn't matter if they just wanted to dance or kill me. Even though I was afraid, I found it all so fascinating. The things I never would have seen from my front yard, all these things across the ocean, changed me. "Thank you, your majesty," I say in a quivering voice.

"So, since we've got that out of the way, I hear that you can control white spirit energy like Ren," the emperor says nonchalantly. When I turn to him, he has the biggest grin on his face. The name of Ren knocks me over. Were all the words they just said to me flowers to cover up the odor of the real, dying problem?

"Telark! The poor child was already shaken up and you go and mention that!" King Vernon yells playfully. The emperor rubs the back of his head with one hand as he bashfully covers his eyes with the other and says "Go-sa," which I assume is Trinity dialect for *sorry* or *my bad*. "Sorry, young King. Despite his image, the emperor is very playful."

Still unsure, I look up at the two old men, who laugh between themselves and lightly roughhouse as if they weren't a day over eighteen. I wipe my face and stand, not very steadily, and as I slip I hear something ruffle beneath me. "Oh right," I whisper under my breath. I stand up and tap my side, where a pocket magically appears on my uniform. King Vernon and the emperor look at me like small children waiting for a piece of candy. However, instead of chocolate in a gold wrapper, I pull out a burgundy velvet letter case with King Vernon's seal.

I bend down on one knee and extend my arm respectfully. "This is for you, grand ruler." I peek up at him and see that the emperor is smiling softly.

"Thank you," he says as he grabs the letter and holds it close.

I jump up, turn to King Vernon, and bow. "Mission complete."

"Well done, soldier." King Vernon winks at me. Both of the old men then pat me on the back with their eighteen-year-old strength.

"Well, now it's time for us to get down to business. Let us head to the situation room. Shall we?" says the emperor as he leads the way to a hidden room behind his throne.

The situation room is filled with high-ranking soldiers and officers from every region. But I am shocked to see Tuy and Sione at the table as well. I hurry to the empty seat beside them and lean in to whisper, "When did you guys get here?"

"Well, after we finished searching, we went back to the room and found a letter for us to go to the emperor's home. We waited for you but you never showed. Eventually a solider from the palace came and told us you were already here," whispers Tuy.

"I see."

"Alright, let's all settle down," says the emperor as he takes a seat at the head of the oval table. "I have called this meeting because I just gained some bitter news of possible future events. I have a few friends with me who will go into further detail. Young King, if you would?"

Tuy looks at me, silently asking if I want him to carry out the briefing like last time. I contemplate it for a moment, since he is the better speaker, but I am not the same King I was when I left Peace Island. I shake my head and confidently stand and begin to speak.

"Good evening, dignitaries. I am here today with a message from Peace Island. Sometime last month I had a vision. It's a special ability I've had since I was young. This vision showed Peace Island being destroyed. Our researchers looked into it and found it to be a possible future event. Many of our elders believe that this destruction would come by the hands of the

Dark King. I agreed with their theory at first, but while we have been on this journey, we've talked with many different people, and I believe it to be true that the Dark King is dead. However, he does have a son." At the word "son," the room starts to rumble with chatter, and Tuy pulls on my sleeve and asks me what I'm doing. I pull away as Sione tells him to let me continue.

"It is true," says King Vernon in a still voice that quiets the room, "for I have seen him." Sione and I jump at his confession. We make eye contact and he nods his head; now I know our theory isn't too far off from the truth.

"After finding out about Ren's son, I knew without a doubt he was the one who would be behind the destruction of our peaceful island. Think about it. He wants revenge for what happened to his father, he is filled with hate without knowing the true story of his downfall. I believe he will stop at nothing to destroy Peace Island, and all of Kasai, in order to avenge his father."

"In conclusion, what do you propose we do? I say we find this child and kill him!" The man who says this wears a sash adorned with small screens that project his medals of honor just like ours, and I know he is from Antenetta.

"No. That will only make the situation worse," I say sternly. "Though Ren is blocked off, I know of a man who escaped. If one has white spirit energy, they can enter through the wall, and news will travel of the prince's death, and we could end up facing another civil war."

The ruler of Antenetta sits down and crosses his arms in front of him, rolling his eyes. "Well, what do you propose we do?" he snaps.

"I want to find him and change his mind."

The old men around the table erupt with laughter. I want to cower in embarrassment, but Tuy pinches me and I hold my head high, not backing down. Then I hear a soothing voice at the far end of the table.

"I agree with King. We spend so much time running straight into situations with guns before we try using our words and talking to each other like human beings. We are a nation that is like an uncontrollable fire, but what happens when fire turns on itself? It combusts and implodes," says the only woman in the situation room. I squint to get a clearer glimpse of her, and once I do, I can't believe my eyes. "Olena?"

"Yes, King. Good evening, everyone. I am the governor of the scattered villages along the land of the Road of Bones."

"Glad you could join us," says the emperor. "I see that you have taken over for your mother. I feel like it was just yesterday that you were born."

"Yes, your majesty."

"Well, Governor Olena, if we do go with King's plan of finding Ren's son and talking him down from his revenge plot, what do we do if talking doesn't work?" With a stern look on his face, the emperor rests his head upon his folded hands.

"Sir, I can answer that." I speak up hastily, without thinking about the weight of what I'm saying. "If Ren's son does not listen to us, then yes, we have no other choice than to deal with him harshly. However, as you know, along the way I've learned that I can manipulate spirit energy, the same type as King Ren."

Before I could get out the name, all types of weapons are drawn and pointed directly at my face, heart, and legs. Tuy and Sione leap up and show their weapons in an effort to protect me, but I motion for them to sit down. I look to the emperor, who just nods for me to continue.

I take a deep breath and face the numerous weapons pointed at me as if they were missiles ready to fall. I clear my throat and take the words from the dignitary's mouths before they can accuse me. "Calm down. I am not Ren's son. The elders who have seen Ren's son say that he has the same grey eyes as his father, and as you all know that is a rare color in this land. So please take your seats and let me finish."

Embarrassed, the dignitaries clear their throats and fix their clothes as they put their weapons back into their sheaths, holsters, and even hidden compartments in their shoes and retake their seats. I look down to the end of the table, where the emperor is practically rolling with laughter.

"I'm so sorry, I know it's not an appropriate time to laugh. But dear Olena was just talking about going in guns first, and what do you all do…?" The emperor laughs so much that he is not even able to finish his sentence. I can't hold in my laughter either as I look down to Olena, who gives me a wink and a nod of encouragement.

"Okay, so I definitely agree with Governor Olena. We must not go in weapons first; it does not feel very good. But in summary, if I can find the grey-eyed prince and talk him down, then we will have nothing to worry about. If not, then I will be able to fight spirit energy with spirit energy."

"Do you think you will win?" questions a deep-voiced dignitary.

"Truthfully, I am not sure; but if that battle does come to pass, I will give my all to protect our land. Another good thing is that the son doesn't know we are aware of him or his plans, so we are a step ahead," I say as I bow my head and take my seat.

"Very well! I think these are all great ideas. However, we must still prepare for the worst. I waited too late to deal with an adversary before, but this time God has given us the upper hand, so I will not make the same mistake again. Everyone, get your militaries ready for war."

"But emperor, sir!" I cry out.

"I am sorry, King. Once you find him you can give him a chance by talking to him, but know this: if we find him first, he will be put on trial for his life."

"But—"

"No buts! I hereby make an imperial decree that the Prince of Ren is a wanted man! If anyone should come across him, they must bring him to me, and I shall decide his punishment." The emperor finalizing his decree by simply walking out the room. The other dignitaries follow behind him, some even stopping and smirking at me.

King Vernon, just shakes his head and says that maybe this is for the best as he exits. I look to Olena, who has buried her head deep into her hands and is yet to come up for air. And all I can do is turn to Sione and Tuy and whisper, "I'm sorry. Maybe I should have let you speak, Tuy."

"Nonsense. You actually said everything I was thinking," Tuy says, sounding defeated.

Feeling defeated too, I tell the others that I need to take a moment to myself before I leave the table and the situation room. I walk slowly and can't help but glare at the emperor's throne. I guess he's not the man I thought he was. Stepping out of the throne room, I come face to face with the butler from earlier.

"Tough meeting, young King?"

"Is it that obvious?"

"I'm afraid so, it's written all over your face. But might I suggest a place for you to clear your mind?"

I chuckle and say, "That would be great, but I haven't had a clear mind since I was ten." The butler just stares at me for a moment. "Sorry, I made it awkward."

"It is all right, nobody is perfect. Now, if you go to door number five, you will enter a hallway and the third door on your right will lead to the palace library. I know you youth don't care too much for books, but it is a great way to escape from reality, even for a while."

"No, actually, I love to read!"

"Magnificent! I hope that our library will be to your liking."

"Thanks…um?"

"Sir Leem."

"Thank you, Sir Leem."

"The pleasure is all mine," he says as he heads off to an opposite tentacle.

The library is beyond my imagination. There are miles of books and antiques like a rustic globe and a gold birdcage along the walls. I walk to the only window at the end of the room and peek through its gothic arch, in awe and amazement at the beauty before me. I seem to be at the back of the castle, for in the distance I can see many valleys filled with the mystical beasts Tuy talked of. Most of the beasts look like your typical animals, just supersized, or have additional characteristic, sort of like The Elk and his spirit energy antlers. Though, the small ones have to be my favorite, I smile, looking at a honey badger standing on a rock near a spring among the other Majestics with his chest poked out, small but full of spunk, with long silver fangs to back up his confidence. Even the elephants who have strange markings, almost like paint on their bodies, avoid eye contact with him as he walks through. It's interesting how they look like animals, but are in harmony. I guess that is why they are Majestics, I shake my head not wanting to know what powers lay behind their façade, as I think back to The Elk. I break away from the window and start to walk along the rows of books, running my fingers across the spines.

My mother use to make me read two hours a day. I hated it until I realized the power of books. I didn't have to think about the bullies at school. Books were my solace. How I wish my mother would appear before me again, even if she doesn't give me a word of advice, just see me and touch my face.

"Right," I whisper to myself as I think of the day she told me about Rania. How she never really mentioned if she was good or bad, just that the princess must go with me on this journey. I think of when Tuy said the only way to figure out if the goddess is good or bad is by finding out her real name. I wonder if they have any information about goddesses in here.

I search the library from top to bottom, pulling down all the books about goddesses and stacking them on a glossy oak table in the center of the room. Once I set down the last stack of books, I wipe the sweat from my brow, plop on a wooden chair, and scoot it to the table. I start with a book called *The Goddess and Her Hair*, sucking my teeth as I see it's a children's picture book. I guess I could have sorted the books better as I was searching. The next book I pick up is titled *Goddesses in the Field*; this is more informative than the last, as it at least has more than pictures, but it still isn't what I need. It only goes into detail about miniature goddesses, almost like pixies, who have small villages in the fields.

I throw the book to the side, frustrated, but for some reason I feel a sense of urgency and I start right back up and continue my search. I go from book to book, but throw each one to the side. I even start to look for the name Luna told me, Tru, but to no avail. Soon the gothic window grows dimmer and dimmer, and before I know it I'm squinting at the words underneath a small lamp. I start to feel twinges in my neck and I give in, finally throwing my head back and letting out a low groan.

This isn't working, I think to myself. I throw aside my final book, titled *Goddesses Reference Book from A to Z*. "If that book had every known goddess's name in our world, and Rania or Tru are nowhere in it, then who the heck is she, really?" I whisper even though I am all alone. I roll my neck from side to side until I hear the door crack open from behind me. I turn around and see Sir Leem peeping his head in. I get ready to speak, but he simply switches on the overhead lights and smiles at me as he slips back out. I shake my head and mumble "Thank you" under my breath.

I get up one more time and start to search again, thinking I might have missed something. I find myself going from row to row and eventually I realize I don't even know what I'm searching for. I walk to the far end of the library and lean on the wall between two bookshelves. I press all my weight on the wall and it begins to move. I know I haven't gained any weight; as long as I have been on this trip, I've probably lost some. I pull away from the wall and look it up and down. There is no way this type of wall would give in, not that easily. I lean back on it, but this time the wall doesn't move. It becomes completely transparent and I fall through it, landing upon another row of books.

I jump up and turn back to the wall, which is fading in and out. It's a hologram. "Why would they be hiding a section of the library?" I say to myself. Oh gosh, what if this is the emperor's private section? I hurry back through the hologram, but come to a sudden halt with one foot in the private and the other in the public sector when a faded letter Z catches my eye. The letter is on the far end of the private sector, on the back wall over a strange door that can only be accessed by an old wooden staircase. I turn around and walk toward the door to get a closer look. I'm able to make out the other faded letters and whisper under my breath: "Zara. Ren's original name."

I walk up the stairs and stand for a moment at the door under the halfway faded Zara sign. I enter a small circular room with books along the wall and one table in the middle.

With shaking feet, I walk forward, running my fingers along the spines of books, until I stop in my tracks and pull out a baby blue book with the gold title: *The Fiftieth Queen of Zara: Tru.* I run my eyes across the title over and over until I lose feeling in my fingers and the book slips through. I quickly pick it up, throw the book on the table, and open its pages. I scan each at lightning speed, so much that some of the pages even rip, until I just yank the book open and it falls to the middle, where I find a beautiful portrait of a woman, not a goddess.

She has thick long black hair and stunning blue eyes. This is not Rania, but she shares the name that Luna told me about. Could this be Rania's true form? But how? I read a little further and fear pierces me in the chest. I read slowly the words, *Tru, the beautiful Queen, does not only have her beauty but is also a renowned chemist of Zara. Through her study of chemistry, she can create many powerful remedies and potions that help with the wellness of her citizens. But just as this queen can lift a healing hand through her chemistry, she can also mix together deadly ingredients, stopping any enemy of Zara with this skill as well as her ability to control time and space. She received these abilities when she was young, after falling into a spring near the mystics' villages while trying to get ingredients for a new remedy.*

So many thoughts begin to swim through my mind, but I know I first must get to the princess, for she is in greater danger than any of us. I jump up from the table, race down the stairs, and rush through the holographic wall. I call forth my sword and exit the library as I take off down the fifth tentacle.

Coming back into the main hall, I start to yell like a madman, demanding to know if anybody has seen the princess. The guards pin me down. I try to shove them away as I continue to scream that I need to find the princess. Tuy and Sione arrive by my side and push the guards off of me. Sione embraces me in his bear hug and tells me to calm down and that the princess is safe. The necklace turns hot as white spirit energy encases my body, stinging him to help me break free.

"Ow! What the heck, dude!" Sione yells.

"I'm sorry. But you all must hear me out. The goddess—"

Bonk! Bonk! Bonk! Alarms blare in the castle as the soldiers scurry outside. The crystal walls become encased with metal as shutters start fall, locking down the castle. I grab Tuy and Sione's arms and shout, "Hurry! We have to get outside!"

We rush into the courtyard, which once was covered in greenery and is now black and filled with fire. It looks like we are in a warzone. There are technological weapons zapping, modified guns firing, swords clanking, and smoke all around. "Tuy, look, The Elk!" Sione yells. I turn in their direction and see not only one but three elk, the same size and kind as we ran into in the woods. Soldiers begin their attack upon them, but it is no use. The Elk ram into the soldiers, lifting them ten feet in the air.

"Ahhhhh!" Sione yells behind me. I turn around and come face to face with The Elk from the forest. He stands tall and looks us three straight in the eyes. I see a scar on his chest that swirls with spirit energy. As I move back slowly, he moves closer to me, so close that I can feel him breathing. "King, don't make any sudden movements," says Tuy.

"Wasn't planning on it." But before I can crouch and hide, he lays a part of his large forehead onto mine. But he doesn't head-butt or harm me. He touches my head just lightly enough that the world around me freezes.

The Elk does not move and neither do I. We just stare at each other with foreheads touching. But then my arm starts to move against my will, and my whole body next. I find myself climbing on top of his head. It is not covered in fur but forms a small valley, with flowers and all the spirit energies swirling through the field that has grown upon his crown. "Pick one," The Elk says.

"What! You can speak?" I almost fall from his head.

"Yes."

"Oh, I see. Well, why did you do those evil things to us before?" I shake my finger in detest, now that I know he has some type of intellect.

"I am sorry, for I was not myself. The one you know now as Tru, had me under her spell. But that is all I can say. Ask me not of how I know of her and your journey. Now, young King, hurry up and choose an energy while you still have time."

"But I already have spirit energy."

"I see. Well, now you will have two. You never know, you might like this energy more than the other; it might feel more personal. Just because something is the strongest doesn't mean it is the best fit for you."

"Maybe," I say hesitantly as I walk from one antler to the next, scanning each point that contains a pure energy—pink, blue, green, white, and so on—but none really piques my interest.

"It seems that you are having a hard time. If none of those stand out to you, why not try the one near my tail?" I look past the elk's grand antlers and walk down his back until I come face to face with a spirit energy that is shaped differently from the rest. I reach for it, surprisingly without fear, and grasp it in my palms. I slowly climb down from the elk's head and hold it up for him to see. "Why is it shaped like a spiral?"

"Simple. There is a jade spiral bondage holding the gold spirit energy in. However, the jade holds its own energy as well. This dual energy is very great, young King. I have only showed it to one other person before. It will sometimes feel that you can't control it, but you must let go of the limitations placed on you by yourself and those around you."

I look to The Elk and back at this great energy I simply am holding in my hands. Is something so easy to hold really that great? It doesn't feel that powerful, especially since it looks like it is being strangled, but nevertheless I bow my head and thank the Elk for his gift.

"Now, young one, you must go. Your life is about to change greatly. But remember this, no matter what comes, guard your heart and mind, for if she reaches them you will surely die, and so will your little island," warns The Elk as he levitates the energy from my hand into the air. He places the jade and gold energy in the center of his head before once again kissing his forehead with mine, and just like that, the spirit energy bursts and the world around me comes back to life and The Elk disappears.

I stand facing the darkening sky, turned away from all the fighting going on behind me. I open my palm and swirls of gold twirl around my fingertips, up my arm, and around my shoulder before seeping into my chest. The pureness of this energy makes me feel so warm and whole, on this unfortunate day.

"The emperor!" a voice cries out behind me. I turn and see that everyone's attention is on the top of the palace. I look up and there she is—Rania, no, Ren's queen, Tru. She stands on a platform at the top of the castle, holding the emperor by the neck and laughing menacingly, threatening to drop him if all of the regions' heads do not bow to her and the region of Ren.

"Luna! Please stop this!" cries King Vernon, who is weeping on the burned ground with outstretched hands to the woman who was once his daughter. We run over to the king and try to lift him up, but he shakes free from us and continues to cry out to his lost child.

"King, what do we do?" questions Sione, choking back tears. I try to think of some plan, but all will likely fail against her, for she is too powerful. She has blocked off any entry into the castle by hypnotizing the elks and using them as a shield. A brave guard scales the castle only to be blown away, literally, as she throws a beam of spirit energy from her free palm, blowing off the guard's arms and legs in every direction.

I look up at Rania as I grab the necklace Luna gave me and squeeze it tight. "I have the strongest spirit energy here. Weapons and strategies will not work on her." I move past Tuy and Sione and place my hands on the king's shoulders. "Don't worry, your majesty. I will save the princess. We protected her this whole journey, and you best believe she will not come in harm's way after we have made it this far."

I tell Sione and Tuy to watch my back as I open my palm and my new little gold friend smiles back at me. I throw the energy spiral in the air and center my emotions. I imagine pulling the jade spiral free from the gold energy, until it grows so grand that it is now before me like a tiny sun. I pull at the jade spiral and the energy busts free and swirls through the courtyard, knocking out the elks and scraping Rania's arm. She loses her grip on the emperor as she yells out in pain, turning to me and clutching her arm. But I cannot look at her; all I see is the emperor, who falls through the sky like a crushed blossom from a dying tree.

"Got him!" Tuy springs into action and scales up the palace walls, finding his footing on gaps in the metal shutters that lead to the top almost like stairs. I follow behind him, only to stop once the emperor falls, which feels like slow-motion, right in front of me. We both reach for him, but Tuy of course, being the cool one, leaves the security of the metal ledge and jumps for the emperor. Now, drifting above me, he catches the emperor and falls with him gracefully through the sky. I should be afraid for the bitter end they seem to be approaching, but I know Tuy, and just like that he grabs onto a broken metal shutter, from Rania's early attack, and makes his way down holding the emperor on his side, all without breaking a sweat.

For so long Tuy has been the hero, but today it is my turn, I think as I turn my gaze to Rania. I climb up the side of the palace at full speed while she moves farther inward until we are both on the palaces exposed platform, right under the Inner Flame. She gazes upon me with cold eyes, no longer Rania but her true self shines through her false forms' eyes. Unsure what she is truly capable of, I creep closer to her.

"Why don't you use the sword I gave you?"

"What did you say?"

"Let's make this fun for the both of us, son." She tilts her head to the side, looking at me with her dark eyes. She holds her hand out and a long spear appears, encased with white spirit energy.

"Who are you exactly?" I stutter.

"Oh, my dear son, you know all about me now, don't you? After your little study session in the library," she says smoothly as she twirls the spear in circles with one hand.

"You're the Queen of Ren?" I ask lightly, slightly nervous about her answer.

This new form of Rania cuts her eyes at me, and unlike the pink and jovial eyes of the goddess she claimed to be, they grow black as night. She whirls and hops around the palaces roof, looking like a joker—or more like a trickster. "Correct. Well now, shall we begin?" She spins her spear above her, creating tornados of white spirit energy that fly in different directions, tearing the palace apart and revealing the crystal underneath the metal shutters.

I dodge and try to throw energy bombs toward her, but she reflects them all and I know I have no choice. I run to a corner on the steeple and hide behind it, trying to remember the emotions I felt the day I was in the valley behind the shack. "Yes, King, show us the powers of the Dark King! A sword so strong it will cut through anything. A power that is only held by the Dark King!" From the distance, Tru's snide comments break my train of thought. I just shake them off, but she goes on and on about the Dark King and proving that his power still lives. I open both of my palms, and white spirit energy sits in one and gold in the other. For some reason, I feel like I am choosing between good and evil. If I reveal the Dark King's spirit sword, I will be further associated with him even if I defeat Tru.

The screams from below get louder and Tru's laughter grows even more menacing as she creates more and more spirit tornados, not caring for the lives that she is taking, and especially not caring for the life that she is holding inside of her. "King! Make a move!" Tuy yells from below, forcing my hand. I jump up from the corner and face Tru, who turns to me with a sadistic smirk and eyes that are seeking blood.

She licks her lips and says, "Oh my, what is that you have there? A new sword, I see. Never knew there was something like jade and gold spirit energy. And my, look at the craftsmanship." She jumps to my side, catching me off guard. I fall back, holding the sword like a shield in front of me.

However, Tru doesn't attack. She just runs her finger along the jade hilt and follows the jade spiral that wraps around the gold spirit blade, looking at it in awe, almost like she is mesmerized. But she finally breaks free and peeks at me from around the edge of the sword's blade. "It looks like my little plan didn't turn out to well. Bell-Ow really needs to mind his business." Tru pouts her lips playfully.

"So, you do have something to do with the white spirit energy?" I ask.

"I know not what you mean," says Tru as she bats her black eyelashes.

"That was cute for Rania, but when you do it, it is disgusting," I snarl.

Tru's playfulness fades as she becomes stern in face and proceeds to try and strike me with her spear. I clasp the jade sword hilt and push myself up before Tru can swing her weapon into my chest. I throw up the gold spirit sword and cut straight through her spear, hearing gasps below.

"My, it seems Bell-Ow must have taken a liking to you. This is very interesting; too bad you wasted all your time training with white spirit energy. Your newfound strength, no matter how strong, can't out beat my years of practice." Tru smirks as she throws out her hand and tenses it up, causing me to fly forward into her grasp. She squeezes my throat tight, digging her nails into my veins.

I gasp for air as she walks, holding me by the throat with one hand. She teleports onto the rim of the Inner Flame. The fire is so hot I feel my skin peel, embers popping onto my face and hands. I wrap my fingers around her arm and try to break free, but it is no use. She dangles me over the rim and threatens to drop me. I slip between a sleeping and awakened state.

"No, no, my dear, you must not die just yet, not until I reveal your truth."

"What truth do you know? You live your life through lies," I manage to choke out.

Tru tilts her head to the side and says, "That might be true, but this, my dear King, is an unfortunate fact that I sincerely wish was a lie."

"Why in the world are you doing this? What will you gain? Just let Luna go!"

"Shut up! This is all your fault. Luna will die because of you. This world will burn because of you. You should have never been born. You shall die a horrible death!" yells Tru as she clasps her other hand over my eyes, covering them. She pushes so hard into my face it feels like tiny needles are sticking me. I cry out in pain as I try to claw at her arms, but she just laughs.

"See here all, Ren's one and only son! The prince of Ren!" Tru yells as she pulls her hand from my eyes and dangles me over the masses below, who are now all gawking and screaming at me, except for some who run away. The alarms blare even louder, and I hear an order over the main PA system for citizens to start evacuating the city. I look around for Sione and Tuy so they can tell me what is going on, but I cannot find them in the growing sea of soldiers who point their guns at me.

"What did you do? Answer me!" I yell, but she just turns me back to face her and gives a winning smile. What has she won? "You can say that

I am the Dark King's son all you want, but your words hold no value, trickster!"

Tru scoffs and finally speaks. "How funny. A man told me the same thing once, but I proved him wrong by destroying everything he loves." Tru cuts her eyes from me, turning back to the soldiers and dignitaries below, and begins to tell of how she will rule Kasai as she tightens her grip around my neck.

How could I have let this get this bad? I should have listened to my gut. I look at Tru and my heart breaks, though I see that her eyes are no longer black but a soft, dark green, I squeeze my eyes shut, tears wanting to fall, but I won't let them. This poor child, it's all my fault. I never should have allowed her to come with us on this journey. I should have done something from the moment Luna told me about Rania. A goddess living in a child's body, it just doesn't sound right! But I did nothing. I doubted her and I should have confronted my inner fears then, but I just left it to fate. Even if nothing changed, I should have done something, now I fear that I must break a promise to my king, queen, and princess.

Looking below, I try to find Sione and Tuy again. I see the king, and there is Sione. His eyes meet mine, as I use the last of my strength, I move my hand by my side to secretly make the numbers; three: God—five: save—zero: the—four: king. Sione immediately sweeps into action and scoops up the king, who is screaming and doing his best to fight to stay, for any glimmer of hope that his daughter will return. But Sione is much stronger and manages to sneak out of the courtyard with our now weary king. Tuy looks at me and, with what appears to be a heavy heart, nods his head before turning and following Sione. Finally I turn to Luna and simply whisper, "Be strong. She might have your body, but do not let her have your mind."

A single tear falls down Tru's cheek. She is still yelling fire and brimstone, but once she feels the tear, she becomes frazzled and slaps her face insanely. "Stay back, little brat!" Tru yells, but unwanted tears continue to flow. She loses focus and eases up some of her hold on me, just enough for me to call forth my new blade and cut it straight across her chest.

Tru yells out in pain, loosening her grip. Her blood splashes onto my face before she completely lets go of my neck. I begin falling to my death, and all I can do is mouth my last words: "Luna, I am so sorry."

The trickster falls back, grabbing her chest, and disappears into the Inner Flame, and I just close my eyes and pray for forgiveness.

—XIII—

ZARA

I wake on a cold cobblestone floor. My head is spinning and I am still covered in blood. I try to move my arm, but I am in so much pain that just to lift it and rest it upon my chest is a grand task. As I move my hand up my body, I feel my clothes in tatters.

For a moment, I just stare at the ceiling and pray that it stops moving in circles. Where in the world am I? I try to turn my neck, pain shooting down the left side of my body, but all I can see are metal bars. I manage to roll over on my belly and push myself up to my knees, but I fall back against the concrete wall when immense pain shoots up my back. I see my body in front of me and it is covered in small burns, cuts, and bruises. I try to take a few deep breaths and regain my composure.

After a few more breathing exercises, the world around me finally comes into focus and I can see that I am in some type of jail cell. "The prince has awakened!" calls a guard who I can just barely make out in the distance.

"Prince? Why the heck would a prince be in a place like this?" I whisper to myself.

The guard turns around and walks closer to me, and strangely, I can sense fear. Why in the world would somebody be afraid of me? And more importantly, what am I doing in a jail cell?

"Here you are, prisoner," says the guard as he slides a tray through the cell door containing only bread and water. "Your trial will take place

181

tomorrow at noon. May God have mercy on your soul." He crosses his arm over his chest and quickly walks away.

An hour passes once the guard leaves, but I have yet to move from the cold stone wall. I lie in confusion, continuously replaying the altercation with Tru. I begin to wonder if any of it was real; most importantly, if I really did strike her. Maybe that is why I am here. My God, did I murder the princess? I throw my hands to my head, hitting it hard and tearing at my hair. I start to sob and wail like a crazy person.

"King, are you okay?" says a familiar voice.

I jump up, even in pain, and reach through the metal bars, Sione and Tuy each grabbing a hand. "What the heck is going on?"

"You really don't know?" Tuy squints.

"Yes. No one has told me anything. The last thing I remember is striking Tru and falling to my death. I didn't mean to kill her. I was just trying to release the princess." I fall to my knees, sobbing again. "She's dead, isn't she? And by my hand. Phoenix warned me, he warned me of this power."

Sione stretches his arm as far as it will go between the tight bars—they have to be cutting off his circulation, but nonetheless he reaches my back and begins to pat it, comforting me.

"King, it will be okay. The princess might still be alive. Rania disappeared into the flame, taking Luna's body with her. But I don't think she will destroy the child. However, King, that's not what is important now."

I look up at Sione. "What do you mean?" He and Tuy look at each other, and I can see that they are very troubled. "Spit it out already!" I yell. "What is it?"

"Have you seen your reflection lately?" Tuy asks smoothly. I stare at him, and he pulls out a small pocket mirror. Cautiously I move my face toward the glass, not knowing what I will find, only to see beautiful but dangerous grey eyes.

I move my fingertips along my face before clasping both hands over my eyes, covering and uncovering them over and over again. "This has got to be some type of trick; she did this to me! There is no way—" I pause for a moment and the tears start again, drowning my newfound irises.

Tuy shakes his head. "Even if this is some type of trick or spell, the royals do not care. They have called for your execution."

The gravity of the situation begins to sink in, but instead of sobbing even harder, I laugh at myself. Tuy and Sione jerk back slightly, probably thinking that I'm about to have a complete psychotic break. "Sorry. It's just that I realized, I created a bounty on my own head. Funny how life works."

"I don't find it funny at all. It's tragic. What am I going to do without my best friend?" Sione cries.

"It's okay, Sione. Maybe this is for the best. I never told you two, but I had another vison after the first. While I was in the Neuro Center I saw the calamity again, but this time I saw myself, glowing and floating above the island, and a voice told me that I was the cause. I kept wondering how would this come to pass, but now I see. If these eyes are real and I am Ren's son, then maybe somewhere down the line something will make me commit treason. I mean, changes of heart seem to run in my family."

I peek at Sione and Tuy, who are taken aback. "Why would you keep this from us, King?" Tuy grits his teeth. "We promised at Dr. Lisa's. If you had told us, we could have done something to protect you."

"Sorry. I just thought it was for the best, and if I am who they say I am, then I don't deserve protection."

Sione slams his fist against the metal bars. "Stop talking like that, King! You are not King Ren. You cannot hold yourself accountable for his sins. We all are our own person, no matter what sins our parents might have committed. Today is a new day and you are in control of your destiny!" His voice roars through the jail.

Sione is right, in every way. But I fear that my father's sins are too great. I lower my head and softly reply, "Unfortunately, it looks like destiny has dealt me a losing hand."

"Even if that's so, we are not just going to throw in the towel. We will get you out of this mess somehow." Tuy places a firm hand on my shoulder and pushes Sione toward the exit before adding, "For there is so much adventure that will come from those eyes, and it can be positive as long as you let your heart lead."

Though I sit at the horizon of death, I chuckle to myself once again, like a madman. I try to think of this new chapter as our exciting new adventure. *I mean, it's not like I can't break free.* They might have disabled my Antenetta uniform, but that's not where my power comes from, I think as I start to play with my gold and jade spirit energy, bouncing it from hand to hand. But I guess I will play along. Rania did say my life was full of lies. Guess it's time to find them and lay them out on the table for everyone to see. "Tomorrow I will get all the information I can from the emperor. He thinks this will be an execution, but I'm going to turn it into a study session before getting free," I say to myself, clasping the energy in my hand to make it disappear.

The sun rises as I pick up my heavy head from the notebook I was writing in all night, which came in handy to release some of my emotions and thankfully a pillow as well. I roll my neck, muttering that they still at least could have given me a pillow and some blankets. They act as if I actually attacked them. How quickly their fears made them forget that I was the one who saved the emperor.

"It is time," says a voice in the shadows.

I jump and turn around to see two well-built guards, all for this Peace Island coward. "Very well," I say as I stand.

"But first, put your hands in these."

"What is that?" I ask, looking at what seem like two crystal boxes with holes.

"These are jade spirit energy chambers. They suppress your energy."

"Oh, I see." I reluctantly place my hands into the boxes losing, last night's fighting spirit.

The guards lead me out to a courtyard, but this one is different from yesterday's; it seems to be in the back of the castle. I'm placed upon a gallows in the center of the flame-shaped courtyard, surrounded by the regions council. I look around frantically for a second, as I cannot find Sione or Tuy. I start to panic. In the section designated for Peace Island, not even the king is present. I've been abandoned. My stomach sinks to the bottom of my feet, but there is no time to clear my thoughts before the emperor reveals himself on the palace terrace. I am brutally pushed down by the guards and forced to beg for forgiveness, for crimes I know nothing of.

"Young King! Let me first start by saying that I am sorry that it had to come to this," says the emperor. I try to look up at him, but the guards push my head even farther down and begin to spit venomous words about how dare I try to look upon the emperor with my eyes. "But for your crimes—"

"My crimes? Are you sure this is what I'm on trial for? Or are you just trying to settle a score with my presumed father?" I cut him off and push back at the guards, lifting my head to look him straight in the eyes. The courtyard grows even quieter as I stare down the emperor, who is no longer the jovial old man I first met. Pursing his lips, he clicks his tongue at me, showing his obvious discontent with my behavior. But I could care less; he does not have my respect.

"Even if I am the Prince of Ren, I haven't committed any crimes. The last time I checked, I saved your life. I know nothing about the land of Ren. All I know is Peace Island."

"So why are you planning to destroy it?"

"What? I would never destroy my home. I had a vision—"

"Yes, we know of your vision, but you also said that you believed the Prince of Ren was the one who would destroy your island and Kasai."

"The prince is still out there—"

"You are the prince! Stop playing these games."

"I am not. The trickster was the one who did this to me."

"Trickster?"

"The woman from yesterday, Queen Tru. She is making you all believe that I am Ren's son. She probably knows where the real prince is and they will try to take over the land of Kasai together. I am the only one that can stop them. So she is trying to get rid of me."

"Enough!" the emperor barks, putting me at a loss for words. "Enough of these foolish stories. You are a clever one, just as your father was. But the point is, we cannot be sure if you just found out, or if you knew of your lineage and hid it in order to destroy Kasai from within after you gained our trust. Even so, the apple does not fall far from the tree. Ren was a great friend of mine, but in the end, he turned into a snake in the garden."

"But grand ruler," I whimper out, "he was not himself at that time. Queen Tru did something to his mind, he believed—"

"King, I said enough." Emperor Telark sternly interrupts my earnest plea.

He paces for a moment before stopping in his tracks as he hangs his head and turning back to me, stroking his beard. "King, I admit that you are an upstanding young man at this moment. However, you did have a vision of something or someone destroying your island, and I believe that by the context of your vision, it will be a someone, someone with great power, someone like you.

"And yes, you are kind now, but what if down the line something bad happens, changing you? Young King, one reason I am able to lead Kasai so well is because I am a firm believer in being proactive. But you are correct. Your eyes might link you to your father's past sins, but that does not mean that you have to suffer because of them. So I will not be sentencing you to death. Instead, we will try to extract this great evil that I know is hiding in you. Bring forth the tools," says the emperor, throwing his hands in the air.

Sir Leem, the butler, rolls out a wooden cart. I jump, as I have never seen so many different types of torture devices in my life. The guards bring a wooden chair, throw me upon it, and bind my hands and legs with leather straps before shoving a white cloth in my mouth. Sir Leem walks slowly toward me and hands one of the guards a long metal pole, He manages to sneak a peek at me and whispers "Sorry" before departing.

The guard throws the pole forward, extending it with an audible pop. This is the same weapon General Claude used on my mother. The guard throws the electric pole straight in the air, and with great gusto, he swings it over my back. I scream out in pain.

The emperor does not flinch as the guard continues to whip me with the pole. He just stares at me, as if he has no feelings or thoughts about what is being done. For the next couple of hours, I am examined, electrocuted, and prodded, and all that can be heard are my screams. I keep trying to clench my fist and use my spirit energy, but the crystal boxes are too strong. After what feels like days, the emperor finally tells the guards to cease, and that my trial will resume tomorrow.

I cannot bear another day like today. Foolishly, I turn back to Peace Island's section, where I see not only Sione and Tuy, but also Olena, sitting in our section as a way to show her support. Tears start to fall as I can tell that Sione is having a hard time keeping it together. I feel so bad for my friend, but more importantly, for the shame that I am bringing to Peace Island. We are supposed to represent peace and neutrality in Kasai, but now a monster like me has come from our island. I look back at the emperor, who is putting on his royal cloak and starting to leave the terrace. The dignitaries begin to clear out as well, not caring anymore for the truth but just believing the stories they have made up in their heads.

How can they be so cruel? King Vernon is so right to keep us locked away from these people, but out of a moment of pride, I rushed into a den of lions. I now lie here beaten, but not broken. For these lions are attacking because of fear. We are supposed to be an uncontrollable fire, but how could we be when all of our dignitaries are being controlled by fear?

An entire region is locked behind a wall because of a deceitful woman. No one dared find the truth or lend a helping hand to a king who changed overnight. They let Ren fall, the king and the region. We all are meant to be one, but they were thrown away. How cruel could our emperor be?

Before he leaves completely, the emperor looks over his shoulder at me. I can see in his eyes that he knows there is more to this story. But instead of letting the truth out, he will allow his people to wallow in fear, not letting them decide their fates. I always thought I was the biggest coward there ever was, but I see now that I have met the biggest coward of Kasai. If he wants his people to be afraid, I will give them something to be afraid of. I will set things right by my own hands.

I turn to Tuy and blink my eyes twice, three times, and lastly five. Tuy jumps up, followed by Sione. Olena tries to grab them, probably wanting to stop us from ruining our lives. Too bad my life apparently was ruined the day I was born. What's a little more?

Tuy bum-rushes the guards, and Sione grabs two of them in a rock-hard bear hug. Tuy grabs the metal rod and twirls it before powering it on and striking the first guard in the head and the second continuously on the back— a small revenge.

The emperor yells out for the guards as the frightened dignitaries flee with their swords and guns dangling at their sides. "A bunch of cowards," Sione spits. Before more guards appear, he and Tuy set me free from the chair. I try to stand but I am at my wits' end. "Tuy, the key," I say, nodding my head at the key that hangs around an unconscious guard's neck. Tuy grabs it and swiftly unlocks the crystal boxes. With no time to waste, I look up at the emperor and extend my hand toward him, but instead of running in fear, he throws off his royal robe and puffs out his chest. However, I'm not buying it.

"I have to say I am disappointed in you, emperor Telark."

The emperor laughs at me as tells the guards to hurry now that I've been freed of the crystal boxes. About twenty more guards show up. Tuy and Sione fight most of them off, but of course the biggest one out of all of them gets to me. He picks me up like a sack of potatoes and throws me into the palace wall. Diving after me, he begins to land numerous punches onto my face and chest. Tuy and Sione try to reach me, but to no avail. I look up and see the emperor smirking as if he has won.

Well, I guess it would appear that I am on the losing end, but I will not give in. I might be weak in body but my mind is still strong, I think as I kick off the giant guard and throw him across the courtyard. It makes everyone else go still. I expect to be covered in gold spirit energy, or even the white energy I am doubtful of, but instead I'm encased in energy that's black as the abyss. The black energy burns my skin, and I let out an animalistic roar as I run for the guards and start to knock them out one by one.

Sione grabs Tuy and pulls him to the side. Though I feel their fear, they do not leave me. I continue to break everything within my reach, but most importantly, I turn my attention to Emperor Telark. I look up toward the terrace, and of course the coward is gone. I yell once again as I jump from the ground to the terrace and begin to break the crystal. I fly through the halls of the palace, punching in walls and shattering windows with a black sword, fueled with negative energy. Everything I punch and slice starts to burn. Near the end of my rampage, I burst through the façade of the palace and fall into the front courtyard. Behind me, the palace is in flames. Sione and Tuy run to my side and I see their mouths moving, saying that we need to get out of here, but I cannot leave. Maybe the emperor was right that something would cause me to change, something would fire up the dark side of my heart.

Once one falls into the abyss, it is hard to find their way out. I reach my hand toward the Inner Flame, which still burns the brightest in the midst of the fire. Tuy grabs me by the collar to stop me from what he knows I'm going to do next, but I push him away. I clench my fist as I did out at sea, and quickly open it up to reveal Kasai's Inner Flame in the center of my palm. Many of the dignitaries, soldiers, and palace staff stand around me now, fearful of my next move. I want them to live in this fear for a while, instead of living in a fake world of happiness. I start to clench my fist as I think of where to throw the captured flame, but before I can, I grow dizzy. This time I am truly at my end. I grab for Sione, who tries to hold on to me, but we fall together, along with Tuy. Instead of landing on the ground, we plummet into a black abyss. I look through the dark matter that surrounds us and the last thing I see is the destruction I have left behind—but more importantly, the emperor, who is smiling. I have to wonder if I really won this fight.

I hear Sione and Tuy's screams as we fall through nothingness. I cannot see them but I feel them holding on to me for dear life. The sky breaks open and we fall through the earth's atmosphere. As I brace myself for the probability of the ground breaking my spine, we stop in midair, inches from the ground. As we hover in place, we look at each other, before we are dropped abruptly onto the dusty road beneath us.

We let out groans in unison as we try to gather our thoughts and pick ourselves up. Both Tuy and Sione stand, but the pain that shoots through my body is paralyzing, and I just make the ground my bed.

When I finally come to, I am able to lift my body without feeling as much pain as I did before. Most of my energy has been restored, though I think it will be a while before I am mentally healed. Sione and Tuy have disappeared. I get up slowly, not from the road but from an old bed that is sitting alone in a house full of destroyed furniture, with black walls and a roof that obviously caved in after some type of fire.

I call out for Sione and Tuy and they reply that they are outside. I lift my aching bones to see where this negative energy has landed us. As I exit the abandoned home, I stand in the embrace of a ruined town. All around me are burned homes that look like they were bombed or torched on purpose. The land is burned and there is no sign of life anywhere. "What is this place?"

Tuy turns to me and nonchalantly answers, "Ren."

"What? But how?"

"We don't know. But I guess it had something to do with that black hole we fell through," says Sione. "We probably can find out more information if we head north."

I look in that direction. Smoke comes from distant chimneys, but more importantly, beyond them I can see a castle. I shake my head and turn quickly, trying to run back into the burned home, but Tuy grabs me by the arm.

"King—"

"No, Tuy. I don't want to go there! I will just live the rest of my life in this abandoned town. You two have done nothing wrong, so you should return to Peace Island."

"King, you are talking crazy. You haven't done anything wrong either—"

"I almost destroyed Trinity. Where will I be able to show my face from now on? My life is ruined. The emperor was right. Evil does lie within me."

"No, King. The emperor was wrong. We all have negativity in us, which is bound to appear if our buttons are pushed. The emperor kept pressing to get the answer he wanted. Just because you lost your cool doesn't define who you are."

"I burned down the palace."

"So what? They tortured you based on the sins of a man that none of us are even sure is your father!"

"But what if he is?"

"If he is, he is!" Tuy yells harshly, causing me to pull back. "I know I told you that if you learned Ren was your father, to turn away from the truth, but sometimes no matter how much we run we have to come face to face with it. If he is your father and isn't dead, the best thing you can do is face him. Even if you're unable to because he has left this world, you should find plenty of answers in his home. Find out why you were living more than a thousand miles away, on an island. If you can face him, question him about the queen, spirit energy, and even his past sins. At this moment, it is your right. King, you have a bright future; don't let the sins of your alleged father dim your light. I know you are scared. But the fact of the matter is we still have to carry out our main purpose, protecting Peace Island. I can feel that Rania is still alive, and after what happened on the rooftop you know she won't stop at anything to destroy our island

and everyone we love. We must find out how to stop her, and I believe the answer is here. You might be some type of tragic prince now, but before that, you are still a Peace Island soldier. So, as your commanding officer, I will ask you one time and one time only: what is your next move?" Tuy asks, lifting his eyebrow and creating a thick tension in the air. I look over at Sione, who avoids eye contact with me. I try to find the words, but nothing comes to mind.

Suddenly my body aches again from the invisible pressure of a decision that I must make, one that won't only affect me. If it was just me who would die and lose everything, I would run, but I keep seeing her face. Her big, dark green eyes. I promised her I would protect her. I promised her father I would not let her die. Yet I drew my sword and might as well have slashed it across her chest. I drop to my knees and finally break. I throw my hands to my face and begin to sob.

I feel Sione's hands on my back and hear him telling me it will be okay.

I am no longer a coward or even a soldier. I don't know what I am, but I do know that I want to protect her and everyone I love. My alleged father might not have answered for his sins, but I will answer for mine, and I will make things right. Even if that means death.

I gently push off Sione's hand and smile at him. I pick myself up and push out my chest as I throw my hand to my head and salute. Tuy does the same, and in a booming voice that can be heard throughout the burned town, I yell, "I shall go!" Tuy smiles at me and nods his head.

We go back into the ruined home and adjust our torn and bloody uniforms, fasten our backpacks, and head for Ren's capital city, leaving behind our fear. From the town, we start up a narrow, rocky road lined with thick bamboo and palm leaves. It's hard to navigate, but we push forward, eventually coming out of the bamboo and reaching a small stream. We take a moment to fill up our canteens and catch a small breather.

I look up at the castle and it's definitely closer. Just beyond a large farm and up a few hills stands the gate to Ren's capital city. I exhale deeply, the last few of my nerves holding on, but I shake them off, for I have made my promise. Actually, I do want my questions answered even if it all turns out for the worse. At least my mind will be at peace.

We pass by the farm, and to our surprise its owner pops his head up from the corn field. We expect him to be mean and rude or some type of monster, but instead he just tilts his hat to us and smiles as he keeps on working. He's kind, just like any of the elders on our island. We all pause for a moment, obviously thinking the same thing, but we just shrug it off and keep on, up three steep hills until we are standing face to face with a soot-covered, giant silver gate. It's a shame; one could tell that before the attack, the gate to the capital city was well-polished and strong.

Sione looks around and starts to rub his belly in thought. "So where are the guards?"

"Good question, but since they're not here at the moment, let's go quickly."

"Go where, Tuy? What do we do, just open the gate and walk through?"

"Exactly."

"What?" Sione and I yell in unison.

"Look, this city is probably pretty much a dead zone. And from what I can see, we still have a few more miles of farm land to get through before we get to thick of the city. Also, see those posts up there? The chairs are all broken and covered in moss. They haven't been sat in for years. Tuy brazenly walks up to the gate and takes hold of it. "See, I told you, it's not even closed." Laughing, he slips into the gate's open crack and begins to run in-between farm houses.

Sione and I look at each other before running after Tuy, who has clearly lost his mind. We have no strategy, we didn't even check out the grounds, yet he just waltzes into the capital of a region that has a leader who is #1 on Trinity's blacklist. After squeezing through the small opening of this huge gate, I scan the area for Tuy, but he's already out of sight.

"Where the heck did he go?" I wonder.

"King, I have a bad feeling about this. Look at this place." I forget about Tuy for a moment and turn to look at the odd city before me. We stand in what probably used to be the outlying district Small stone cottages hug valleys, streams, and farms for miles. Though farther up, taller cobblestone buildings that look like parliament buildings as well as rich folk's homes start to make a city outline. I could see how beautiful this place might have been before the war, but now most of the buildings are burned down. Only a few remain in good standing, but many are charred black and have roofs missing or holes in the walls. The more elite buildings ahead are in a little better condition, but they too have been burned and bruised.

"I don't even want to imagine the battle that happened here," I whisper under my breath.

"Yeah. You can tell many people died here. I mean, at least 20 years have gone by since that day, yet its scars still remain. This is a broken city."

"More like a broken region." I lower my head to the ground and rub my eyes, causing Sione to jump.

"Uh, King," he says as rummages through his backpack and takes out his cloak, "I think you should wear this and cover your face. Mine is a lot bigger than yours, so it is enough to cover your new set of eyes." Sione treads lightly with his words, which is surprising from him. I reluctantly take the cloak, trying to become accustomed to my new life thanks to these eyes.

Not wanting him to feel burdened, I smile and say, "Thanks for looking out, man."

Sione lets out a quick sigh of relief that he tries to hide. "No problem. Just looking out for my brother. Now let's go and find Tuy." I nod and we head deeper into the city.

As Sione and I start our search, we are surprised to see that people actually still dwell in this burned town. And unfortunately, we're sticking out like sore thumbs, especially Sione, who is walking around in his tattered uniform. He leans over to me and says that we should get out of the people's line of sight. We slip off into a side alley, away from the main road.

"Why are there so many people still living here?" Sione exclaims, frustrated.

"Well, this is their home. If Peace Island were to be destroyed, we would become just like them, with nowhere to go. Think about it, our people know nothing about the outside world. It's better to suffer in one's own region than to suffer in a foreign land. And once the storm is over, you still will have each other. These people went through a great ordeal because of their king, but that doesn't mean they have to throw in the towel. If you are still breathing, you can still fight and keep going. But, it could also be the fact that there is a giant spirit wall keeping them in?" I shrug my shoulders cutely making Sione laugh slightly at my sarcastic yet heavy comment. However, He becomes solemn in mood again.

"These people have strong wills. Just like you." His words hit me in the chest, and at first I'm not sure how to take them, but then I find myself smiling from ear to ear. For the first time I feel like I belong. "Yeah, just like me." I say as Sione and I walk farther into the city.

"Alright, we have been walking for a whole thirty minutes. I'm starting to get nervous," Sione says.

"Same. But this city is too large. We need to split up."

"I don't think that's a good idea. Remember what happened at Trinity?"

"Yes, but at first everything was okay, and we eventually found our way back to each other."

"Yeah, but we were searching around a peaceful nation, with a peaceful ruler."

"Well, depending on who you're asking, Trinity isn't really that pure."

At my words, Sione bites his tongue and looks to the ground. "Sorry. And yeah, I guess you're right, but at least put this on your wrist." He digs in his bag and pulls out a silver bangle that lights up with three blue lights when stroked.

I peek my head in Sione's bag. "What the heck is that? How do you have extra things in there?"

Sione chuckles. "Let's just say Dr. Lisa and I hit it off. She told me all about these different types of technologies, and I figured a tracking bangle probably would come in handy." He clasps the bangle on my arm before I can protest.

"Whatever you say, but this is the last time I am accepting any jewelry." I bust out in laughter, as does Sione.

"This place is so strange," he says. "All our lives we were told this was a place of destruction and a home for criminals, but we are laughing as much as we were at Ms. B's."

"Yeah, funny how that happens sometimes. Guess you've just got to see some places for yourself. Now, how does this electric bangle work?"

"Easy," says Sione, clasping one onto his arm as well. "First I will sync them—"

"Sync?"

"It's like connecting them over electromagnetic waves. Just listen, King. Okay, so now that they are synced, inside of this bangle there is a GPS." Sione laughs at me as my eyes grow huge. "Think of it as an electronic map, okay? Now watch this." He taps the bangle and a hologram of a map appears with red and green dots.

"Those dots are us!" I exclaim excitedly.

"Exactly, very good. Thus, with this we'll always know each other's locations. Also, as we move closer to each other, the bangles will start to make a beeping sound. Now, if you are in danger, this option can be turned off by pressing on the bangle three times. That puts it in vibrate mode, so it will shake to let you know I'm nearby," says Sione proudly.

I just look at him in amazement. "Very interesting." I say.

"Very." Sione's smile slowly fades and he pulls me into a hug. I wrap my arms around him as well and pat his back, but before I can say anything, Sione steps away, throws his hand to his head, and salutes before he runs off deeper into the cobblestone city.

I drop my head once again, but swiftly pick it back up and look toward the castle. Without a second thought, I head in its direction. I run through the streets, catching many wary eyes because of the cloak I'm wearing, but I do not care; I must reach the castle. Even if I'm pushed back, I will let nothing stop me. I run past the last row of cottage themed shops and cross under an archway, entering the streets of tall beige cobblestone buildings. This part of town is filled with fancy people sipping afternoon tea on their patios. I snarl to myself, starting to notice a sickening pattern of Kasai's regions.

I continue to run even if my feet feel like they're bleeding and daggers shoot through my lungs. I don't care, I can't feel a thing. I have become numb with a strange mixture of pain and wonder. Leaving my weaknesses behind, I run under another archway and enter into a large valley on the outside of the city, filled with hills and the mountain terrain that hides the castle in the distance. I look up and see the peak of the castle's roof sticking out from the side of one of the smaller mountains. The city's outer grassland has a few secluded houses spread out among its burned grass. I see farmers who are inspecting their small crops, and even some small children, despite tough times, playing a game of chase. Thankfully none of them notice me, and I continue toward the castle without any interference—until I hear a voice that stops me dead in my tracks and instantly makes my eyes well up. I turn slowly to the voice, now steadily calling out my name.

I turn and see first a perfectly kept, medium-size house. Then I see an orange tabby cat taking in the sun, lying on the stone path leading up to the house. I gulp, as this cat looks oddly similar to the one I had as a child. All the while, my name is being called in a voice that has long gone. My tears fall non-stop now, and I swing my head high and turn fully in the direction of that voice, using all the strength I have within me.

My vision is blurred from crying, but there she is: unique silver hair, ebony skin, and purple eyes. And she is flesh and not spirit; she is my mother. Before I know it, I run to her and fall into her embrace. She cuddles me in her arms, telling me she is so sorry and that everything will be alright.

I look up at my mother and hold her small face in my hands as I stare into her eyes. I gently squeeze her cheeks to make sure it is really her. She chuckles for a moment, but soon becomes serious. "King, you should not be here."

I lower my head, sacred of the direction this conversation might go. "I know. But let's just say I sort of just landed here accidently."

My mother gives me a smile that says she does not fully believe me. "Very well. Come inside, son, I am sure we have lots to discuss."

I follow my mother into her perfectly designed home. It is very feminine; almost everything is pink or a light blush, frills cover much of the furniture, and all types of little trinkets line the walls. I walk around and look at everything, trying to get back a piece of my childhood memories. But as I continue around the home, I notice that it doesn't really contain the things I would expect my mother to own. For one, I see no pictures of me. She disappeared when I was young, but she still should at least have a baby picture or my first day of middle school. Maybe she's hidden it somewhere because she couldn't live with the sorrow. I shake my head, trying to feed my mind with all the excuses in the book. I break from the war in my mind as my mother calls me from a back room. I enter into a sunroom, where she has prepared some tea.

"Let me guess, Cosmic Lotus Tea?"

"Why yes, how did you know?"

"Let's just say I've met some interesting people on my journey."

"I see," says my mother as she lifts the teapot in the center of the table and pours us each a glass. She takes the first sip.

I sit down next to her and cool off the tea that I have now become accustomed to. When I take a slow sip, it warms my body and I fall back into the comfy straw chair.

"So, Mom, what are you doing here?" I finally blurt out, tipping over the elephant in the room without even feeding it a few peanuts first. But my brash words do not surprise my mother. She calmly places her teacup back on the saucer before turning to me with a loving smile that is starting to drown in tears. I lift my hand to her cheek to wipe them away. I drop my head, though, for she doesn't need to say a word.

"I figured this much." I pause for a moment, a moment whose passing will rip my heart straight from my chest. But no matter how much I wish to remain in this moment, I know I cannot, because this lie that surrounds me will continue to eat me alive. I avoid my mother's eyes, but somehow, I find the courage to speak the words to a question I've known the answer to all along. "You're not my real mother, are you?"

"I am so sorry, King. I wanted to tell you so badly, but I was obligated not to. But King, don't you for one second think that I did not love you as if you were my own. No matter what happens from this moment, you will always be my son," she says as she moves her hands to stroke my hair.

I push her away, rising and glaring out the window at the castle behind the mountain. "Does this have something to do with King Ren?"

"Unfortunately, everything. King, please have a seat."

"Yes...Mother."

"One day I was called to the castle. The king was holding a small child, you. He told me to take you to Peace Island, but that I must keep our identities a secret. I left the castle and changed any resemblance you had to, um..." Looking at her, I see she is starting to sweat.

I exhale deeply and finally let the truth roll off the tip of my tongue. "The words you're looking for are, 'your father.'"

My mother leans forward and grasps my arms. "How long have you known?"

I smirk and reply, "Since right now."

My mother playfully hits my arm and crosses her arms. "You always used to do that as a child. I guess I didn't scold you enough."

I rub the back of my head and say, "No, you actually scolded me too much," causing us both to laugh softly and letting up some of the tension in the air. "Please continue," I say.

"Yes. So, your father ordered me to change your name and appearance. I decided on the name King."

I furrow my brow, trying to hold back a wail now that I've finally learned where the name that brought me so much bullying and pain came from.

"I know, King, I'm sorry. But you know I have a playful side. And at the end of the day you are a king, no matter how much you want to deny it. Anyway, before I left I went out into the field of dreams and picked a Pepper Rose, a black and white rose that releases a grey, salty slime, and I placed it into your eyes, changing them to brown."

"Why not purple, to match yours?" I ask, amused.

"I was going for that, but I sort of picked the wrong flower." My mother throws her hand to the back of her head, laughing awkwardly.

"So, did you change your eyes with a flower too? I mean, purple is a weird color."

"Why yes. I used the blue slime of a Spike Lily."

I scrunch up my face. "That sounds painful. So why didn't you just use that one on me?" I scoff sarcastically, forgetting that the woman I'm sitting with was my mother for ten years, but it quickly comes back to me as she swats my mouth with her hand and exclaims, "I was young, okay? Twenty-one to be exact and it was a very hostile situation. Most people don't have babies thrown upon them. No offense, of course, but I just wasn't thinking straight. We might not be connected by blood, but I am still your mother, got it?" She points her long, painted fingernails straight in my face, and even with the heaviness of the story, her flamboyant personality brings a genuine smile and I say, "Yes, ma'am."

The room grows quiet again as thousands of questions spin in my head. I try to sort out the less evasive ones, with no luck. I sneak a peek at my mother and she is still smiling at me. I turn away quickly, but I know she is reading me like a book right now.

"Son, go ahead and be sure to choose the hardest one. The one you lose sleep over and the one that could change you. It is better to live with the truth than a lie. And quite frankly, you deserve the truth. You are a bright young man whose light is being dimmed because of foolish adults and that is not fair. I always told you, with everything you do, face it head on, and that includes right now."

I stare her straight in the eyes, but she just continues to smile. I guess it's time to break through all the lies. I clear my throat and finally ask my question. "So, if you are not my real mother and if King Ren is my father, does that mean Rai—I mean Queen Tru, is she my mother? And if she is, why was she trying to harm me and my friends? Also, weren't you the one who told me to trust her?"

My mother's smile fades, but she doesn't look angry or sad. She looks content as she wraps me in her arms and whispers in my ear. "To answer your last question, it was my mistake, and I am so sorry. I saw a woman who is very special to you; I didn't know who she really was. Now, I think it's time we go see your father."

"Wait! King Ren is still alive?" I exclaim.

"Yes," my mother says in a firm tone, accompanied by a reassuring nod. With her words, I no longer feel uneasy, ashamed, or afraid at the mention of King Ren. Instead I am overjoyed to finally have found the door to unlock to the truth to my life. After this is all said and done, my only hope is that I will finally belong.

—XIV—

FAMILY

I now walk next to my mother through the valley leading up to the castle. I expected to walk in awkward silence, but instead we spend the next twenty minutes chatting about what we have been up to. I tell her interesting childhood stories, how I became a soldier, and even what happened at Trinity. She tells me about the wonders of Ren and what she has been doing during our time apart, though I can tell she's leaving things out. Nonetheless, I'm just glad to have my mother back by my side, even if it's only for a moment.

We finally arrive at a wired trolley that could have come from Peace Island. "Wow, this looks pretty old," I say.

"Being a restricted region does have its downfalls. But we were able to reap some technological advancements thanks to that Dr. Lisa."

"Dr. Lisa?" I shout.

"Um, yes. She helped smuggle in new technology, saying that the good people of a nation shouldn't suffer because of the wayward ways of their king. Now of course, we had to be her test dummies in return. But being one of the first to try out new technologies was fun." My mother pauses for a moment as she tries to read my facial expression. "Why do you look like that? Did you meet her along the way?"

"Yeah, I actually did. I know it looks shabby now, but she made these uniforms for us," I say, holding out my arms and showing off my clothes.

My mother nods in amazement before saying, "Small world. We fight each other over trivial things but we are all connected. Oh well." She sighs and hops on the trolley, and I join her only for my jaw to drop again.

The trolley might be old, but its operating system is lightyears ahead of Peace Island's. Now I know my mom is telling the truth because this type of system could have only been thought up in Antenetta. My mother smirks at me and flips her hair. "See, son, Ren is much more than a burned, barren region. We found the right blend of tradition and advancement and merged them together, all while keeping a perfect harmony with the environment."

"Wow, that's really cool. Sucks, though, that the environment had to suffer too after the fall," I look at the barren and burned spots in the valley.

"Yeah, it did. Especially since the environment was of great importance to the king. When one tries to destroy you, they don't just stop with you. They even want to take away the things you love," says my mother as the tension in the air returns.

The trolley travels quickly toward the mountain thanks to the high-speed Antenetta system. We enter a cave of trees that still have some fight left in them. Their freshly changed red leaves twirl through the sky, painting the tracks a unique blend of orange and red. For a moment, I just stare at the leaves, trying to shake away a thought that has been plaguing my mind since Dr. Lisa was brought up. But no matter how hard I try, I can't shake the anxiety in my chest, and I decide to set it free. "So, Mom, back to Dr. Lisa. Did she ever bring her brother with her?"

"Why yes, all the time! He was such a handsome little helper. Did you also meet him on your journey?"

I click my tongue at the fact Tuy had been lying to me, but I can't get completely upset at him, being as I have kept things from him as well. Come to think of it, even though it wasn't clear, he did say he saw the Dark King once, just not how, and foolishly this whole time I thought it was in a picture or he was just lying. "I know him. Not because of this journey, but he is the commanding officer for this mission as well as my best friend."

"Oh, I see."

"Yeah. Life just keeps getting more interesting."

"Well, sometimes friends keep things from each other to protect one another. Think about it. If you knew of his families' dabblings with a restricted region, he would have been putting you in danger. Don't think too hard about it. He was just a child; truthfully, he probably forgot."

"I guess you're right. Also, I can't act all holy as I have too lied in order to protect those I care about," I say as the trolley travels farther along the tracks, scaling the mountain to the biggest elephant in any room of my life.

We now ride in silence. The red leaves fade and barren branches encase the trolley; but swiftly pink florals surround us and my mother tells me we are almost there. The trolley halts in a dense cloud of blossoms, so dense I can't see anything in front of me. I can hear the tracks changing before the trolley submerges deeper in, entering a cavern on the other side of the cloud of flowers. At the end of the stone tunnel, we push through more pink flowers, and there it stands, right before my eyes: Ren's castle comfortably nestled between the mountain terrains.

I look to my left and with a sting in my heart, I see a hurting city in the distance: Trinity. Though, the palace has visible damage, I feel a little easier because they have relit the Inner Flame.

My mother places a reassuring hand on my shoulder. "It's all right, son. The way you were treated, they had it coming."

I ponder her words, but I still can't shake the sour feeling in my stomach. I should have maintained my composure; that is what a true king, prince, or whatever I am would have done. "Well, at least they relit the flame, so our people won't lose hope."

"Yeah, but it makes you wonder."

"What do you mean?"

"How they just relit something that is supposed to be eternal. Wouldn't the people have fallen into great turmoil?"

I chuckle to myself despite my agony. "The people probably didn't even realize it went out. That place is so full of lies and corruption, it makes Ren look like a walk in the park."

"I see. Well, we are here, son." The trolley comes to a screeching halt right at the front of the castle's marble stairs.

My mother swiftly exits and heads up them. She says something, but I do not answer, making her turn around. "Son, what are doing?" She extends her hand. "It's time to meet your father."

I grab ahold of the trolley's railing and squeeze it tight, so much that my fingers turn red. I feel lightheaded and as I look up at my mother, it feels like I will fall over at any moment. I'm afraid to see the destiny before me. Tears well in my eyes as the false mask of bravery I've put on starts to break.

My mother runs back down the stairs and pulls me into her arms. Tears continue to try and escape, but I bite down hard on my lip, breaking the skin, to keep myself from showing my true face.

"I know this is hard, King, but you have come too far. Don't give up. Look at me," says my mother as she pulls away from me and places her hands on my cheeks. "If you do not confront this lie that has shrouded your life in hardship after coming this far, what will that make you? A fool? A trader? Or a coward?"

I throw my head up as my mother questions my bravery, but I say nothing, as she is right. I am acting like the very person I wanted to leave behind once I stepped away from Peace Island. Peace Island—an island that will be split in two if I don't find more information about Queen Tru. An island that will never see their princess again if I don't face my fears. I must remember that this is not about me, but about protecting everyone I love.

With my mother's help, I take baby steps off of the trolley and begin to climb the marble stairs even though I feel I am walking to my end. I look to Trinity and think of the princess, the fear in her eyes on that rooftop, the same fear she had when we started on this journey. I wonder what was real and fake. Was all her bravery just a façade created by the queen? A queen who dragged a young girl's helpless body across the world in the name of destruction?

At the battle of Trinity I disgraced our island, which preaches of peace. I lost sight of what was really important. But at this moment, I remember that I am a soldier first. If I am to save Peace Island, I must find out who I really am. In war, one must know their enemy from head to toe, even if the enemy is themselves.

"I don't know what happened in the past, mother, but I feel that once I find out, it will be the key to saving my home." I turn to my mother with a huge grin on my face as I extend my hand to her. She reaches for it and we head up the marble stairs with fingers clasped. My mask of courage is left behind, but not forgotten. Its imprints still lie upon my skin, engraved into my heart, as I walk the stairs to my truth. Not as King the coward but as a soldier, and the son of a king.

My mother pushes open the large metal door and peeks in, scoping out the castle's foyer. She enters first and then signals for me to follow her. Though it's bright as day outside, the castle is dark, and the rips in the window's thick curtains are the only way light can sneak in. "This place is a mess," I whisper as I look around at unpolished trinkets, dusty furniture, and cobwebs on the grand chandelier that hangs above us. "Are you sure King Ren still lives here? Maybe he did die and nobody knew it."

My mother pops me in my mouth. "Watch your words, son!" She makes a tiny cross over her chest as if to cancel out any bad vibes.

"It's quite alright. I just had my monthly check-up and I am in perfect health," says a muffled baritone voice from above us.

I look up and see a man sitting on the castle's silver second-floor banister. He has unkempt black hair and is dressed in a black silk robe that covers his hands and feet and ties in the front. I squint to try and get a closer look at him, but my mother jumps in front of me as the man leaps from the banister. I gasp, but he flows through the air gracefully and lands on his feet with a slight spark of white spirit energy. He moves from the shadows and the creeping light hits his grey eyes, and I finally come face to face with the most dangerous man of Kasai.

He approaches until he is basically towering over the both of us—he must be at least six foot five. He slowly lifts his hands, flexing his bulging muscles as he runs his fingers through his long hair and lets out an annoyed sigh.

"Kema, you better have a good explanation for why you allowed an outsider into my home," Ren says in a stern tone that sends chills down my spine.

"My lord, I'm afraid that she is causing problems again," my mother replies, making him click his tongue as he rolls his neck.

"I see. But there is nothing I can do about it." He turns to me and tilts his head to the side, rubbing his thin beard. "Young soldier of Antenetta, you are a brave one to seek my help, but I have washed my hands of our queen years ago. May God bless your souls, and I offer you my humblest apologies," says the king as he lowers his head toward me.

I jump back in shock, completely confused once again. This was supposed to be a man who would kill you just for speaking his name, but yet he has lowered his head to an outside soldier without hesitation. I clear my throat, getting ready to speak. My mother turns to me shaking her head but I just smile at her. She returns my smile, putting her trust in me, even though her eyes show she is slightly worried.

With a hand that shakes, I tap the bowed king's shoulder while calling his name…big mistake. He swiftly looks up and knocks my hand from his shoulder, then leaps back, calling forth the powers that made him a king. White spirit energy cracks through the castle like lightning bolts, burning the curtains and letting in the banished light. The energy encases his entire body and burns away his silk robe, revealing bloodstained and broken battle armor. He then throws his hand forward, and there she is in all of her greatness: his legendary seven-foot-long spirit sword.

I quickly move in front of my mother and try to yell over the thunderous popping of spirit energy, "Your majesty, I didn't mean to startle you. I was just going to say that I am actually from Peace Island and I'm not looking for your help to fight. I was just hoping you could give us some information about Queen Tru and some other personal things!"

The king does not budge, but instead looks around, paranoid, before completely checking me out. Finally, he stares me straight in the eyes and I can see him tremble slightly.

"Who the hell are you?" yells King Ren as he points his free hand to my face, still on the defensive. "Tho…Those…eyes?"

My mother comes to my rescue as she shouts for the king to calm down, but he does not lower his sword. I bite down hard on my lip as the marks left from my mask of courage start to sting. I glare at King Ren. "I am your son. Now please, put that sword away, I am running out of time!" I yell as the princess's face flashes in my mind.

Ren's eyes grow large with shock. He directs his attention to my mother, staring so hard he could burn a hole through her soul. He begins to mumble obscenities under his breath as he moves closer to us. My mother pulls my arm and motions for me to follow her. She starts to run, but her foot gets caught on a burned curtain and she trips and falls. King Ren leaps in the air, ready to strike her with his sword. I yell out for my mom as I stretch my hands out, revealing my gold spirit sword. I swing it around my head and leap in front of her, blocking the king's sword in midair and making him fall back. My gold energy and his white now bounce off of one another, creating a thunderstorm without the rain through the foyer.

King Ren starts to breathe heavily. His sword disappears, but I continue to guard my mother. He glares at me for a moment before turning around and heading down a hallway. However, as he's about to turn the corner, he nods his head for me to follow before disappearing into the shadows.

What in the world was that all about? My sword vanishes as I quickly turn to my mother, who is now by the door. She smiles at me one last time with her hand over her heart. Whispering, "Good luck, my son," she too vanishes as if she never existed.

A sharp pain shoots through my chest as I cover my mouth and try to catch my breath. I have to remain strong, for Peace Island. I turn to the corridor that King Ren went down and head after him. At the end of the hall there is an open door. Cautiously I head toward it. The room beyond is a library like the one in Trinity, just bigger and dustier. Through its giant window, I can see the emperor's palace in the distance.

"You did a lot of damage over there, huh?"

I jump as I see King Ren sitting on a wooden stool, reading from a notebook on a podium. He turns to me, looking over his reading glasses, and he is much different from the man who was swinging a deadly sword just minutes ago. I also notice that he found another robe and now looks more like...a father.

I clear my throat, moving farther into the library. "Uh. How did you know?"

"This is my favorite part of the castle. I saw the whole thing right from this window. You've got to be careful when dealing with our two-faced emperor."

"Our emperor?"

Snickering, Ren rises and places two strong hands on my shoulders, and I feel paralyzed. "Just because he turned his back on my region doesn't mean he isn't still the emperor." He releases his hold on me to go to the window. "The emperor can be a good man! But he sometimes sees things in only black and white, and unfortunately that is not how life is. Life is full of many different colors. I hope one day he will understand."

"I don't think he ever will," I say as I take a seat.

King Ren approaches, grabs me by the chin, and turns my face to him.

I squirm, not sure what he is doing. He raises one eyebrow as he turns my head from side to side. "She changed your face too much," he says, clicking his tongue and hovering his large hand over my face.

I see a small mirror on the wall and run to it. I tilt my head and say, "I look the same."

The king comes behind me and lightly taps my cheeks, making me jump. "Your cheeks are a little higher."

I turn my head from side to side but I don't see anything different other than my eyes, but I just shrug it off and turn around to give an awkward thanks.

"What are you thanking me for?"

"I don't know, for turning me back into who I really am."

"Let me see. I guess you should be about twenty now. I cannot change you into who you really are. The life experiences you have are what makes you, you. I know you were seeking me hoping that I will give your life some profound meaning, but that is not so. I can tell you about the past, but that will only help answer a few questions about other people and your mission. If you are looking for who you really are, you have to look inside. Family does not dictate who we are. It can define our looks, class, and early personality, but once you get older you start making your own decisions about what you will and will not tolerate, because you are now experiencing the many colors of life through your own eyes."

"I see," I whisper.

My father shakes his head as he motions for my backpack. I slowly hand it to him. He rummages through it for a while before pulling out the black leather notebook from the shack. He throws it on the table, turns to the last page I wrote, and reads it out loud. *"As the princess faded before my eyes, I felt like I had lost my entire world. A great injustice was committed. I cry in this cell that holds me. I am at my lowest and I fear death is near, but I hope I don't hear his call. I now see that Kasai is a beautiful painted picture, but scratch at the canvas hard enough and holes will break through, showing its rugged maggot-infested beams, the truth that the paint tries to hide from the people. If something isn't right, we cover over it, hoping no one will find out, but eventually a lie will implode on itself, the truth busting free. I must not die here. For the people of Kasai deserve to know the truth so we all can decide our own fates."*

207

My cheeks grow warm at hearing my travel diary being read aloud.

"At this moment, you had a rebirth within yourself alone in a jail cell. You did not need mine or anybody else's fancy words. You are a lot stronger than you believe."

I look up at Ren, but quickly look away, snatching my notebook and shoving it deep into my backpack. "How did you know about my logs?" I cross-examine the king.

"Simple," Ren says as he gets up and walks to the podium he was sitting at earlier. He grabs the book there and places it on the table. "I have the same one."

"But how?" I stutter.

"I'm sure Phoenix told you about our relationship. I gave it to him so I would still have some connection to the outside world. This notebook isn't your regular notebook. It has the ability to store all the words written in it at one main location," says Ren, tapping on his notebook.

"Then everything I wrote was transcribed into this notebook, virtually somehow?"

"Exactly!"

"Antenetta technology?"

"Nope. Magic!" Ren snaps his fingers.

"Huh?" I tilt forward, unsure of why I am surprised. Maybe the answer I was looking for was spirit energy, not magic.

"Get comfortable, son. It is now time we talk about the past. Excuse me if I become weak in voice at some points. This story is not one I long to remember." Ren leans back in his chair and sticks his glasses in his robe pocket. "Before I begin, let me apologize. The predicament you and your island are in is all my fault. I passed on my sins to others, became weak, and failed to stop a certain someone when I had the chance. I should have ended her life, but no matter how evil I had become, I couldn't find it in my heart to slay her. Also, if I had it would have destroyed Ren even more…" The king pauses for a moment before making an expression of disgust. "Ugh. I hate that name."

"You may call your region by its original name if that makes you comfortable," I say.

"After everything that happened, who am I to be so lucky as to have such a compassionate son?" Ren moves his hand toward my face, but I jerk away, knocking it from me. Ren looks down in sorrow and I feel sort of bad for him. "My apologies. I guess I would be frightened of me too with all the rumors floating around about me, but I assure you, the events that occurred in the thirty-fifth year of my life were not caused by me.

"Phoenix was completely correct when he told you of how a trickster made her way into my heart as she blinded my eyes. She ran my region into the ground by doing her evil bidding disguised as me. As you found out in the library and saw on Trinity's palace roof, I will confirm with my whole heart that Queen Tru is the trickster Phoenix warned you of. You read how this woman is a great controller of time and space and a very knowledgeable chemist. But that book you read didn't mention her most venomous skill: to control others and use their bodies as her own, as she is doing with the princess. But it is much worse, King. You should have seen the look on my face when she showed me who she really was."

I pause for a moment, fearful of opening the king's old wounds, but in the end, I press forward. "So how did Queen Tru become this evil trickster?"

The king's eye twitches as he fights back tears from demonic old memories. "Do you know what it is like to have your lovely wife feed you lies? For forty days and forty nights, she spoke of Trinity's plans to up rise against me. She stole half of my powers without me even noticing. I'm sorry." The king shakes his head furiously as he tries to regain himself. He clears his throat and takes a deep breath before continuing. "She hid as a messenger with a different face from her own. That poor soul she used has probably long been consumed. She smiled at me day by day as another woman, and at night she would lie next to me smiling at me with her blue eyes."

"So how did she end up with her current form? She now has amber eyes and long, curly brownish blonde hair."

At my words, Ren leaps up and covers his mouth, trying to stop himself from sobbing. He leans on the bookshelf beside him as if to keep from falling.

"Your highness, are you all right?" I ask, standing up.

"I am sorry. I am so sorry. The woman you described is not the queen. That is your mother."

"What? But if you are the king and Queen Tru was the queen, then shouldn't she be my mom?"

The king wipes the tears from his eyes roughly as he turns back to me. "I am a horrible man, son. The truth is, I had an affair with your mother, and from that affair you were conceived. Now I see that the last person the trickster took control of, before I banished her from Ren, was your mother. She took everything I love. She even tried to take you, but I hide you away just in time."

Tears start to well up in my eyes as I try to find the words. "But...how? Is my mom still alive? If she is using my mother's body, then what does she need with the princess?"

Ren exhales deeply and turns to me with a look deeper than sorrow and grief. "This evil woman," he whispers under his breath. "She had told me, before I erected the barrier to keep her out, that your mother killed herself because she couldn't face the shame of our affair.

"Now I know that was a lie—to cover up how Queen Tru stole your mother's body—but that had to have been about twenty years ago. Unfortunately, when she lives inside of her hosts, she claims she is giving them power but she is really sucking out their life energy. This keeps her young and strong. Energy draining is a type of vegetation spell that is supposed to be used as a non-invasive extraction tool when extracting ingredients and oils from plants and produce for remedies, but she uses it for evil. She becomes the tool, entering inside the persons being as she controls them. The person she is controlling can usually only last for three years, five if they are strong. Therefore, it breaks my heart to say, there is no way your mother is still alive. This woman is so evil she was taunting you with a face that you will never get to see full of genuine life. A face that resembles your own."

"So, Rania was never a goddess only the trapped soul of my mother?"

"Yes, the fact that she presented her as a goddess should have tipped you off. Goddesses do not exist, there is only one God."

"But the library in Trinity has books full of information on them."

"Those are just fables, there are only messengers in our world. You must understand this, that woman is an impeccable liar. If you separate her from the princess, she will not look like the goddess she claims to be;

that was just an illusion. The woman you are looking for has blue eyes and long black hair."

I try to pull myself together after learning that my biological mother is dead, and by the hands of that woman. No doubt the affair was wrong, but did she really deserve death? I lower my head and stare at the table. So many thoughts are flying through my head. "If the queen already destroyed Ren and my mother, what is she after? She said that she wanted to become supreme ruler of Kasai. But you said she stole some of your powers. Then maybe is she after mine as well?"

The king finally composes himself as he sits back down in front of me. He tells me that the queen does not desire power but revenge. Because of his affair, she is trying to destroy everything he loves. The king pulls out a small amulet from under his robe. I wince as I notice it glows the same color as my necklace. He holds it close and says that it was a gift from Queen Tru, a jade dragon claw amulet. At the time, he did not know that jade was a conductor that can extract spirit energy from a weak mind. The king laughs at himself and says it was insane that he didn't realize he was being drained of his energy. When he looked into the mirror, he still appeared full-fleshed and healthy, not like hollow skin and bones. She deceived his eyes with an enchantment, using the pink spirit energy she received from falling in the springs of the Majestics (a power that was never really hers either).

"No, she does not desire this power. She destroyed your mother, my region, and my mind. But there is one thing or person that she has not been able to dig her venomous claws into."

"Me?"

"Exactly. All she desires is to destroy you, a creation of my infidelity. I knew she would come searching for you one day. That is why I asked Kema to take you far away from this place and pretend to be your mother."

"So that's why you chose Peace Island?"

"Well, your real mother was born there. The scary general you met is actually her brother."

"General Claude is my uncle?"

"Yes. I have eyes in many places. Though at the time I smuggled you from our region I was being labeled as a traitor and tyrant, General Claude still went ahead and got all the necessary papers together to make it look like you were a child of Peace Island."

"But why? No offense, but I was the son of an evil king."

"Dear Baris, blood is thicker than water."

"Baris? I know it's been a while, but how could you forget my name that quick? My name is King, remember?" I say, flustered, but king Ren only chuckles.

"That is your real name. King is your fake name, remember?" he says, mocking me. "I have no idea why that Kema chose King. The name Baris means peace, which is all I ever really wanted, but somewhere down the line this crown became too heavy and I made too many mistakes. Yet I have hope in you. May I?" the king asks as he points to the chain under my shirt. I hesitate for a moment before I reveal the butterfly hidden under my uniform.

"ow cuHjjjHow cute, and discreet, I might add. No one would think anything of a sweet, childlike butterfly necklace given by a princess. However, Baris, that necklace around your neck is pure evil. It contains my spirit energy but she has tainted it with negativity. You were very smart to stop using it. Bell-Ow found you just in time."

"You know about the Elk too?"

My father chuckles again, pointing at his notebook.

"Oh right. I forgot. So, was he the one who gave you your spirit energy also?"

"Um, not exactly. God has many messengers, but you met a very pure one, and you have an energy that not many are blessed with. The last person to have your energy was Emperor Vince Zyel."

I almost fall from my seat after hearing our first emperor's name. I can't believe I possess a gift so great. But deep down the burden of it sits at the bottom of my stomach. "To a degree, is my energy stronger than yours?" I question lightly, moving back in case the king becomes offended.

Instead he just throws his hand to the back of his head, and for the first time since we have met, he smiles. "Actually, yes. I know I am in no position to say this but, I am so proud of you, son. If you would allow me to call you son."

My body grows hot and I find myself looking down at the necklace, but it is as cold as ice. I contemplate if this is a man I want to allow into my life. Honestly, I want to say no, not because I am afraid, but from anger at being given away. Though I know he was only trying to protect me, it doesn't change a thing.

Then again, as Tuy says things are not always as they seem. I finally lift my head and look this strange man who is my father in the eyes, for what feels like an eternity. I place my hand on my heart and let everything go, nodding.

King Ren smiles from ear to ear, but quickly hides his excitement, putting back on his cool demeanor. "I am sure Queen Tru did not calculate you would find your own power, your own inner strength. You can stop her. The gold sword you stopped mine with has a jade spiral wrapped around its blade . You must get to her mind first, weakening it, and then attack her with the jade part of your sword, extracting her spirit energy and destroying her."

"Then my vision of me destroying the island?"

"Is actually her. She will break the spell on your amulet setting free all of my energy, which at this moment is too great for you to bear. You will be overwhelmed, and even if you are able to carry the remaining bits of my power, the negative energy she has infused it with will destroy you. You will become blind and do her bidding. What happened at Trinity will also happen on your island, but it will be much worse."

"The island will split in two, destroying everyone."

"Yes. Everyone will die if you allow her to get to your mind before you get to hers. Remember, spirit energy relies on a strong mind. For the mind speaks to the heart—"

"And the heart nurtures the soul," I say, finishing King Ren's sentence.

"I see that Phoenix has taught you well."

"Yes, he did. Oh! And he asked me to pass on a message to you: he says he is sorry."

King Ren lowers his head as his cool façade breaks again and he starts to smile from ear to ear, obviously thinking back on old times. I use this moment to take in everything I have just learned. I move my hand to my necklace and run my fingers over the butterfly's broken wings. It is still cool to the touch. I tug at it with false hope, hoping somehow, I can remove this weight that I was forced to bear. I pull and pull until I am yanking at the necklace, causing it to come alive and grow hot.

I jump up and lean forward so the burning amulet won't touch my skin. Ren moves to my side, placing a firm hand on my shoulder while tapping the necklace with the other and stopping its lava show. I look to him and he smiles, telling me that Queen Tru might have stolen part of his powers, but he can still control them.

"Then can't you come with me? If the amulet breaks, you can stop the destruction and you will regain all of your powers!" I blurt out with eyes full of tears.

This man who is my father just shakes his head. "Young Baris, I cannot go with you. Many believe that I died years ago. But don't worry. You are not alone, you have your two comrades."

"But what if I fail?"

"You will not fail, for God is on your side. But if it be his will that you do, make sure you fall with dignity after giving it all you have. Do not become like me, son. Now hurry! The waves are shifting near Peace Island. She is coming. You must go now and finish my fight!" King Ren says in a booming voice as he turns, his robe trailing behind him and fluttering in the wind as he exits through a door at the back of the library.

I grab my chest when the room starts to spin, but I quickly slam my hands on the table, regaining my balance. Luna. I must save her. Queen Tru has already consumed my mother and I will be damned if I let her take our princess as well. I hastily leave the library and sprint back down the dark hall. The chandelier in the foyer glistens above me as I push the front door of the castle open full-force and head straight for the trolley.

Once back in the city below the castle, I run through the streets, shouting for Tuy and Sione, not caring about the strange looks I receive. I only stop yelling at the top of my lungs as I feel a hand on my shoulder. It is my mother. I take a moment to breathe as I hug her. I didn't think I would ever see her again.

"Are these the two fellas you are looking for?" my mom asks playfully. She holds both of her hands out to her side and Sione and Tuy pop out from behind her. The overwhelming emotions from the castle still brewing inside of me make me melodramatic as I lunge at both of them, wrapping them in a strong embrace.

However, my soap opera continues up the dramatic scale. I break free and turn my attention to Tuy, lightly punching his arm. We make eye contact, not saying a word, until Tuy lowers his head with an ambiguous smile. Sione looks at both of us, but shrugs his shoulders as he interrupts our moment. "Why are you in such a rush, man? You were sprinting through the streets like a superhero."

"We must hurry! Queen Tru is on her way to Peace Island. This will be our only chance to stop her and save the princess!"

"Why would she go back to Peace Island?"

"I will explain later! Just trust me, okay?" I yell, slightly agitated.

Sione and Tuy look at each other and nod. "Okay, but it will take us over a month to get back to Peace Island," Tuy says.

I rub the back of my head. I had forgotten that we were over a thousand miles away from home. "Well, how in the world did she get back to Peace Island so quickly?" I ask through gritted teeth.

"Don't mean to butt in," my mother says, "but she probably teleported."

"Teleported?" Sione and I blurt out. Sione grabs the back of his neck and groans. "King, I can't take this anymore. Why did you put my name on for this mission?" He punches at my arm until he completely gives in to his dismay, as he throws his head on my shoulder.

I turn to Tuy and furrow my brow, but he just shrugs. "Hey, my sister has nothing to do with this. She is a genius, but she hasn't developed teleportation yet."

My mom is grinning. "That's because it's not technology, but magic."

"Magic?" Tuy and Sione exclaim.

"Is that the same as spirit energy?" asks Sione.

"Not quite."

I turn around and throw my hand to my head. "Not this again," I groan under my breath. "Look, guys, I will explain later. But we really need to hurry."

"Alright, you three stand real close together," says Kema as she huddles us together like sausages in a can. "Now, how did that teleportation spell go again?" She ponders as she taps her temple with her finger.

"Uh, Mom, do you know what you're doing?" I ask suspiciously, causing her eyes to snap at me.

"Why, yes. It's just been a while since I used this teleportation spell, as I learned it from a book."

"A book?" we all exclaim, but too late, as my mother starts to mumble some sort of enchantment and twirls her fingers in a counterclockwise circle.

We hold each other tight as orange lines are drawn around us. Soon we are encased in a cube and being slowly lifted in the air. I look down to my mother, who is waving her hands at me and smiling. The people of Ren have even gathered around and are looking at us in awe. "Good luck, Prince Baris, Sione, and Tuy!" my mom calls, still frantically waving.

"Baris?" Sione snaps this head to me, followed by Tuy. "Prince?"

"I told you two I will explain later!" I yell over the increasing sound of the orange-lined cube, which has started to twirl rapidly. In the blink of an eye, Tuy and Sione disappear, and before we know it we are falling through the sky. Just like last time, we stop and hover inches from the ground, before falling completely upon the soft sand of St. Royal and Antenetta's shoreline.

— XV —

PRINCE BARIS

"Ahhhhh!" Sione jumps up from the ground and starts to run around in circles like a madman.

"What's wrong?" Tuy's eyes frantically follow Sione's unpredictable movements.

"I'm just tired of everything! Falling through the sky, technology, giant elks, creepy old men and women in robes. I just want to go home!" he cries as he falls over, his bottom hitting hard on the sand. Sione covers his eyes with his thick hands while Tuy goes by his side and pats his back. I shake my head, for he has yet to meet his biggest test.

I turn to the sea and look out at Peace Island, where dark clouds have begun to gather. Then it happens. A giant thunderbolt falls from the sky, setting the distant castle ablaze, and the alarms start blaring. Sione and Tuy jump up, joining me. We look to each other and take a simultaneous deep breath before turning back to the burning horizon before us.

"Guess we'll have to get filled in on the situation later, but let us know our plan of action." Tuy looks at me attentively, and for the first time I do not feel beneath him. I finally feel like we're equal comrades. I see that he has put his pride aside. "Rania is actually the Queen of Ren; her name is Queen Tru. She is the one who will cause the calamity by trying to take control of me through this cursed necklace she tricked the princess into giving me. But the good thing is, I know how to stop her. So, all I need from you two is to have my back, understand?"

Sione and Tuy don't even hesitate, nodding their heads in unison.

217

"Okay, one more weird adventure, but I am down for it! We have to save our island and the princess!" Sione exclaims with flaming eyes.

"That's the way, Sione! Now let's go save our little comrade and everyone we love," I say as another lightning bolt strikes, this time setting the market in the village on fire. We don't say a word, just run toward the monorail that leads back to Peace Island. Tuy jumps on it and Sione tries to follow, but I grab his arm and whisper something in his ear. His eyes grow large, but nonetheless he mouths the word, "Okay."

> *If only I could be back on the unburning Peace Island after*
> *I open my eyes, but here I stand, my father's tainted energy*
> *seeping out and my island on the brink of destruction.*

Unfortunately, I must come back to my reality. My island has split and just as I envisioned, I am the cause. Queen Tru might have been the source, but I failed because of a weak mind.

"King! Get it together. Weren't you just the one who told me to be brave?"

I turn and look back at Sione, who is trying to help fallen citizens, and warm tears start to run down my cheeks.

"The whole village has not split! Look, it was only the upper half. The royals usually evacuate first, so I am sure they are okay," Sione shouts, trying to get through to me.

"But what about all these dead bodies?" I say frantically, snatching at my hair.

Sione runs toward me, grabs me by the shoulders, and starts shaking me frantically. "Snap out of it, man!" he yells even louder, slapping my cheek, but I still see nothing but dead bodies and hot lava all around me.

"King! Listen to me. What did Phoenix say? You have to protect your mind."

Sione's words flow slowly into my ears and find their way to my subconscious. I exhale softly as the last remains of the negative white energy fade and turn to gold. Now three small jade beads are spinning in a circle before me. They stop without notice, changing their trajectory from spinning, to flying so close to me they are out of my line of sight. However, I feel the beads slightly pinching my forehead at three different points. I raise my hand to my head but the beads have disappeared, not even leaving a scratch, and finally my world becomes clear.

I remove Sione's arms from my shoulders as I turn around in a circle, reorienting myself. I see now that Tru only caused damage to Royal Town, and the people of our lower village have only sustained small injuries from the aftershock of the torn earth above us. I move my hand to my head, shuddering at the lies that filled it. She truly is an evil woman to have invaded my mind with such images. My friends and neighbor's dead, everything in flames, and me at the center of it all. However, she has miscalculated again. After experiencing the authentic emotion of my home being destroyed, there is no way I will allow her twisted illusion to become a reality.

"Are you alright, King?"

"Yeah, sorry, man. This woman is beyond evil. I heard her laughing before she put me in a trance. I never told you, but while I was in the Neuro Center and on this trip, I constantly heard a soft voice giving me all this weird information and showing me different visions. This whole time I thought it might have been a guardian angel, but now I see she has been picking the lock to my mind this whole time."

"We have to stop this woman!"

"Yes, and there is no room for failure. Her lies and destruction end here!" I yell, calling forth my gold and jade sword and running toward the broken Royal Town.

In many ways it reflects the fake world I saw. But thankfully there are no bodies on the ground, as it seems everyone has evacuated in time. We creep slowly through the broken streets whispering Tuy's name, but we hear no answer even as we move closer to the burning castle.

"Looking for me, boys?" Tru coos coquettishly from above.

She sits cross-legged on the edge of the tailor shop's half-caved-in roof, running her fingers through my mother's stolen curls.

"Take your dirty hands out of her hair," I growl at her, but she just smirks and laughs.

"I see that you have met your father, son."

I roll my eyes. "You really wish, don't you? But no matter what you do, in the end I will always be the sole heir to the throne of Ren. I was created beautifully by the woman you wanted to be so much that you stole her body. But you will never be her. You will always just be an heirless queen and a queen that was never good enough!" I yell, taunting her as I throw my dice and start to pick at her mind.

"Cute. You think it will be that easy to get into my mind? Honey, I put the game in mind games," says Tru, smirking.

"But don't you ever get tired of playing games?" Sione chimes in.

"Aww, the fatso wants to play. Shut it before I torture you like your friend," snarls Tru.

"What did you do with him?" we yell simultaneously, but Tru just smiles as she raises her finger, whispering words under her breath. Her chanting and the twirling of her finger stop suddenly. She winks at us as she snaps her finger and Tuy appears out of nowhere, falling from the sky.

We recall our weapons and run toward him, catching him inches from the ground.

"Nice catch," Tru says sarcastically, throwing the tail of her long scarf in the air and disappearing. We turn our attention to Tuy, who is beaten badly. His face has already started to swell and he is covered in blood and wounds. We call out his name and he eventually opens his eyes. He tries to give his heroic smile, but it quickly fades and he shakes his head. Tuy then tries to lift his bloody hand to my shoulder, but he has no strength so it falls back to the ground just as quick as it came. He closes his eyes, releasing his soul. I scream his name at the top of my lungs, beating at his chest. I frantically yell for Sione to give him CPR, but it is no use.

"Move out the way," yells a familiar voice.

"Sidney!" I exclaim.

She pushes past me without a word, carrying a small, dirty white box with a sunflower on the front. Opening the box, she reveals tiny needles connected to clear long tubes. Without hesitation, she cuts open Tuy's uniform and sticks ten of the needles evenly across his chest. From deeper in the box, she pulls out a strange purple rock. She flicks it along the backs of the tubes, causing electrical currents to flow, delivering doses of them to his heart. She flicks the rock once, twice, and on the third time his eyes fly open and he catches his soul back before it leaves.

"He will be alright! Now, go after her!" Sidney shouts.

Sione and I exchange glances. I look back at Tuy, who seems confused, but is only catching his breath. I nod my head at Sione and we jump up and head after Rania. But for a moment I stop, Sione leaving me behind, and I turn to Sidney. "About what happened at the market..."

"I know you didn't try to hurt me intentionally, King. I forgive you," Sidney says as she strokes Tuy's hair and starts to tend to his wounds.

"Thank you." I lower my head.

"Don't mention it. If you had not done what you did, our island would be in a lot of trouble. I remembered what you said, about 'knowing what to do if things look bad on the home front.' Those words saved many lives today." I smile back at her and construct a golden spirit barrier around them before I run after Sione.

I arrive at the castle, where Sione is waiting for me, looking uncertain. I'd guess it has something to do with half of the castle being on fire, but of course Tru is inside, for we hear her maniacal laughter.

"Well, the fire is in the west wing so it should be okay to enter, but just in case, can your spirit energy help somehow?" asks Sione.

"Yeah, I can actually make barriers."

"Like father, like son." He shoots hand guns at me, clicking his tongue, but he notices the unenthusiastic look on my face and slowly lowers his hands. "Too soon?"

"Yes. But it's all good. In the end I'm hoping that's what will save the princess," I say as I create another gold barrier and we run headfirst into the castle. Thankfully the foyer is fine, but smoke is starting to filter out from deep within the castle. "Do you hear her?" I whisper.

"Unfortunately, yes, and figures it would be coming from that direction," says Sione, pointing toward the hall that leads to the west wing of the building, which is also the hall emitting the most smoke from its corridors. Yet we do not hesitate as we head inside.

We walk until we are no longer surrounded by smoke, but unruly flames. Thankfully they do not hurt us, but we still can feel their heat as our progress becomes sluggish. Sione stops and places his hands on his knees in the center of a room that appears to have been a ballroom but now is nothing more than broken glass from the chandelier, melting gold, fallen pillars, and burning rubble.

"Hold on a moment, King," he says, catching his breath. I do the same as I wipe the sweat from my brow in this dome of flames. "King..."

"What?"

"The laughing stopped," Sione says, concerned, as he stands straight up and my eyes grow wide. We are out of time.

A sharp pain shoots up my back as I am kicked from behind, through my barrier, so hard I fly halfway across the room. I manage to fall backward, avoiding the fire. Sione, however, is falling straight for it. I throw a barrier in front of the flames, catching him just in time, and he lands safe on his tummy. But there is no time for thought, as we both are kicked again. We flail through the flames, trying to avoid their depths. I am kicked, slapped, and even cut at the shoulders by Tru, but I cannot see her. I only hear her laughter.

I fall to the ground, grabbing my stomach and bleeding from the mouth. I look at Sione, who is now running in some sort of weird pattern that doesn't keep him from getting kicked around.

I try to stay down, but she finds me and lands blow after blow, each one more powerful than the last, until she knees me straight in the face. I fly back, landing hard, coughing up blood and phlegm. Sione still runs in weird zigzag formations, now heading toward me. He falls next to me and places his hand on my chest, frantically asking if I am all right.

Rising slowly, I pull at my collar, slightly revealing the breastplate underneath. "Yeah. This thing sure is coming in handy," I huff.

"Good. But look, man, I figured out how we can attack."

"How?"

"Just wait for it." Sione looks intensely at the flames, counting in a weird number sequence until he yells out, "The spark!" He picks up a piece of flaming wood with his bare hands and swings it into a section of the fire, causing Rania to fly from its embrace onto the floor of the ballroom. Her top alight. "Every time she was getting ready to attack, a slight spark would burst," Sione says, breathing heavily with burned hands.

Tru beats at her blouse, which has caught fire, but it does no good, so she rips it from her body. Sione and I are startled. We've been uncertain what she really is, but as I take a closer look, I see now. She has the face and long, curly hair of the goddess we thought was named Rania, but I guess it was all an illusion as well. As my father said, she tempted me disgustingly with a face I would long for, but never see full of life. Her appearance is now like when I saw her in the upside-down world, but the jewels that covered her breasts have tarnished. I guess they were fake, just like her.

She's nothing but skin and bones, so much that a piece of her lower rib could be seen through a gaping hole in her flesh. Her veins all over her body are stressed and poking out as they glow a deep red color. This poor woman is doing nothing but holding on to the body of a corpse.

I clutch at my chest, where the cursed necklace grows hot. I claw at it and beat at my body. The sight of my biological mother, trapped to the point of death and decomposition by a woman scorned, is too much for me to bear. I find myself whispering for my "Mother," repeating the word over and over again until I feel Sione's hand on my shoulder. He kneels down next to me and tells to me to keep it together, that this is my only chance while we have the upper hand.

I look up at Tru, who is stomping on her torn uniform, each stomp filled with anger on top of anger. This woman has so much hate in her heart. How can she have lived so many years with the face of her husband's mistress? I pull at my hair, thinking of all the lies she fed us. I still wonder what was real and what was fake. Rania was a jovial soul, Luna is a lost child trapped, my mother is ashes, and all the while Queen Tru continues to hide behind her comfortable mask.

She spreads her venom, mixing lies with truth, and when the time is right she is so evil that she does not allow you to choose your fate; instead she acts in your stead and destroys cities, relationships, families, and lives. Twenty years of sadness have come from this woman and my birth, but after today she shall spread her lies no more. I pause for a moment, looking up at the shattered chandelier, as one last tear escapes.

As I lift myself up, I stumble, but Sione catches me. I pull away from him and I take a few steps closer to Tru. "Why?" I yell causing the queen to regain her composure. She turns her attention to me slowly and softly says, "Why what?"

"Why are you doing all of these things? The destruction of Ren, murder, manipulation, and worst of all, torturing a mere child! Release her, please! I even beg you to release my mother's soulless body so she may finally be at rest. Has she not suffered enough for her sins?" My voice grows hoarse with tears, not of fear but of anger, rolling down my cheeks. I throw my hands out wide, stumbling closer to the queen, not in my right mind. "Take me instead. Direct your anger toward me. What will you do with a small child? I am much more powerful than Luna; you will have more use from me. Please just let her go!" But my pleading is in vain, as I hit a nerve.

Tru's nails grow long and turn black, as black as her eyes now glow. She bites down on her lip, breaking the skin. "Power, power, power! If I was really after power, I would have murdered Ren long ago. I had him right where I wanted him, but I foolishly still loved him! Yet what did he do? He continued to break my heart! Even after you were born, he still would sneak away in the night to be with her! No, having all of my husband's powers would not heal my broken heart. So instead I decided to have my revenge and take away everything he loved, as he took away his love from me."

Tru's breathing grows shallow while she tries to hold back tears. "I hate looking at what I have become! Seeing the woman who stole my husband every time in the mirror—but I'm not letting her go. She will not get to rest peacefully in death! You," says Tru, extending her hand to me, "were supposed to be my son, but you were foolishly born to that hussy! Everything is your fault! If only you had not been born, then I could have forgiven Ren. Baris…I am so sorry, but you must die. Then everything will go back to normal. I will be the woman Ren desires and we will produce a rightful heir to his throne." She laughs and pulls at her long curls.

Sione nudges me and whispers for me to pull myself together. That she is starting to snap and now is my chance. "The best way to destroy a trickster is to beat her at her own game," He says with a heroic smile that reminds me of Tuy.

Somehow I find a way to snicker in the midst of these flames. "You look just like that idiot right now," I say to Sione, who just continues to smile and says with a wink, "Go get her."

I turn my attention back to Tru and stand tall. She has played with my family's minds long enough; this time I will go for hers. "You're wrong, your majesty. Even if you kill me, Ren would not take you back. He has already moved on," I say tauntingly.

Tru sticks her nose in the air, not taking the bait yet, but I am just getting started.

"Honestly. You have been gone from your home too long. King Ren has already gotten remarried to my foster mother, Kema."

"Lies. You think you can beat me at my own game?" She laughs wickedly.

"No, I cannot beat you with a lie, but I can beat you with the truth. He is living happily with her, especially since she was able to do what you never could: take care of his child as well as give him another heir."

Queen Tru snaps her neck back from the sky and her glowing eyes fade, irises flickering blue for a moment. "He would not have another child."

"But he did. Think about it. Why would Ren give his child to an unknown woman in the village, unless they had something going on?"

"Lies!" yells Tru at the top of her lungs, stumbling over. Her exposed veins glow more vividly as she pulls even harder on her curls.

"Reel her in," Sione whispers from behind me.

"I am sorry, Tru, but you have already lost this fight. No good will come from killing me. Kema and Ren are living happily in your old home with their daughter, who has beautiful grey eyes just like me. The people of your homeland that you tried to destroy are already starting to rebuild."

Tru throws her hands to her ears as she starts shaking her head frantically.

"The Elk you sent to kill us! I know you saw the flash of white spirit energy from the mountains of Ren. Who do you think sent that? It was my little sister. I'm slightly jealous, but she inherited my father's energy. Poor Tru, you are nothing more than an outsider now. I even found my place where I belong, after so many years away, but you, you will never be able to return. You are nothing more than a random woman running around in this fantasy world of yours with stolen faces and spirit energy!"

I yell the last sentence at the top of my lungs, and the flames part and run up the wall, encasing us in a box of fire. "Shut your mouth!" yells Tru, but there is no way I am stopping now. I continue to mock her with lies and truth wrapped together. Just like how she manipulated my father, Luna, and me. She will now have a dose of her own medicine. I drill in the fact that there is no place for her at Ren. I tell her King Ren will never take her back after all she has done, and that even if she kills me, she'll have to start all over and kill his new heir as well.

Queen Tru screams for me to stop with my words as she shoots her spirit energy sporadically. I dodge each shot, as her accuracy fades once she begins to snap. She finally lets out a strange cry and starts to twitch uncontrollably. Sione pulls me back and I materialize my spirit sword.

Tru's skin crack along her legs and arms and even her face. Pieces of her skin break, not like flesh but like porcelain as they fall to the ground and shatter. She raises her head, slowly laughing, twitching insanely as my mother's left eye flakes away and breaks on the ground into a million pieces. Tru's blue eye is revealed, and part of her olive skin sits contrastingly beneath her ebony mask.

I turn to Sione and tell him that this is it. "If she will not let Luna go, then I will dig inside of her and pull her out. She is nothing more than a nesting doll. Be on guard, Sione," I say as I center my energy into the jade of my sword. It grows longer, extending past the blade and curving in a spiral with a small point and three rotating jade beads at the end.

Tru is frantically picking up the fallen pieces of her skin, completely distracted, as she is trying to put herself back together. Bingo! I run for Tru, leaping a good length in the air. She notices me just as I am about to land my attack and tries to dodge, but I grab her arm and pull her to the ground, then point my sword directly at her heart.

Tru squeezes her eyes shut, one brown and another blue. For the first time I can feel her humanity. I hover my sword over her heart but I do not follow through. The small beads rotate, building up to a rapid pace, but they stop suddenly, making a straight line and slowly disappear into the center of her chest. Once they do, her fake body completely shatters. I feel a tug in my heart, as that was the last time I'll see the face of a mother I never knew, but at least she can now be at peace.

A dark-haired woman with stunning blue eyes kneels before me in the broken pieces of a woman that died long ago. Queen Tru still wears her royal robe. She looks to me, and I have never seen so much sadness and heartbreak in anyone's eyes. Her make-up is smeared and her arms filled with slashes. This poor soul. But those sorrowful eyes flicker dark green for a second and it brings me back.

"Release her," I say in a stern tone, my sword still pointed directly at her heart. And slowly the evil of this woman returns as her sorrowful lips curve into a sadistic smile. She knows that I cannot kill her without killing Luna as well. She throws her arms out, taunting me, but I make no move.

Before I can react, she throws herself on my sword, pressing it into her heart. I pull back just in time so it won't cause any fatal damage, but she grabs me by the throat, wrapping her long fingers around my neck, pulling me closer, and driving my sword an inch deeper. I have to get Luna out of there!

I try to pull away, but her grip is too tight and it's starting to become hard to breathe. I try one last time to plead with her through my crushed throat and demand she release Luna, but she still does not budge, and I know now that it has come to the end.

I look Tru in the eyes and mouth the words, "I'm sorry. I hope you find some peace." With my free hand, I materialize a jade glove. I know that Tru sees me and she could stop me, but for some reason she does not. Her face just grows soft.

Nonetheless, I hold nothing back as I dig my jade-gloved hand through her chest. Once inside this strange space Tru has created inside of herself, I feel a soft, tiny hand grab on, and with no hesitation, I pull Luna free from this cursed energy spell my father spoke of. The moment the princess materializes in front of me, I want to cry, but I know I must act fast. Throwing her toward Sione, I simultaneously stab Tru straight through the heart, again.

And there we are in the center of this ballroom that is on fire. Tru kneels with my sword pinning her to the ground. As her power weakens, her hand slowly slips from my throat and falls to her side. She looks up at me and I dare not take my eyes from her. I am shaken and honestly sad that it had to come to this. Though she had done so much evil, at one point she was Rania, our strange friend and comrade. This poor, powerful woman, blinded by revenge but most of all scorned with a broken heart. Tru smiles at me in her final seconds and a small tear escapes from her. Right before my eyes, she turns to dust and disappears as if she had died long ago. I cross my hands over my chest as I whisper, "Sorry" under my breath one last time.

I wipe the sweat from my face and run to Sione, who is swaddling Luna. "Will she be okay?" I ask frantically.

"Yeah, her breathing is shallow but she will be fine once we get her to a doctor," Sione says as he wipes the sweat from Luna's forehead.

"Thank God! Well, I think we should get out of here." I look at the fire surrounding us. Sione nods and quickly gets up, but as we start to move, things get strange again. The fire begins to disappear. The chandelier is no longer broken and the pillars no longer burned. The air inside of the castle is fresh, not suffocating. We move quickly from the ballroom, and most of the smoke has cleared from the rest of the castle as well.

But the biggest surprise comes when we push open the doors and are blinded by blue skies, our noses tickled by the fresh scent of salt in the air. I look out and everything is back to normal. Royal Town is unharmed, the village below is filled with people cheering, and even on the distant island the refugees join our celebration. The dark clouds have rolled back, but most importantly, our peaceful island is in one piece. I thank God it was all an illusion.

EPIL⊕GUE

Five days later

I look out at a sea of people all cheering our names. I never thought some of my greatest bullies would finally give me applause. Though truthfully, I could care less about winning their approval. I won this time for myself. I found something so much greater than a king inside of me.

Sione nudges my arm. "Look alive, man!" he whispers to me.

"Oops! I got lost in thought," I say, straightening atop of the wooden podium in front of the castle.

"Daydreaming like a little girl," Luna says mockingly beside me.

"Well, I see she hasn't changed," says Sidney.

"Leave her be. She is still just a kid," Tuy preaches before he and Sidney start a side conversation. Luna twists her face, since she is able to still hear their conversation and it's obviously about her.

"A twisted face will make for an ugly picture," I warn her. "Also, I don't think being a little girl is a bad thing. You showed more bravery than this grown man right here. I am so proud of you, Luna. You think, fight, run, and are brave like a girl, and maybe one day I can act just like a little girl too."

My words cause Luna to laugh immaturely. "You wish," she whispers under her breath and I can't help but smile.

General Claude finally finishes his speech and walks by each of us, shaking our hands. The king follows behind him and pins Medals of Honor on our newly designed Antenetta-inspired uniforms. They finally get to me and the general stares at me for a moment. He never did mention being my uncle, but as he shakes my hand, he squeezes it firmly and I know he is proud.

I turn to King Vernon, who is on the brink of tears. "And to our young

King! For saving Peace Island and my daughter, I bestow upon you the Medal of Honor, the Medal of Sacrifice, and the Medal of Bravery!" he declares in a booming voice across the land, and the crowd's cheers erupt once more.

"Where are you going?" Sione asks as I sit in my room trying to stuff a few more socks into my bag along with my Medals of Honor. I exhale as I swing my backpack over my shoulder and stumble out of my room, heading for the front door, with Sione quick on my heels. He calls once more and I turn to him with a big grin on my face, catching him off guard.

"Nowhere important. I just have some business to attend to in a distant land."

Sione pauses for a moment, rubbing the back of his head, but quickly returns my stupid grin with his own and simply says, "I understand, Baris."

I nod my head to my friend one last time before turning on my heels and heading for a very special place where I can finally live up to the name *King.*

About the Author

L. STITT is a rising author and poet. Her previous releases include the self-published collection of poetry, Escape. L.STITT was born in Charlotte, NC but her heart is in Owings Mills, MD where she spent 13 years of her life making Owings Mills (Baltimore) her hometown at heart. She enjoys the feeling of creating new worlds and characters, which is why you can find her spending her free-time watching Marvel movies and dancing all night to music. Find out more about L.STITT on her website: ariah-alana.com.

Printed in the United States
By Bookmasters